Audrey Hepburn's Neck

SCEPTRE

Audrey Hepburn's Neck

ALAN BROWN

First published in 1996 by Hodder and Stoughton
A division of Hodder Headline PLC
A Sceptre Book

10 9 8 7 6 5 4 3 2 1

British Library Cataloguing in Publication Data

Brown, Alan
Audrey Hepburn's neck
1.English fiction – 20th century
I.Title
823.9'14[F]

ISBN 0 340 64936 4

Typeset by Palimpsest Book Production Limited,
Polmont, Stirlingshire
Printed and bound in Great Britain by
Mackays of Chatham PLC, Chatham, Kent

Hodder and Stoughton
A division of Hodder Headline PLC
338 Euston Road
London NW1 3BH

for Carolyn Doty,
John Kander,
and Donald Richie

and for my cousin Sue

Acknowledgements

I would like to thank Sarah Blake and Gen Watanabe for their steadfast attention to my manuscript. Thanks also to Jane Brox, Glenn Finch, Louise Quayle, Louise Steinman, the MacDowell Colony, Yaddo, and the Banff Centre for their support and encouragement.

Prologue

Toshiyuki Okamoto was born at the end of the road.

He was delivered into this world in a bare room upstairs from his father's noodle shop, halfway up Shiretoko Peninsula on Hokkaido, the northernmost island of Japan. A few meters past the shop the gravel road tapered off to nothing, like a Zen conundrum, a calligrapher's brush stroke on a sheet of handmade birch bark paper. The steep slope behind the noodle shop was covered with scrub bamboo and white birch, and with ladder fern whose roots his mother dug up and boiled like potatoes, and was inhabited by a family of red foxes.

Across the road from the noodle shop, fishermen sat on the seawall like seals, smoking Hope and Peace cigarettes; their nets the color of dried persimmon strung up behind them in the cold sunlight; their boats, fat and ungainly-looking as white-skinned foreigners. Then the sea itself, and only a little farther on, close enough so that as a child Toshi always thought he could swim out to them if he had to, were two lumbering islands that belonged to Russia but which in his schoolbooks were clearly labeled part of Japan.

The hand-painted sign that covered the front of his father's shop advertised soup noodles with bear meat, and sea lion meat, and a special crab ramen *with, if one could believe the weathered painting, giant red crab legs that rose up out of the bowl like the limbs of a movie sea monster rising out of Tokyo Bay, breathing fire on the Diet building, and stomping on Ginza's department stores. But in truth, Toshi's father mostly served the same selection of dishes – miso* ramen, *pork* ramen, *fried rice,* gyoza *dumplings – as did every noodle shop from Hokkaido to Okinawa. The shop was on the edge of the village of Rausu, and his customers were the Hope and Peace-smoking fishermen, weekend hunters, and, in the summer months, tourists.*

To reach the end of the peninsula, a traveler would have had to continue on by foot, searching out the deer paths that cut through the forested hills, or scrambling along the rocky beach, scattering the pale yellow, the deep purple, the spotted red sand crabs. Or hire a fisherman who had the time and inclination to guide his boat up a coastline of gray cliffs washed smooth and shiny as pachinko balls. In winter, passage by land or sea was unthinkable. The snowpack reached up to the treetops, concealing boulders bigger than cigarette vending machines, bigger than 7-Eleven convenience stores. From January through mid-March, the coastal waters froze into trembling sheets of ice.

Toshi was born upstairs from the noodle shop in the six-tatami-mat room that faced the sea. Until his mother left them when he was eight, he slept every night between his parents, their three mattresses laid out side by side, edges touching. After his mother went to live at the inn in Utoro across the peninsula, Toshi slept next to his father. There was a second room in the back that faced the white birch-covered slope. Six mats. A television set, a low wooden kotatsu *table, and a gas burner for making tea. The bath and the squat toilet were downstairs behind the shop.*

The day before Toshi was born, his mother, Hiroko, swept and vacuumed, then wiped down the tatami in the front room with a damp cloth. His father, Fumio, hung the mattresses and quilts out over the window ledge to air in the cold light, turning them every hour and beating them with a soup ladle. They did all this without speaking.

There was no doctor in Rausu, and the closest hospital was a two-hour drive. So, while his father was downstairs frying up plates of rice with egg, pork, shrimp, and green onions for seven weekend hunters from Sapporo who'd arrived drunk in a Mitsubishi minibus, Toshi was wrested into that speechless world, pulled in through eddies of soy sauce, cooking oil, and cigarette smoke, by Mrs Uchida, a cheerful, retired midwife who had just months before moved up from Yokohama to live with her eldest son, Taro. Taro owned the inn in Utoro where Toshi's mother went to work and, eventually, to live. So, growing up, Toshi saw Mrs Uchida almost every weekend. He, as did everyone, called her 'Granny.'

After he was born, Granny carried Toshi over to the front window to get a better look at him in the light, or perhaps to give him his first glimpse of that world at the end of the road. And, to the fishermen sitting on the seawall who happened to look up, his tiny blue head appeared to float between the two giant crab claws, to bob like a blue balloon in the painted steam that rose up from an enormous and delicious-looking bowl of noodles.

1

According to its brochure, The Very Romantic English Academy occupies the third and fourth floors of the Hysteric Glamour Building, upstairs from My Charming Home interior furnishings, a Häagen-Dazs ice cream parlor, and the Cherry Blossom Discount Camera Center, and is only a seven-minute walk up Dogenzaka Hill from Tokyo's Shibuya Station, where the Ginza, Hanzamon, Inokashira, Toyoko, Shin-Tamagawa, and Yamanote train lines all converge on top of a Tokyu Department Store, two *soba* stands, the Love Bun German bakery and coffee bar, and a branch of Williams-Sonoma.

Twice each week, Toshi hurries up Dogenzaka Hill, checks his Swatch watch in the lobby: six minutes. He never misses Jane Borden's Intermediate English Conversation class. He raises his hand and asks and answers more questions, and in better English, than anyone else except for the Ishikawa sisters, who lived for three years in Hawaii, where their father owns a papaya plantation.

'Jane Borden. Borden, like the ice cream, like the cow, like Lizzie who chopped up her father with an ax,' she tells her bewildered students on the first day of class. She throws open all the windows, as if she is freeing caged birds, and they can hear ten thousand angry rice farmers chanting at a rally in front of Shibuya Station: 'No

American rice. No American rice. Keep the market closed. No American rice.'

'I want you to forget that you're in school when you're in this room with me,' she says, rearranging their chairs so that they circle her like planets around the sun. She perches on the edge of her desk and she beams. She drinks coffee from a huge white mug with her own initials painted on it. She writes her name on the blackboard in English and then again in phonetic Japanese.

'Jane Borden. I'm thirty years old. I come from New York City in New York State in the United States of America,' she tells them proudly, as if these are things she has achieved rather than accidents of fate. 'No, I'm not married. You can call me Jane. We don't have to be formal in here. I want you to think of me as someone you can talk to about anything. I'm always available. I'm here for you.'

Toshi is sure she is looking at him when she writes her home phone number on the blackboard, each successive numeral larger and loopier than the one before.

She is as slender as a Japanese girl, but she moves constantly and talks too quickly. She wears red tights and red cowboy boots and antique silk sarongs from Thailand, she tells them, which she drapes around her neck like voluminous scarves. Jewelry: Hoops and pendulums, sharp daggers, pots and pans, and cloisonné tigers dangle from her salmon-colored ears; bead and bone and silver necklaces from Sri Lanka hang down between her breasts. Jade and feather fetishes flutter in the breeze that always seems to accompany her even when the windows are closed.

'Language is communication, it is social intercourse,' she says, prancing around the classroom.

'You're standing in front of Courbet's *Woman with a Parrot* at the Metropolitan Museum of Art in New York City and you see a beautiful woman all alone.' She pauses in front of Toshi's desk and stares at him. 'Your eyes meet. Your heart beats fast. Your palms sweat. She waits for you to speak. What do you say to her?'

The class is silent, waiting. Toshi's heart beats fast. New York. Courbet. His palms sweat. Jane brushes her dark hair out of her seaweed green eyes. She reaches out her hand to him, and her bracelets spin, rings from Bali and Katmandu on every finger.

'It is nice to meet you,' Toshi says, but the words come out stilted, badly inflected. Someone giggles.

Is this American-style education? He is confused and seduced. The next week he wears his tightest jeans to class. When the weather turns warm, he wears his gym shorts. He smiles and nods his head constantly when Jane speaks.

Toshi is fascinated by American women.

Two days before his twenty-third birthday, she stops him in the hallway. Classroom doors open and shut, flutter like eyelids.

'I was impressed with the talk you gave today about your job. You expressed some very deep feelings.'

'Thank you,' Toshi says, backing away slightly. Jane always encourages them to express 'deep feelings,' but no one in the class, except for the Ishikawa sisters, seems to know what they are or how to express them.

'Comic books are such an important art form in Japan. You must be a very talented artist.'

'Yes,' he says, then, too late, realizes his mistake. He should have said no. He is mesmerized by Jane, she makes him thirsty when she smiles.

He recovers. 'I work for another *manga* artist. I only draw what he tells me.'

'Still, it's special. I'd love to see some of your drawings.' She moves in closer. In her boots, she's as tall as he is. 'You know, I'm not just an English teacher. I'm an artist, too. An actress.'

'Really? In movies?'

She laughs, and her red lips part to reveal small, even, white teeth, then beyond, wonderful darkness. 'No. On the stage. The theater. You know?'

He nods, too nervous to speak. Is she famous in America?

'I have this script, in Japanese, that a director gave me, and I need help translating it. If you're interested, I'd pay you. It could be fun.'

'Yes. Fun,' he says, but he isn't sure in response to what. Her words dart past him like startled birds. Around them, the buzz and whirl subside as students move on to their next classes and the hall empties. Then they are alone. Can she see that he is shaking? American women still do this to him.

'So, do you have plans for your birthday?' she asks, and he is so astonished to see her turn red with embarrassment that he feels himself blush too.

'No plans.' He scrambles for something else to say, but all that comes to mind are learned phrases: *America is a wide country. Japan has four seasons. Do you take traveler's checks?* He wants desperately to impress her, but she isn't giving him time to put his words in order.

'Well, why don't I take you out to dinner and we can talk about the script?'

Now he thinks of something to say. 'How did you know it was my birthday?'

'I looked up your records in the office. You were born in the Year of the Monkey, right?'

'Yes! The monkey! Yes.' He relaxes. At last, something he knows. Monkey. He once saw monkeys at a hot spring resort in the snowy mountains of Hokkaido. The monkeys came down and bathed in its pools. DON'T LOOK IN THEIR EYES OR THEY WILL ATTACK YOU the posted signs warned.

'I was born in the Year of the Tiger,' Jane says. 'We should work well together. You know: The monkey riding on the tiger's back.'

Before he can reply, she turns and walks into the classroom, and shuts the door behind her.

Toshi is out of breath. He staggers like a drunken salaryman on a midnight commuter train out of Tokyo Station. This is what he likes best yet dreads most about American women: You can never tell, even with the ones you think you know, what they're going to do next.

The restaurant was designed by a famous British architect, Jane tells him as the tubular glass elevator descends eleven floors below street level. The doors open, and they step out into flashing red and yellow lights, Chinese gongs, a wall of carved African masks. The menu is Thai and Italian. The Japanese waiters wear bicycle shorts.

They never talk about the script that Jane needs translated, for she has invited along two American friends. Hugh, who is making a documentary film about the rice riots, smiles at Toshi relentlessly, as if he is trying to make him feel comfortable. It has the opposite effect. He likes Hugh's wife, though. Lucy is a composer. Tall and broad-shouldered, with hair as short as his, she looks like someone he'd want to talk to if he saw her at a party. Every time their eyes meet she leans almost imperceptibly across the table, as if she has something fascinating she wants to say to him. But he looks away, flustered. He's never met a composer. What are they like? he wonders as Jane refills his wineglass, then rests her hand on his thigh. Romantic? Moody? Unpredictable, he guesses.

It is Jane, though, whose behavior bewilders him. Twice she bursts into tears and excuses herself from the table. Is she sick, or has something terrible occurred? Hugh and Lucy stare down at their plates and say nothing. Then, when they are all being served their salads, a strolling guitar player stops behind Jane's chair and strums 'The Tennessee Waltz.' She starts to cry again.

'I know what you're thinking,' she sobs. 'I invited you and now I'm ruining your birthday dinner. You must think I'm awful.'

Before he can say anything, she runs off to the toilet.

There's a long, uncomfortable silence at the table.

'She probably has a flu or something,' Lucy says.

'Oh, she's not sick. Physically, anyway,' Hugh says. Lucy gives him a sharp look, which he doesn't notice. 'She's just freaking out because she was having a wild affair with her *ikebana* teacher.' Hugh smiles widely, exposing shiny gums.

Toshi smiles back. 'Yes, I understand,' he says, even though he doesn't, can't connect flower arranging with Jane's troubles. He pretends to examine the pile of greens on his plate. This is something his best friend, Paul, taught him about dealing with Americans: Never act surprised.

'Hugh!' Lucy says abruptly. Are they going to argue? But the room lights dim. Four waiters carry a candlelit cake to the table and sing 'Happy Birthday' in English. When they are done, everyone in the restaurant applauds. Toshi is embarrassed by the attention.

'Now blow out the candles, all at once,' Lucy says. She leans over the green tea tiramisu cake and purses her lips to demonstrate, and she looks so funny that Toshi laughs. She laughs too.

'No, really. It's an American tradition. You blow out the candles, then you close your eyes and make a wish. But if you miss a candle, your wish won't come true.'

A wish? Japanese make wishes at Shinto shrines and Buddhist temples, before school exams or the birth of a child. At the beginning of a new year. Americans make wishes on the most unlikely occasions. When blowing out candles. Looking up at the stars, and crossing their fingers.

When breaking dried chicken bones – something his last American girlfriend, Wanda Williford, taught him.

He blows out the candles and closes his eyes, but he is so drunk that he is unnerved by the sudden darkness and by the images impressed on his eyelids: Lucy puckers her lips, Jane weeps. He opens his eyes before he can think of a wish, and Lucy and Hugh applaud.

A waiter takes the cake away to be cut. Jane returns dry-eyed from the bathroom, and apologizes again. Then she and Lucy and Hugh all start talking at once, very fast. They race to tell one another stories of their own birthdays, the parties they had growing up, parties their parents gave them.

Toshi doesn't tell any stories. His English isn't that good, and he still hasn't mastered the skill most essential for talking with Americans – how to interrupt. Jane and Hugh and Lucy talk as if they are playing sports and someone is keeping score. Toshi chases after familiar words – *mother, awful, divorce* – and strings them together. Drunk, he struggles for connections and for meaning, constructing scenes from American movies he has seen. Fat white children in pointed hats. Bursting balloons. Cakes as big as tatami mats. A silver rocketship you could slice with a knife and eat. And birthday presents. So many presents to unwrap and hold up like prizes.

But at the parties Jane and her friends recall, and in the movies he's seen, there are also arguments. Between children and parents, between parent and parent. There are drunken uncles. There are broken toys and sobbing aunts.

'And they put him in jail overnight,' is how Hugh ends one of his stories as the slices of cake arrive. Hugh crumples his cloth napkin and puts it on the table. Lucy's is still on her lap, but Jane's is folded neatly next to her plate. Toshi's napkin is still spread on his knees. What should he do with it? Sitting stiff-backed as a schoolboy, he feels awkward and ignored.

The stories continue over cups of Viennese coffee topped with swirls of whipped cream that sag from the heat. Disappointments pile on top of disasters. It seems to Toshi that while Japanese take pains to present cheerful pictures of their families to strangers, Jane and her friends offer up their unhappy childhoods like movie plots, or like gifts: They unwrap and display them with something resembling pride.

After dinner, they ride the glass elevator up eleven floors – past an underground batting center, past a blowfish restaurant of thatched-roofed teahouses set in a subterranean forest of bamboo and bathed in artificial moonlight – and surface on a narrow street lined with pachinko parlors and karaoke bars.

'Look!' Lucy says, peering in the window of a beer hall with a Swiss chalet facade. Inside, two women in strapless dresses snowplow down a tiny ski slope.

Jane rises up on the silver toes of her cowboy boots and presses her lips to Toshi's ear. Startled, he is instantly erect, waits for her to stick her tongue in. But she only whispers, 'I have a special birthday present for you, but I couldn't bring it to the restaurant. Why don't you come back to my apartment?'

She reminds him of the red foxes that wander out of the Hokkaido woods at the end of winter. The famished yet tentative look in her eyes. He thinks he knows what the present is.

'If you're sure it's okay,' he says.

'Don't be so Japanese. I wouldn't have asked if it wasn't.' She raises her bare arm and flutters her fingers. A taxi door springs open.

While the driver is watching the news on the dashboard

TV – two more rice farmers and a Buddhist monk starved to death at the hunger strike in front of the Ministry of Agriculture – he sails through a red light and bumps a Pizza Hut delivery boy off his motor scooter. In the backseat, waiting for the police to arrive, Jane and Toshi kiss. But when he sees her face in the flashing red light of the police car, his erection melts like spring snow. And that's when he wonders if she will be his new American girlfriend.

Jane wouldn't be Toshi's first American girlfriend. He has had two since he moved to Tokyo. Before Jane, there was Wanda Williford. Before Wanda, Sally Youngblood. In Sapporo, where he went to college, there was, in his last year, the exchange student Patty Shapiro, who had a cat also named Patty.

He has never had a Japanese girlfriend, not even when he was in high school and there were only Japanese girls to choose from. He never wanted one. What Toshiyuki Okamoto has wanted, has desired, has dreamed erotic dreams about since the day of his ninth birthday, is a girlfriend who looks like the movie star Audrey Hepburn – Audrey Hepburn in *Roman Holiday*, beginning with the scene in which she walks into a barbershop and gets her long beautiful hair sheared off.

Toshi's ninth birthday fell on a Saturday. After school let out, he took the bus across the thawing peninsula to Utoro. From the bus window he looked down on the small fishing village where his mother lived – a cluster of low, steep-roofed buildings on a dark fist of granite that curled out into a darker sea.

The inn was quiet. His mother was in the kitchen washing rice for dinner. Sunlight and cold air poured in the open windows. Pushing her sleeves up past her elbows, she plunged her hands into the glassy water. She asked him to go to the movies with her in Shari.

He leaned over the sink and watched chalky powder swirl up through her fingers. The water clouded, and stray grains floated to the top. 'But I'm going up to the hills with my friends, to catch foxes,' he said.

After the winter, the red foxes walked out of the woods and sunned themselves along the roadside. They were half-asleep and still stunned from the cold. You could walk right up to them, pick them up, and they went limp in your arms. You could drape them around your neck.

'The snow's almost all gone. It's too late to see a fox in a tree.' Smiling, his mother lifted her red hands out of the water and shook them over the sink.

She'd told him this story often when he was younger: In the winter the snow was so high that the foxes walked across its surface and slept in the branches of the soft pines, nesting like birds. While they slept the snow melted, and when they woke up they couldn't get down.

'What's the movie?'

'An old American one. It's very famous.'

'But it's in English. I won't understand it.'

'Movie subtitles are easy. And it will be fun to go together, won't it?'

She turned on the tap water. She plunged her hands in again, and her fingers disappeared into the pearly grains like bare feet into wet sand.

The movie theater was cold. They passed a thermos of green tea back and forth while up on the screen Audrey Hepburn walked into a barbershop in Rome and had her beautiful hair cut off. In the seats around them, middle-aged women and high school girls opened wooden lunch boxes of grilled eel, rice, and pickled radish. They reached down into shopping bags for their potato cutlet sandwiches, grilled rice balls wrapped in seaweed, and damp cakes filled with sweet red bean paste.

'Oh, her neck. Look at her neck. Isn't it lovely?' his mother whispered while the Italian barber fell in love with Audrey Hepburn and asked her to go dancing with him down by the river.

Toshi looked up at his mother and, turning around in his seat, at the chattering women in the theater, the wives and daughters of fishermen, farmers, and loggers. Their broad, weathered faces tilted up toward the screen, their mouths filled with gold and silver teeth, stuffed with potatoes and rice. Their flat faces lit up by flickering light, brought to life by a shimmering Audrey Hepburn. Audrey happy. Audrey mad. Audrey dancing by the river with her barber. Audrey so sad it almost broke Toshi's heart.

He took off his shoes and squatted on the seat, stared so hard at Audrey Hepburn that his forehead hurt. Whenever she disappeared from the screen, even if only for a moment, he couldn't sit still, rocked from side to side looking for her. Where was she? What was she doing?

'Do you need to go to the toilet?' his mother asked.

Toshi was only nine years old, but he could see the difference between those women in the movie theater and the woman up on the screen. And he knew, and his little penis knew, which he preferred. On his ninth birthday, Toshiyuki Okamoto experienced the first important, the first truly rhapsodic, erection of his young life. It sprang to attention in the haircut scene and beat like a heart for Audrey Hepburn throughout the entire second reel of *Roman Holiday*, waning only slightly during the credits.

* * *

'It's the milk,' his mother told him. She took her handkerchief out of her purse, unfolded a daisy chain of Mickey and Minnie Mouses, and smoothed it out on her lap.

It was still early, and they were the only customers in the restaurant. Behind the counter, the chef watched TV as he lifted dripping slices of green pepper and sweet potato out of the batter bowl and dropped them into hot oil, where they sizzled.

'Foreigners drink lots of milk growing up. That's why they're so tall and good-looking.'

Her dinner arrived, two giant tempura prawns on top of a bowl of glossy rice. She picked at it with her chopsticks without really noticing it.

'After the war, we didn't have real milk. There was only powdered milk from the Americans. And it was so expensive.'

Toshi listened carefully, for his mother rarely talked about her life before he knew her.

'When we first got television – Can you imagine, there was a time when we didn't have television? – almost everything we watched was from America. On American television, people drank milk all the time. They drank it like water, they drank it from big glass bottles, like it was free.'

She rested her chopsticks on her pickle plate and absently wiped her mouth with her Mickey and Minnie Mouse handkerchief. 'I used to cry when I watched Americans drink milk on television.'

The waitress brought Toshi's dinner, and the Coca-Cola he'd ordered.

'Mother,' he whispered, embarrassed that the waitress might hear him. 'I don't want Coke. I want a glass of milk. Ask her to change it. Please.'

'They don't have milk here. Drink your Coke. I'll buy you some milk later.'

'Mother?'

'What?'

'What about before the war? Did you have big bottles of milk to drink before the war?'

He watched as her face abruptly turned pale, and she spread her fingers out on the table's edge as if to steady herself. Toshi braced himself for an earthquake, but none came. She didn't say anything, and it seemed to him as if everything else suddenly went quiet too. The TV on the counter, the trickle of early evening traffic outside. Just when he thought he might have done something wrong, she spoke.

'Before the war there was nothing. There was no "before the war." Now eat your dinner before it gets cold.'

She turned to watch the TV on the counter.

The street door slid open. The blue curtains parted, and Audrey Hepburn walked into the restaurant. Her hair was short.

'Hello,' she said. 'My, what a handsome young boy you are. And your tempura looks so delicious. May I try some?'

She sat down in the empty chair next to his, gracefully, like a princess.

'I'm so lonely,' she said. 'Do you think I could come home with you? I could come and take care of you.'

Audrey Hepburn smiled at Toshi. She was so beautiful it took his breath away.

'I could bathe you, and I'd scrub your back. We could take a bath together.'

Toshi looked at his mother. She was removing a prawn's tail from her mouth with her fingers as she watched TV: The studio audience applauded as a girl in a bikini poured cartons of milk all over her body, then stepped inside a glass booth filled with kittens.

'Oh, yes,' he said to Audrey Hepburn. 'Yes, please come home and take a bath with me.'

'Now that it's your birthday, I don't know what to do . . .'

Jane sings as she slips down under the sheets.

Her soft head of hair vanishes as she nibbles her way down his chest and stomach.

'Can't give you a Cadillac or a penthouse with a view . . .'

Still serenading him as she disappears. He thinks, A fish. A cat. An animal from America I don't know yet.

She keeps singing, but now she slurs the words. Anyway, Toshi isn't listening anymore. A red scarf is draped over the lampshade, and a quivering light reveals framed woodblock prints on the walls of Jane's apartment: Geishas draw back the folds of their kimonos. Curtains of colored silk. Green, yellow, plum. Tempting. The skin of ripe fruit peeled back to display the pulp. The geishas smile with blackened teeth as they are entered by samurai, swords unsheathed, robes and sashes flung back and suspended in midair.

He is having drunken visions. Jane's futon is crowded with naked women – pale breasts, sweaty triangles of blond hair, damp darkness behind the knee where he buries his head. The powdery fold of an arm envelops him. Toshi feels Jane's fingernails tear at the skin on his backside, as they roll off the futon onto the kitchen linoleum and crash into a shopping bag of empty beer cans. And there's Audrey Hepburn! Young, bare-shouldered Audrey. Sabrina. She runs across a sweeping lawn at night toward the lights and the music, her cranelike neck stretched forward, her neck white as milk.

* * *

'Oh, what I've done,' Jane laughs. 'This must be against the rules.'

They are lying side by side in the dark. It's the middle of the night. Toshi, exhausted, tentatively explores his own body, discovers bruises, scratches, and bites. He winces each time he touches a new one, yet he is more astonished than disturbed by sex with Jane.

'What's against the rules?' he asks. His eyes are open, but he sees nothing in the darkness. He is aware of the greasy smell of her tiny kitchen behind them, and of her voice. And then a thought flickers briefly: Could she hurt me? Could sex with Jane be dangerous?

'A teacher seducing her student. If the school finds out, they might fire me.' She turns on the floor lamp and smiles at him. 'Or maybe all of my students will want to sleep with me.'

He shuts his eyes, opens them, and reaches out to touch the albino tiger on her breast. He's never known a woman with a tattoo.

'Students and teachers often sleep together in Japan. Even in high school,' he says.

Jane laughs. 'You're lying to make me feel better.' She picks up a pack of Cheerful cigarettes from the floor, shakes one out into her mouth. 'Jane, Jane. She's an evil seductress. A corrupter of children.'

'I'm twenty-three. I'm not a child.'

She lights her cigarette, snaps the lighter shut.

'Jane is thirty. A cradle robber.'

He pictures her running across a dark landscape with a baby under each arm. 'Why did you get a tattoo?' he asks, purposely distracting her, disturbed by the image, and by her use of the third person. Is this proper English? Does sex change usage?

'You don't like it?' She shifts her weight to her elbow so that the tiger rests on his arm. Her breast is cool.

'It's my animal. The Year of the Tiger. My last boyfriend forced me to get it. He got me drunk and then dragged me to this tattooist. He ordered me to do it.'

'He ordered you?' The way she's smiling, is she making up a story for him?

'I often find myself with men who order me to do things.'

He doesn't say anything. She exhales smoke in his face, then puts out her cigarette. He shuts his eyes.

'Would you order me to do things?' she asks, stroking the inside of his leg. His penis flip-flops onto his thigh like a fish. Once he and Taro were fishing, and Taro caught a salmon so big it flipped over in the boat and landed on Taro's foot, breaking a bone.

'God, you have the most incredible skin. I can't stop touching it. It gives me goose bumps. Feel?' She leans over and presses the tiger against his face, and he does feel the bumps rising on her breast. He gasps for air. She slides down and bites him hard.

Just before dawn, Toshi wakes up, and for a moment he thinks he is back in Rausu, above the noodle shop. And he remembers: three narrow mattresses laid side by side, the edges touching, Toshi in the middle.

The pillows were hard, stuffed with buckwheat husks. In the winter, the three of them shared two old wool blankets that crackled when his mother took them from the closet each night. Asleep, his parents rolled toward the middle, toward him, for warmth. His father snored, exhaling tobacco, soy sauce, and beer. His mother sweated green tea and miso. Sometimes she'd sigh a name. Toshi. Fumio, his father. She'd murmur nonsense words he didn't understand, another language. And she wept in her sleep. Dreaming, she'd toss about as if at sea, her restlessness waking him. Toshi drifted in and out of sleep, back and forth between his parents. Away from his father's stink into his mother's moist sadness and back again to his father.

In the summer he and his father slept in their cotton underwear. But even on the hottest nights, his mother wore a nightgown and pulled the sheet up to her chin. He never saw her body. Some nights, his snoring father's penis poked out of his shorts and bobbed like the mast on a fishing boat. Once Toshi awoke to see his father erect, his hand sliding up and down. His eyes were squeezed tightly shut, and from the terrible expression on his face and from his loud breathing, Toshi thought he was having a nightmare. He looked as if he were running away from something.

At twenty-three, Toshi's childhood memories of his father are as remote as Shiretoko Peninsula is from Tokyo, where Toshi now lives – images from an old film he might have seen on television. His father stands at the end of the road, the flat sea on one side, the noodle shop on the other, bowing as a customer drives away. He wears a white apron, and his hair is cropped close as an athlete's, the sides shaved right down to his skull. His wristwatch flashes in the sunlight like a gold tooth. The road is gravel, and the departing car stirs up dust. The car is white. Back then, all cars in Japan were white.

The white car and white apron. Dust. The masts of the fishing boats bobbing and nodding. The hills of the Russian islands dim as dreams. His father bows and shouts, 'Thank you. Drive carefully. Thank you. Please come again. Thank you very much.' He bows over and over again as the driver, who cannot possibly see or hear him any longer, disappears down the road.

Toshi's childhood memories of his mother are both more vivid and more troubling. Sometimes they are illuminated by dazzling winter sunlight. They walk together along plowed roads after the first snow, following the skittering tracks of antelope. The world has been turned upside down, she tells him as she points out a stand of white birch whose leafless trunks and branches stretch up out of the snow like frosty roots into the blue sky. Under the snow, where the black bears sleep, fantastic trees are in bloom, she says. And he believes her. But on many other days: a slate sky over a colorless sea. His mother sits motionless and silent at the back window while the teakettle whistles on and on.

Toshi was eight when his mother left them to go live at the inn in Utoro, where she had been working weekends for a year. His father closed the noodle shop to drive her to the bus stop, and Toshi went along, sitting in the backseat of their shiny white car. His father kept the car washed and polished year-round.

'I can take you over to Utoro. There's time before dinner,' he said as they drove down the coast road, passing three naked old women. The mother of the butcher and the sisters who ran the laundry waddled like sea lions over the dark rocks toward the narrow strip of beach, where bubbling pools of hot spring water sent up clouds of steam. Toshi could smell the sulphur through the closed windows.

'That's too much trouble. The bus is fine,' his mother said.

They didn't say anything else until they reached the bus stop and she opened the car door.

'Better to wait in the car. It's cold out,' his father said.

'It's all right. The bus will be here soon.'

She opened the trunk and lifted out her big suitcase and shoulder bag. His mother was a strong woman. She'd lifted mattresses, cartons of radishes and onions. Buckets of water. Toshi. She carried her luggage to the bus shelter, and her green rubber boots broke through the thin ice, made a crunching sound. Each step she took away from him, Toshi winced with pain.

She came back to the car, opened the door, and looked hard at him. He wanted to turn away.

'You help your father in the shop.'

'Yes, I will,' he said, holding back his tears.

In the front seat, his father turned around to watch them.

'And do your schoolwork.'

'Yes.'

'Saturdays, after school, you come over on the bus and spend the night. Your father will bring you to the bus every Saturday, all right?'

'All right,' he said. What choice did he have? Who decided that his mother should leave?

She looked at his father. 'Thank you for driving me.'

'Take good care of yourself,' he said. 'If you need anything, you call me.'

His father's face was so rigid it looked like it would break if he moved it. Toshi couldn't bear to look at him. He turned to his mother. Her lips trembled, parting slightly as if there was something she was struggling to say. But no words came out. Snow clouds over the Russian islands moved quickly toward them. The three of them waited – for the bus, for the snow, for their lives to change – under a mute winter sky.

At last, she spoke. 'I'm sorry.'

His father's head fell forward so suddenly it startled Toshi. It was as if the weight of it was intolerable. He shut his eyes and didn't answer her.

She turned back to Toshi, in his bright yellow school cap

and red mittens, pressed tight against the seat. She was crying.

'Bye-bye, Toshi-chan.'

His mother waited but he, too, refused to reply. She closed the door and walked back to the bus shelter, her boots cracking the ice. His father turned the car around and they headed home. Toshi waved from the back window until he couldn't see his mother anymore.

He tells Jane the story, how his mother left, how he still remembers details: Driving home without her. Toshi alone in the backseat, waiting for his father to say something. His father silent. The smell of sulphur as they passed the hot springs again. He climbed the stairs to the front room while his father stayed down in the noodle shop. Looking out the window at the falling snow and the sea, he listened to the steady rocking of the knife blade on the cutting board, like waves breaking on the shore.

Jane shakes her head. 'That's so sad. That's an awful story. I think I might cry.'

They are sitting naked at her *kotatsu*, their bare feet touching under the thick quilt. She pours strong coffee into Japanese tea bowls. Dusty sunlight streams in through the high windows, lighting up the room and the framed woodblock prints. He wasn't imagining them last night. Toshi pulls the edge of the quilt up to cover his bruised chest.

'You mean your mother didn't even kiss you or hug you when she left? She just walked away?'

'My mother never kissed or hugged me,' he says, and he

tries to remember, Did his mother ever touch him at all, for any reason? Jane is rubbing the inside of his thighs with her warm feet, so it's difficult to concentrate, to think about his mother.

'But didn't you want her to? That day? Wouldn't it have made you feel better?'

She slides over to stroke his hair, then his hard penis, as if to comfort him, so many years later. His American girlfriends always do this for him: try to make up for what they decide he's missed in his life. Briefly he remembers the shame of a schoolboy whose mother left him behind. He shivers as Jane bends over and takes him in her mouth. He feels her hand slide up the crack in his ass, then her finger tap, tap, tapping. He tenses. This is something new.

'If she had touched me that day,' he says, his voice tight and high, 'I would have known for sure that something was wrong.'

The abrupt transition into bright sunlight. Three children on bicycles ride up and down the narrow lane in front of Jane's building, laughing. A girl in a pink dress skips down the lane, towing a unicycle.

'Yumi-chan! Good morning!' her friends shout.

'Good morning! Good morning!' She mounts her unicycle confidently, and they all ride circles around Toshi as he walks toward the main street.

He is startled by the light, by the cheerful children, and by the potted red geraniums and powdery green aloe vera, by the flower boxes of tulips lined up in front of each house. Morning glory vines stretch up a homemade wire lattice. High above his head, mattresses and quilts float like clouds out of bedroom windows. White undershirts flap, scattering sunlight.

Toshi is troubled by his night with Jane. He feels uneasy, as if he has made a mistake, or has unintentionally done something he shouldn't have. Suddenly, he longs for Hokkaido's wide, clear skies. Even now, scattered clouds threaten to end this spring morning's sunshine. He doesn't want to go home, so he walks past the subway station, keeps on walking, in and out of unfamiliar neighborhoods, looking for distractions. Pretty housewives in jeans and aprons hurry along the streets with grocery bags, their white sneakers smacking the pavement.

He still doesn't know Tokyo above ground, how its parts relate, so he follows distant landmarks. The hotels of Akasaka, the metallic skyscrapers of Shinjuku. He passes doughnut shops and noodle stands. A shopkeeper washes down the sidewalk with a bucket of water, then hangs out his blue curtain. Toshi turns corners to be delighted: yellow plastic clothespins clipped to a fence top like a row of tropical birds. The scaffolding of a new building wrapped up in blue netting. Web-footed construction workers, their flaring pantaloons like wings. A tall black man in brilliant African robes sits in the window of a McDonald's drinking coffee. Abalone shells piled waist high outside a fish restaurant.

A heavy truck screeches to a stop. 'Turning left. Turning left. Turning left,' the truck's speaker squawks. He crosses the street to a grassy slope lined with cherry trees. Down below, on a tennis court, girls in white dart around like petals scattered by the wind. He can hear the pleasing *thwack* of the balls. Behind the court, a subway train emerges from a tunnel and pulls up to the station platform.

Toshi has never been in this part of the city, and he feels like a tourist, like he did the first time he saw Tokyo. Excited yet uneasy. Waiting for something to happen. This morning, he senses, is caught just between the seasons. The train doors open to reveal small groups of schoolgirls chattering and laughing, clusters of blossoms, their white uniform shirts ruffled by sunlight and breeze. Toshi stands above them, unsure of himself, trying to decide which way to go.

2

When he was seventeen years old, Toshi traveled to Tokyo to take the entrance examination for the National Art University.

'Tokyo is a big city. Be careful,' his mother said on the telephone the morning he left.

'Please don't worry.'

'You've never been out of Hokkaido. You don't know about life. People aren't all nice.'

Her warning didn't surprise him. His mother had always been suspicious of the world. There were things about her he accepted but would never understand.

His father drove him to the airport in Nakashibetsu. They drove in silence down the peninsula, then inland. They watched the mountains disappear behind them and the land flatten out. The forest ended, replaced by farms and ranches, and in every direction there were only silver grain silos on the horizon, and tight herds of rice white Hokkaido cows stomping up dust clouds. The fields were cleared for the winter, the dark earth deserted except for scarecrows clothed in old baseball uniforms, flapping uselessly in the cold wind.

'I've never been on an airplane,' his father said.

'This is my first time,' Toshi said.

It was always awkward when they found themselves together outside of the noodle shop or their rooms upstairs. They stood inside the small terminal, waiting for Toshi's flight to be called. The concrete building seemed to float on the frozen prairie below the blue sky. His father bought a can of hot coffee from a vending machine. Toshi's blue and white school duffel bag hung around his neck on a wide strap. He rocked back and forth on his heels, and the bag bounced against his stomach, a comforting weight.

His father handed him an envelope. 'Your life will be much different from mine. It already is, I guess.'

He opened it. It was filled with ten-thousand-yen notes.

'Father, this is too much.'

'No. You'll need it. It's very expensive in Tokyo, people say.'

He put the envelope in his pocket and bowed. 'Thank you.'

'Do your best.'

'Yes. I will try hard.'

'And after the examination is over, go out and have a good time.'

His flight was announced. Toshi and his father looked at each other. Neither of them smiled.

The Emperor was dying. The plane was filled with passengers clutching tiny Japanese flags, red suns on white. As they approached Tokyo, the rice fields and dense clusters of houses and apartment buildings abruptly ended and gave way to rolling turf and narrow stands of trees. Golf courses surrounded the city like a brilliant green moat. Toshi watched from the window as Tokyo itself came into view, an absence of color like the insides of an enormous machine. The immensity frightened him. He felt the plane suddenly drop down, and he grabbed the armrests, thinking something had gone wrong. But the flight attendants walked up and down the aisle with plastic bags, collecting paper cups and candy wrappers, and chatting with the passengers. The no-smoking sign lit up.

Pushing through the crowds and commotion in the terminal, Toshi fought off unexpected feelings of loneliness and confusion: so many faces, and dialects he barely understood. The Emperor's gaunt visage was on the cover of every magazine and newspaper. TV monitors showed crowds waiting in the rain outside the Imperial Palace, praying, and waving their tiny flags. An old farmer and his wife prostrated themselves in front of a monitor and shouted, '*Banzai! Banzai!*' Passengers and baggage handlers and counter clerks bowed, their flags falling forward all at once like a flock of seagulls alighting. Confused, Toshi bowed too. His duffel bag swung out into space.

White-gloved hands shoved him in through the doors of the airport monorail, and he pressed his face to the glass as the train emerged from the station, then sped past factories and smokestacks, a deserted race track, muddy baseball diamonds. A multitiered driving range where golfers in rain slickers balanced on the edge of space and swung their gleaming clubs. Gray canals crisscrossed under gray, congested roads under a gray sky. He looked for trees. He suddenly felt homesick. Nothing was familiar except for the names, huge letters on the roofs of warehouses and glass and steel office buildings: Sony. Panasonic. Coca-Cola. The train glided into the station, and Toshi was unnerved: There were more people waiting on the platform than all the people who lived in Rausu and Utoro combined.

Toshi wore his high school uniform as required: black shoes polished, new white socks, black pants and jacket freshly pressed and buttoned up to the neck. In his pants pockets, he fingered a good luck charm that Granny had ordered from a shrine in Tohoku that specialized in amulets for school entrance exams. Before he entered the auditorium, he removed his black cap, bowed, and had his head shaved and his underwear checked.

'Regulation white.' The guard nodded and stamped a sheet of paper.

The girl just ahead of him was rejected because her braided hair had red highlights.

She burst into tears. 'Please. I beg you. I live in Okinawa. It's from the sun.'

'Go dye it black and come back next year,' the guard told her.

Except for English and art classes, Toshi had never been much of a student. Halfway through the examination, he knew he wouldn't pass. Still, there was something reassuring about sitting in a huge auditorium with students from all over Japan dressed exactly as he was. They wore name tags pinned to their jackets. There were dozens of Yamamotos, Ishikawas, Tanakas, Matsudas, Muratas. He had counted at least six other Okamotos. Could they be related? His parents had told him he had no relatives.

When the exam was over, four students carried a giant photo of the Emperor onto the stage, and they all stood in a groundswell. He stood, too, then knelt and pressed his forehead to the gritty floor.

A few students stayed in their seats.

'The flag is a symbol of the military. The Emperor is responsible for the Pacific War,' one boy shouted. A monitor slapped him repeatedly on the face, backing him down the aisle past Toshi. Watanabe, his name tag read. The big metal doors slammed shut, echoed through the cavernous hall.

'What an idiot,' someone whispered. 'Now he can't go to college.'

Toshi felt the same way. What difference did it make?

He didn't care about the Emperor one way or another. The Emperor was just an old, sick man.

He explored the city. In Seibu department store, people shopped for clothes and furniture, had their teeth fixed, bought houses and Hawaiian vacations. There was a wedding chapel on the seventh floor. In the basement, housewives crowded around bins of fresh crabs flown in from Alaska, mangoes from the Philippines, melons packed in velvet that sold for ten thousand yen each. And they bought them!

There was an art gallery on the fifth floor. All the department stores had galleries. He recognized the French Impressionists' paintings, but most everything else – a glass-enclosed ant farm modeled on the Japanese flag; six-foot-high, chrome rabbits; a room webbed with rope – confounded him. At Parco department store in Shibuya, an American photographer's pictures of naked black men and longstemmed flowers. This was art? Toshi drew pictures of fishing boats, forests, his father. The gallery was crowded with people, but still he felt he was seeing something forbidden, and that excited him.

He was fascinated by the mammoth train stations, bigger than towns, millions of people passing through them every day. Ueno. Tokyo. Ikebukuro. The morning after the examination, he ate his breakfast in Shinjuku Station. He stood at a coffee bar with a bean paste-filled doughnut in his hand and watched commuters pour out of the trains with their briefcases, comic books, newspapers, and rolled umbrellas. How could he go back to Rausu? he wondered.

Out on the streets, smiling girls in jackets emblazoned with cigarette brand names – Shiny Stars, Clean Spirit, Lark – pressed sample packs into his hands before he could say, No, thank you. Men in sunglasses stuffed his pockets with packets of facial tissue – pictures of bare-breasted girls, advertisements for hostess bars and saunas. Passersby poked him with umbrellas and lit cigarettes and stepped on his new shoes. He hobbled back to the hotel on swollen feet.

In his tiny room, he hung up his jacket, which was flecked with cigarette burns. Now he wanted to go home. He bought a beer from a vending machine in the hall, turned on the TV, and sprawled on the bed. A group of children dressed as cockroaches scurried around onstage chased by a giant can of insect repellent. Running across the bottom of the screen, the day's body count of dead office workers followed by a warning: 'If you are working more than sixteen hours a day and experiencing chest pains, headaches, or shortness of breath, call this number.' Outside his window, packed commuter trains crisscrossed a clogged freeway. The afternoon sky was crowded with blimps – Fuji Film, Nissan, Sapporo Beer – that flashed the dying Emperor's blood pressure and rectal body temperature.

He bought *ramen* from a vending machine. Exhausted, he looked down into the steaming Styrofoam bowl and saw his father lean over the stove. His mother, before she left them, came through the back door of the noodle shop, her arms filled with ladder ferns, tears streaming down her face. He slept. In his dream, Audrey Hepburn and his mother ran hand in hand through a rice field.

There were English words everywhere, in store windows, on neon signs, on billboards: WOMEN'S. FASHION. SPAGHETTI. FASHION. PIZZA. COFFEE. WHISKEY. AMERICAN JEANS. LET'S KIOSK. And restaurants and clubs: YES CAFE. CASUAL HOUSE. LOVE BURGER. PIT INN. And there were foreigners in the streets. They darted through the crowds like sleek, dangerous fish, appearing suddenly, startling Toshi with their sharp faces and bright eyes. Their blue-tinged complexions and long noses seemed assertive, conscious choices, along with their loud voices and exaggerated hand gestures. They pushed through Tokyo's crowds carelessly, with shocking self-assurance. Seeing them up so close made Toshi giddy. He followed two middle-aged women for blocks, in and out of Mitsukoshi department store and through an underground shopping arcade until a poster advertising an English-language school brought him to a sudden stop. A smiling young woman with long blond hair leaned against a surfboard and opened her arms to him. CALIFORNIA KATHY IS ONE OF OUR TEACHERS said the ad for the Very Romantic English Academy. He stared at her picture while rush-hour crowds jostled him. He imagined himself dazzling California Kathy with his command of English. 'I like American movies. Do you eat raw fish? Can you use chopsticks?'

At the souvenir stand inside Tokyo Tower, he bought a guidebook, *Where to Spot Foreigners in Tokyo*. It fit in his jacket pocket. He sat in a red booth at a spaghetti restaurant and read the bold-print warnings on the inside cover:

1. Avoid Caucasian and black men with very short haircuts. They are American soldiers. They often get drunk and violent.
2. Beware of Asians who try to sell you foreign rice at low prices. Foreign rice is illegal. Also, it is treated with many pesticides that cause serious health problems.
3. Foreigners carry AIDS and other diseases from abroad that are easily transmitted by sharing food and utensils, touching, and, of course, sexual activity. Please be careful!

In high school history class, Toshi had learned how Japan, closed off by law to the rest of the world for centuries, had remained pure while Europe had been devastated by waves of deadly plagues. And in hygiene class, he and his classmates had gasped and tittered when the teacher told them: Foreigners sit in their own dirty bathwater.

His spaghetti arrived, topped with sea urchin and shredded seaweed. He sprinkled on grated cheese.

Saturday night, he took the subway to Roppongi, where, according to the photographs in his guidebook, foreign models danced in the discos. As the train sped through dark tunnels, he stared furtively at the pictures: exotic women under mirrored lights, their long bare limbs shimmering like wolf willow. Nature studies. Cranes in flight. Heat rose up from vents under the velvet seats and made him sweat.

A rowdy group of foreigners scrambled aboard, and the other passengers backed away to make room for their extravagant bodies and raw laughter. Toshi started to move toward them, when he noticed that two of the women were staring at him. He stopped, afraid that something was wrong. But their crayon-colored eyes wandered over his body, and they looked at each other and raised their eyebrows. He didn't mistake that look, for he'd seen it in many American movies. He felt his face redden. Woozy, and suddenly emboldened with a sense of possibility, he stared back.

'Roppongi. Roppongi is next,' the conductor's voice came over the loudspeakers.

A small earthquake shook the station, and three sumo wrestlers came crashing down the stairs like a tidal wave. Toshi, frightened, ran past them, up toward the exit. He burst out onto the street under the roaring shadow of an elevated freeway. A giant TV screen flickered like summer fireworks, illuminating the crowds. Two stories high, the new prime minister announced his resignation, then bowed low as a stream of numbers raced across his knees: the dying Emperor's vital signs, followed by the weather. Cloudy. Occasional rain.

Instead of his map, Toshi followed light, constellations of

bar signs, video screens, traffic signals, the headlights of taxi cabs and motor scooters. The lights of a TV camera crew held high on poles like festival lanterns.

'Here's one!' the announcer shrieked, and she thrust a microphone into the face of a tall, red-headed foreigner.

Red hair! He'd never seen red hair before except in cartoons. His hair reminded Toshi of something. A flash of color in a sunlit meadow. A spring bird.

The lights blinked. The announcer moved in.

'Excuse me. Excuse me. You from America? Yes? You are?'

'Yes, I'm American.' He smiled warily.

An American! He didn't know that Americans had red hair. He watched the foreigner's hand go up to brush the hair back from his forehead, and the pale underside of his arm was incandescent in the lights.

The announcer turned to the camera, spoke Japanese: 'This man is a genuine American. But look at his hair color. Do you think it's real? Maybe he dyes it, I think. We've just come upon him walking the streets of Roppongi. Perhaps he's searching for a Japanese girlfriend. I'll bet he's headed for a disco right now to pick up a Japanese girl.'

The American looked past the announcer, right at Toshi, and rolled his eyes. Startled, Toshi backed away, out of the lights. Why did he do that? They didn't know each other. The announcer was being rude, but what was he expected to do?

'Excuse me. Excuse me, but do you have AIDS by any chance? Do you bring AIDS to Japan?' she shouted, grinning.

Everyone looked at the American and waited. Why was everyone so interested in this AIDS? The American didn't look sick. He looked healthy. He had a kind, handsome face, Toshi decided. And that hair! He edged closer again.

The American spoke excellent Japanese: 'You're a foolish

girl. And very rude.' He leaned over and kissed her on the cheek. 'If I have AIDS, now you do too.'

She screamed. 'I'm infected!'

The lights clicked off.

'Get me a hot towel, quick! Get me some antiseptic!'

The cameraman lit a Marlboro. 'Just our luck. The producer said no Japanese-speakers. Let's go look for another foreigner.'

The American turned and walked away, past a French bakery, a Korean barbecue restaurant, a branch of the famous Ginza coffee shop, Cozy Corner. Toshi ran after him.

'Wait for me, please,' he shouted, amazed at himself. What was he doing?

They stood in front of the station.

'I apologize. It was a terrible way to treat a visitor to Japan.' Toshi bowed, light-headed, his first real encounter with a foreigner. He couldn't believe his own courage. Is this what happened to people when they came to Tokyo: They turned into different people?

'It's not your fault.' The American bowed. 'My name is Paul Swift. I'm pleased to meet you.'

He was about twenty-five years old. Maybe thirty. Foreigners' ages were difficult to judge. Toshi bowed again. 'I'm pleased to meet you. My name is Okamoto, but please call me Toshi.'

'And you should call me Paul.'

'I like foreigners,' Toshi assured him, still worried that he'd been offended by the TV announcer.

'Is that so? Well, I like the Japanese. We're very lucky to have met then, aren't we?'

'Yes. I like Audrey Hepburn. Do you know her?'

Paul Swift rolled his eyes again.

A dozen Indian women in blue saris swept into the

station, a breeze on their backs. Toshi turned toward them, astonished at how quickly his life was changing.

Paul took him to a small bar in Shinjuku where Japanese and English conversation floated through the air, mingled with the cigarette smoke, and made him dizzy. The master brought over hot towels and a plate of peanuts and dried squid.

'I like this music,' Toshi said in English, not really hearing it but knowing he should say something.

'Ella Fitzgerald.'

'Yes.' Was that a kind of music?

'She's a black American singer.'

'Yes. I like American singers.'

'Really? Like who?'

'Yes.'

Their beers arrived. Paul sipped. Toshi gulped his. He'd never been in a bar before. He'd never talked to a foreigner. Everything was moving so fast.

'So, what sport do you play?' Paul asked.

'Sport?'

'Judging from your shaved head, you're either a Buddhist monk, which seems unlikely, or an athlete.'

'I am a student,' he said, hoping it was the right answer.

Paul smiled. 'Which university?'

He felt himself blush. 'I am in high school.'

Paul slapped his forehead and spun around on his stool, said something in English Toshi didn't understand.

'What?'

'Jailbait,' he repeated slowly. 'Two syllables.'

Toshi had gone to Roppongi that night looking for foreign women to draw. He had his sketch pad in his day pack. But there were only men in this bar. So he stared hard at Paul, memorizing his features – his wide, smiling mouth, his deep-set eyes – imagining him in pencil and charcoal. Suddenly he realized that Paul was staring back at him. He looked away, embarrassed, and scrambled for something to say.

'What is your job?'

Paul grinned and passed him his business card. Densu. The biggest advertising agency in Japan. Copywriter.

'This is a very great company. You are a smart man, I think.'

Paul grinned. 'That's true.'

He thought of another question.

'Are you married?'

'No.'

'You have a girlfriend?'

'No, no girlfriend.'

'You like Japanese girls?'

'I like Japanese boys.'

Toshi laughed. Americans were funny.

Paul looked at his watch.

'It's after midnight. The trains have stopped running. You'll have to take a taxi back to your hotel, and they're very hard to get at this hour.'

'That's all right. The hotel is nearby.'

'Oh. Just my luck.'

'Yes. Very lucky.'

'No, that's not . . .'

'Yes?'

'That is, if you wanted to, you could stay at my apartment. It would be a new experience for you. A foreigner's apartment.'

'Really? I could?' He didn't understand why so many people were scared of foreigners. Paul was kind and generous. Toshi finished his fourth – or was it his fifth? – beer. 'Yes, please. I'm looking forward to it.'

'So am I. It should be an interesting night.'

Paul signaled for the bill, then took out his wallet.

* * *

He was afraid to walk across the thick carpeting, to touch the white furniture. The chairs and the sofa were so big and soft that when he sat down he felt like he was being swallowed up. But there were surfaces he had to be careful of too. Glass and metal, table edges that could cut him. He couldn't plot a straight line across any of the rooms. And he might lose himself in the apartment, he realized, already confused by the number and spaciousness of the rooms, and by their foreignness. Unfamiliar shapes and textures like new ideas.

There were two bedrooms.

'You live here alone?'

'Yes.' Paul turned on the stereo. Japanese music. Shamisen. He collected Asian art. Chinese scrolls and Japanese woodblock prints hung on the walls. Toshi recognized a Hokusai.

'Is it real?'

'Yes. Real.'

'Expensive?' He had seen Hokusai only in books.

'I suppose.' Paul poured him a glass of white wine.

Here was something else: He'd never held a wineglass. It was shaped like a stemmed flower. He lifted it with two hands, as he would a sake cup, one hand cupping the base, and swallowed the wine all at once.

'No, no, no. Wine, you sip. Like this.'

Paul showed him, then poured him another glass.

Over the toilet, there was a framed photograph of a Japanese man in a loincloth, his muscular body tensed, the red sun flag behind him. The grim expression on his face and the sword in his hand disturbed Toshi.

'Who is he?'

'That's Mishima.'

'Who?'

'You don't know Yukio Mishima? The writer?'

Toshi shook his head. There was so much he didn't know, even about Japan, it seemed. He was tired and drunk, and he walked through a dream of colors: Paul's red hair, his own blue-socked feet sinking into the gray carpeting. Paul's bed was as big as the room he slept in with his father, the blanket the color of squid just pulled from the sea. Toshi took off his pants and slid between two cotton sheets. Had his parents' heads ever rested on such soft pillows? Paul's arm slipped around his waist, and Toshi supposed, half-asleep already, that this was how Americans showed their friendship.

'You know, when I first saw you on the street, I thought you were so handsome,' Paul whispered. 'And then you turned out to be so nice, and smart, too.'

No one had ever complimented him like this before. He was in one of the American movies he and his mother often went to see. He sat on white sofas and sipped white wine. His own skin was white. Toshi saw himself laugh as Americans laugh: uninhibited, his head thrown back, a flash of even, white teeth. He fell asleep.

When he was a boy, his parents once took him to Sapporo for the Snow Festival, and they ate breakfast at Denny's, an American restaurant: fried eggs with strips of bacon, a tomato salad with mayonnaise, corn soup, and a scoop of fried rice with a tiny American flag planted in the top. So the breakfast Paul served disappointed him. Bananas and strawberries and orange juice in the blender. French toast, which Paul explained wasn't French at all but American. The maple syrup, though, was thick and sweet, the way he imagined all American food to be. Paul told him it came from trees, and Toshi laughed at this. He wanted to fill up a glass and drink it.

Then Paul said, 'I like men.'

Toshi nodded and reached for the syrup again.

'Do you know what I mean?'

He shook his head, confused.

'I'm attracted to men, not women,' Paul said. Toshi stared down at his plate and pushed the last piece of toast around in the syrup. What was Paul telling him? It was probably just another one of those foreigner things. He wanted more French toast.

Then Paul said, 'I'm gay.'

Startled, Toshi looked up. He knew *gay*. It was the same word in English and Japanese. Paul was staring at him, and it made him uncomfortable.

'I brought you home expecting to have sex with you. But don't worry. Nothing happened last night. We just went to sleep.'

Sex with Paul. He couldn't imagine it. Toshi had never had sex, but he knew who he wanted to have sex with. A foreign woman. Audrey Hepburn. Certainly not with Paul. It was such an absurd idea that he almost smiled. But he stopped himself.

'Please forgive me. I still think you're handsome and smart and nice, and I'd like to be your friend.'

He didn't answer. He didn't know what to say. Paul's words, and the bitter coffee, and the sweet maple syrup made his head hot.

In his hotel bathroom, there were illustrated instructions above the Western-style toilet: A stick-figure man squatted on top of the toilet seat – with a big red *X* through it. Below, another man used the toilet correctly, sitting on the seat as if it were a chair. But there were no stick figures in Paul's bathroom. He wasn't sure what to do. Shower, then fill up the tub and soak, then leave it filled for Paul? Or wash in the tub as Americans did? If he did that, how would he get clean? Paul's confession had made him uneasy, and unsure of himself. He wished that there were instructions for dealing with foreigners.

He looked at himself in the mirror. Paul had told him he was handsome, and those women had stared at him on the subway. But Toshi saw only his Japanese face and his hairless chest. At least his teeth were white and straight like an American's. His skin was too dark, though. And his black hair stood up in spikes when it was wet. He unwrapped his thick bath towel and looked down. His legs were as smooth as a girl's. He sighed.

When he was twelve years old, Toshi had met a foreigner at the inn in Utoro, and had seen the face and body he wanted to grow into. He memorized it. He drank milk, played on the school football team, and joined the judo club, willing a transformation of pigment, of features, and of size. Every morning he woke up and looked in the mirror. But now he was almost a man. He had grown up and nothing had changed.

His first glimpse of a foreigner disturbed him. A white rental car heading down the mountainside like a fleeting, troubled dream. Crossing Shiretoko Peninsula on a Saturday afternoon, Toshi sat behind the bus driver and gazed out at the soggy spring landscape through a haze of cigarette smoke. The bus pulled into the parking lot at the top of the ridge.

'Toshi-chan, look! Foreigners!'

A white rental car swung out of the lot and disappeared around a curve.

'Did you see them?' the bus driver, Mr Goto, asked.

'Yes, I saw them,' he lied, confused first by desire, then by shame.

'Scary-looking, weren't they?'

He opened the bus door. Two bird-watchers stepped down to the asphalt, their black binoculars swinging from their necks. Then the bus was on the road again, heading down the mountain, Toshi's face pressed against the window, his breath on the glass, visible, invisible, then visible again. Impatient, he could already see Utoro, a patch of gray scooped out of the coastline.

The rental car was parked in front of the inn, its tires splashed with mud. He ran up the stairs and stepped out of his shoes. His mother and Granny were in the kitchen, bent over a wooden tub of rice.

Granny laughed at his agitation. 'Oh, the foreigners. Yes, they're staying here. They just went off on a sightseeing boat.'

Three Australians, a man and two women. Granny had spoken to them.

'The man spoke very nice Japanese. I was surprised.'

'Do you know where Australia is?' his mother asked. She fanned the rice with a magazine while Granny poured on the vinegar.

'Near America?' He dipped a finger into the rice. 'Are we having sushi?'

'It's a special day. It's Granny's seventieth birthday.'

'Is it really your birthday?'

'Yes. I'm getting so old. And can you believe it, I have to make my own dinner.'

'I can help, and you can go rest.'

'No, no,' she laughed again. 'I enjoy cooking.'

'But what will the foreigners eat? They can't eat raw fish.'

'Oh dear, that's right,' his mother said.

'Well, they told me they could eat anything at all, and that's what they're getting.'

'In any case, we'd better give them forks and knives,' his mother said. She put down the magazine and started opening drawers.

'Did I ever tell you? I once delivered a foreign baby in Yokohama,' Granny said. 'About 1950, it was. I'll never forget. The parents were American. It was the most beautiful baby I'd ever seen.'

Granny made a cradle of her arms and rocked it, remembering. Toshi saw a perfect, pink-skinned, blue-eyed, smiling baby.

Taro said it made no difference to him, Japanese or foreigner, they were all the same, what was the fuss about? And he went off fishing. Toshi stayed behind to help his mother.

'I hope they understand that we don't have beds for them,' she said as they vacuumed the tatami, then carried the mattresses and quilts up to the roof to air. 'Maybe we should give them two mattresses each, so they'll be more comfortable. Of course, it will still seem primitive to them, won't it?'

It was the first time he ever heard her talk like this. Was the way they lived really so bad?

'And what shall we do about the bath?'

'What's wrong with the bath?' The inn had a nice bath. No one had ever complained.

'Foreigners wash themselves inside the bathtub, not outside. And they refill the tub for each person.'

'You're joking, aren't you?'

'No, it's true. Granny will have to explain to them.'

She lifted the last load of quilts, then stopped in the doorway and looked around the room, as if searching for something.

'I asked Taro to pick up meat and eggs, so we can make them a Western breakfast. Have we forgotten anything?'

The presence of foreigners at the inn had disturbed Toshi's mother. He watched anxiously as her face darkened. She turned and stepped off the tatami and into her slippers. From the back, she was twice divided by white apron strings, at the neck and at the waist.

'So many Australians were killed in the war. Terrible,' she said. He knew she was talking to herself.

'It's okay, Mother. The war was a long time ago, wasn't it?'

She didn't turn around, only repeated what he'd said. 'A long time ago. The war was a long time ago.'

She was already drifting away. He wanted to grasp her apron strings and pull her back. But he stayed put.

She sighed, and left the room. He listened to her slippers on the wood floor, then her slow, steady footfalls on the metal staircase to the roof.

Alone in the room, Toshi felt the shift in both mood and light. Outside, he knew without looking, the village of Utoro, the sea itself, had somehow altered. He could make no sense of what his mother had said, so, instead, he considered this: In *Roman Holiday*, Audrey Hepburn took a bath in Gregory Peck's apartment. If what she said was true, then Audrey Hepburn sat in her own dirty bathwater.

Toshi lathered the rough washcloth, dipped it in the plastic bucket, and scrubbed his body hard. Sitting on a low stool, he shampooed his hair, then filled the bucket with hot water and poured it over his head again and again. When he'd rinsed all the soap from his body, he stood up and walked across the bathroom. Cold air and afternoon sunlight poured in the open window and illuminated the gleaming stainless steel tub. He edged in, his ankles, then his shins. The ache entered his skin, seeped into his muscles and bones. His body absorbed the heat all the way up to his neck.

Outside, the five o'clock siren sounded. When he stood up, his dark skin was too tender to touch. He crossed the room and squatted in front of the mirror, watched the steam rise from his skin. He poured a bucket of cold water over his head, then pursed his wet lips, unsure of his own reflection.

The glass door slid open, and banged against its metal frame. In the mirror, he saw long, hairy legs and the hem of the inn's blue and white robe.

'Is it all right to use the bath now?'

He turned. The Australian stood in the doorway, obscured by shadow and steam, the dressing room's fluorescent light and green tile walls behind him. He was as tall as a tree. Toshi was too astonished to reply.

'Hello. Is it all right to use the bath?'

Light shone through his pink ears and shock of blond hair. The wall fan rotated and disturbed the cotton sleeves of his robe.

Toshi realized his rudeness and stood up. 'Yes. Please come in.' Bowing, he saw fragments of his own body – his knees, a shoulder, his penis – scattered on the wet tile like pieces of a puzzle. He kept his head down as the foreigner untied the sash of his robe, folded up the blue and white material, and stepped into the bathroom. A shrinking rectangle of sunlight traveled up past Toshi's head and glowed on the wall like a movie screen. Water dripped from a faucet into a yellow plastic bucket, each drop startling him.

'Hello,' the foreigner said, extending his hand.

Toshi couldn't stop himself; he reached out and ran his fingers up the man's thick arm to the elbow, turning the dense blond hair over like autumn grass.

The Australian laughed and stepped closer.

Toshi jerked his hand away, ashamed of what he'd done, then gasped when he saw the foreigner's penis – absurdly long, and thick as a matsutake mushroom. Dizzy, he looked down at his own hairless, translucent body. The landscape transformed. He crossed his hands over his tiny genitals.

'What's your name?' the Australian asked.

Toshi darted past him, tumbled out the door, and slammed it shut. He stood under the fluorescent light, shaking, swallowing air like a landed fish. And when he caught his own reflection in the mirror, he swooned. For he had become insubstantial, a phantasm of steam.

'I have a stomachache,' he told his mother.

She was surprised to find him under the quilt, his damp hair framed by the white pillowcase.

'You won't meet the foreigners if you don't come eat.'

'I can't eat.' He wouldn't tell her about the bath. She'd say he'd been rude.

'Granny will be disappointed.' She bent down and felt his forehead. 'You don't have a fever.'

'Really, I'm sick. I'll make Granny a drawing for her birthday tomorrow.'

'That would be nice.' She looked at him, uncertain, then closed the door behind her. Light from the street lamp hit the frosted window and broke into thousands of pieces.

Voices drifted out of the second-floor dining room, carried on the steady current of Taro's constant laughter. Alone in the dark, Toshi listened to the English words that flitted in and out of the dinner conversation like hummingbirds. The language of movies, of Audrey Hepburn, it hovered outside his door. He was hungry and miserable, ashamed of himself. He felt the heavy quilt press down upon his narrow frame until he almost disappeared into the mattress. Hummingbird wings beat furiously in his chest, and they stirred up a scene he would carry with him into the future:

The foreigner washes himself inside the bathtub, shampoos his blond hair, and turns the water dirty. Toshi, standing by the tub, draws his picture. The foreigner is impressed. Toshi's own arms and hands are thick and muscular. Using brilliantly colored crayons, he sketches faster, draws marvelous pictures of things he's never even seen: Palm trees. A koala bear. The Imperial Palace. He draws Audrey Hepburn. The foreigner applauds.

Then Toshi explains to him in grammatically perfect English how to take a Japanese bath – how to wash and rinse before stepping into the tub. Apologetic and grateful, the foreigner stands up, naked. But Toshi doesn't run away. No, he looks right at him, and he holds the drawings out to him. 'A gift,' he says.

The foreigner replies in the kindest voice imaginable, 'You are such a talented young man. Why don't you come back to Australia with me? You're much too smart and handsome to stay here in Japan. Yes, Toshi, you can be a foreigner like me.'

3

The doorbell interrupts a dream of his childhood: Falling snow. A white car stops in front of the noodle shop. Audrey Hepburn steps out, her legs bare. Toshi blinks himself awake and shuffles to the front door. It's eight in the morning. A long-faced mailman in a motorcycle helmet holds out a clipboard. Toshi stamps his seal on a document, and the mailman hands him an express, registered letter. A square rice paper envelope tinted a delicate red. Jane's name, unexpected, embossed on the back in phonetic Japanese, startles him.

He leaves the unopened envelope on the *kotatsu*, lights the burner, and puts water on for tea. He sits down and stares at the envelope, then out the sliding glass doors. He gets up and waters the plants on his balcony. He likes Jane, but he has a bad feeling about the letter and doesn't want to open it. He's learned from past American girlfriends that when they have something nice to say, they simply say it. But when they have something unpleasant to tell him, they like to write it down.

Toshi lives in a six-tatami-mat room with no bath, on the tenth floor of a rickety old building that sways alarmingly in typhoons and earthquakes. He looks out his balcony doors at an old washing machine left by the previous tenant, and on three potted azaleas given to him by Wanda Williford.

When the apartment building went up almost forty years ago, it was the first in the neighborhood. There's an old framed photograph in the lobby taken from this, the top, floor: a patterned landscape of dark tile roofs, rice paddies, and vegetable gardens, wood smoke rising out of bathhouse chimneys. But today's view: across the street, another dreary, concrete apartment building, then another, and another, like endless ocean swells.

Toshi sips his scalding tea and, finally, opens the letter. It is handwritten and long. After only one date, how could she possibly have so much to say to him?

Dear Toshi,

It's been more than twenty-four hours and I haven't heard from you. Maybe you did call. Sometimes I forget to leave my answering machine on. When I'm feeling confused, like I am right now. There are things I want to say to you, need to say, about the other night. About my life.

When I was a girl, I had long, stringy hair. I wasn't pretty. No, she wasn't pretty or nice. Other girls teased her.

He puts the letter down. He's not sure he wants to read the rest. Did he do something wrong the other night? Say the wrong thing? His girlfriends always want something from him, only they never tell him what it is. They expect him just to know.

Dressing, he examines his body, oddly fascinated by the scratches and teeth marks that adorn his flesh like tattoos. He'd been wrong about Jane. She's so funny in class, so energetic, so American. He'd imagined that sex with her would be exciting. But it wasn't exciting, it was scary. He had no control. On her futon they traveled forward, fast, but only she knew where they were going and how to get there.

*   *   *

Before he leaves for the studio, he reads the rest of the letter.

> *The first time you walked into my classroom, I felt the incredible sexual current that flows between us. You felt it, also, I know. I got wet just looking at you, at your beautiful legs. This is what I want: To get down on my knees, right there in front of the class, and lick your calves and your thighs, to stick my tongue up the leg of your shorts. I know why you wear those shorts.*

Toshi can't believe this letter. But as he imagines the scene Jane describes, he unzips his jeans.

> *I had no idea it would be like it was. After making love with you – how many times was it? Four? Five? Six times? – I'm stunned, dazed. Exhausted. I can barely speak or eat.*
>
> *She peels an orange, and she sucks out the juice. In Florida, where her father lives, the oranges are incredibly sweet. The white flesh of the orange is under her fingernails as she writes this letter. Can you smell it? The juice runs down her chin, her throat, between her breasts. She presses her breasts to the paper. Her body is sore from you, but still it craves you. She thinks only of this. Your skin. To touch it. And now look: Her head, her hair is on fire.*

Toshi closes his eyes.

Shinjuku Station.

On platform twelve, trains arrive and depart every forty-three seconds. 'Move quickly! Don't fall off the platform! Work hard today!' a recorded voice booms as the crowds are herded along by a battalion of white-gloved men, shoved through the doors of cars already filled to twice their capacity. The doors shut behind him, and Toshi turns to look out the window. On the platform, stooped Korean women wearing surgical masks sweep up shoes, briefcases, umbrellas, and magazines, drop them into bins marked LOST AND FOUND.

Inside the car, everyone watches the morning news on the TV monitors over every door: The Minister of Agriculture's suicide. The burning rice fields in Niigata Prefecture. The schoolboy next to Toshi falls asleep standing up, his head resting on Toshi's shoulder, saliva seeping from the corner of his mouth. At Yoyogi Station, a pretty, dark-haired foreigner is shoved through the door, wedged in two bodies over from Toshi, who shifts slightly so that he faces her. Her hair, piled on top of her head, trembles in the slight *whoosh* of air from the ceiling fan. He waits for her to look his way so he can smile, but she is surrounded by salarymen, and they hold their comic books and newspapers up to their faces, form a circle around her, and press in. She closes her eyes, lets out the tiniest cry of pain, like a little bird, and then sinks out of sight.

While everyone else he knows takes snapshots, Toshi doesn't even own a camera. He prefers to sketch the places he visits and the people he meets. Soon after he started to work at Nakamura Studio as a *manga* illustrator, he sent envelopes of sketches to both his mother and his father: the five-story, stucco Tokyo Refresh Building, which houses, on the ground floor, the Paris Esthetic Salon, with its facade of marble columns and nude statues; and, on the second floor, the Fly Sexy Snack Bar and Karaoke Lounge, where his boss, Nakamura, took him for drinks after his first day of work. The hostesses wore topless stewardess uniforms and served them their beers on airline trays.

On the third floor, 'Nakamura Studio.' Toshi sketched in the dirty green door and, just inside, the coatrack and the crowded umbrella stand. He drew in blue, green, and pink plastic umbrellas. The 'Hello Kitty' umbrella, the American-flag umbrella, and the Tokyo Giants umbrella. Now, almost a year after making those drawings, the same umbrellas are still there. And the room has hardly been cleaned in all that time either. Cigarette smoke long ago stained the walls and ceiling yellow. Faded posters of Nakamura's most famous *manga* character, Chocolate Girl, in her various incarnations – uniformed office lady, high-priced prostitute, super-heroine in black leather boots and helmet – are peeling off the walls, so that she seems drunk, or dead, her arms and legs akimbo.

Fifty pages of Chocolate Girl's serialized adventures appear weekly in *Business Hip Hop*, a best-selling comic book, and have turned her creator, Tetsuya Nakamura, into an unlikely media celebrity. Every time Toshi turns on the TV, there's his boss – his eyeglasses smudged, a cigarette hanging out from under his untrimmed mustache – on interview shows and quiz shows, in cameo roles on detective dramas. Once he was cast as a murder victim, and Toshi watched his boss plummet from the roof of Takashimaya department store.

Nakamura Studio also produces other comics, but Chocolate Girl, who stands tall and big busted behind Nakamura's desk in a life-size cardboard cutout, pays the rent and the salaries of Toshi and his two co-workers. Each week, Nakamura draws a rough storyboard and writes the dialogue, then Toshi, Akira, and Mami finish the drawings. *Manga*s are as popular as newspapers, and Chocolate Girl's battles with rapists, child molesters, gangsters, and rice smugglers are followed by most of Japan. And Toshi likes his boss. Nakamura is an odd and funny man. When Toshi comes to work, he never knows what to expect.

Today he walks in to find a big sheepdog trotting in circles in the middle of the room, kicking up dust. Mami follows it around, trying to pet it. Nakamura stands by his desk, smoking and grinning.

'Look, Toshi-chan. A dog. Come touch it,' Mami says.

'Go ahead. Don't be shy. Try it,' Nakamura says.

'Whose dog is it? Akira-kun?'

Akira is, as always, staring at his computer screen, his gold earrings and dyed blond hair hidden inside his sweatshirt hood. The beeps and groans of a computer game fill the room.

'Me? How could I have a pet? I live in a four-mat room.'

'It's ours, for one hour,' Nakamura says. 'I rented it. We have a year's contract. One hour, once a week.'

'Rented it? You're joking?'

'Isn't it wonderful!' Mami kneels down, adjusting her white leather miniskirt, and squeezes the dog around its waist, but the dog squirms out of her grasp. 'I feel so lighthearted.'

'You'd better hurry up and pet it. There's only forty minutes left before they come back to pick it up,' Nakamura says.

The dog sits down and barks. Mami backs away.

'Don't worry. That was a happy bark,' Akira says without looking up.

'How do you know?' Mami asks.

'I understand dogs. I have a way with animals,' he says. On his screen, two Japanese farmers poke pitchforks into a sack of rice with an American flag on it. Each time a pitchfork scores a hit, grains of rice fill up the screen, and the farmers' hats fly off their heads.

'If this dog causes us any trouble, next week we'll get a different one,' Nakamura says.

'You actually rented a dog?' Toshi asks.

Mami tentatively approaches the dog again.

'That's right. With so many people dying from overwork,

I thought we should do our part to stay healthy. Having a pet around the office helps you to relax. It improves office efficiency, government studies show.' Nakamura says. 'Nobody in Tokyo has the time or space to care for a dog. So this friend of mine started a pet rental company. It's become very popular. He's getting rich.'

'I do feel so much happier,' Mami says, but just as she leans down to hug the dog again, a strong jolt shakes the room. Pencils and ashtrays rise into the air, then fall back onto the desks with a clatter. The coatrack tips into Toshi's arms. The dog growls and lunges at Mami. She screams and runs behind Toshi.

'Wouldn't you know it, a dog scared of earthquakes.' Nakamura backs toward the door, puffing hard on his cigarette.

Akira jumps up and holds his chair in front of him like a lion tamer. 'Everybody get back. Take it easy, dog. Relax. What's this dog's name?'

'I don't know. Look on the rental receipt.'

'You call the police, Toshi-chan, while I keep him under control,' Akira says.

'The police? Why? The dog doesn't look dangerous, only confused. This room is too small for a big dog.' He feels sorry for the dog. How many offices does he visit every day? How many strangers pet him?

'They can bring a tranquilizer gun or something,' Akira says.

'Oh, look!' Mami says.

The dog lays down, puts its big round head on its paws, and closes its eyes. Nakamura lights another cigarette and sticks it in his mouth next to the first one. They all watch silently as the dog starts to snore. Its tail twitches, swatting the dusty floor.

'How sweet,' says Mami. 'It's dreaming.'

* * *

Two gigantic television screens flood the plaza in front of Shibuya Station with bright, High Definition images: An army of armored samurai ride their horses over a cliff and, banners waving, plummet into the sea. Mickey Mouse and Donald Duck lead a parade of high-stepping baton twirlers through Tokyo Disneyland. Toshi is swept through the ticket wicket and out of the station on a wave of spring colors and flower-patterned umbrellas. The crowd splits before a Caucasian street musician strumming a guitar, then comes together again like seawater swirling around a reef. Toshi breaks free, finds himself in front of a girl who holds out a clipboard and a pen to him.

'Free cigarettes and a doughnut if you sign,' she says in stilted Japanese. She's dark-skinned. Possibly Thai.

He glances at the petition. Something about Cambodia and the UN Peace-Keeping Force. 'I'm sorry, but I don't have time. I'm late.' He signs without reading it and takes his doughnut.

'Peace,' the girl says, holding up a pack of cigarettes of the same name.

'No, thank you.' Swallowing his doughnut, he threads his way through the procession of shoppers heading up Dogenzaka Hill, past window displays of Italian furniture, digital rice cookers, Burberry coats, gleaming plastic models of salmon-egg and tuna-belly sushi.

When he arrives at the Very Romantic English Academy, classes have already started, and the hallways are deserted. What he really wants to do is leave right now, go back to the studio. Passing each closed classroom door, he hears snatches of CNN news broadcasts, language tapes, and conversation drills: 'Take my wallet. Take my wristwatch. Take my leather coat, please. Please don't shoot.'

Pausing outside Jane's classroom, he hears nothing. He takes a deep breath and opens the door. The room is empty, and there is a note on the blackboard: 'Today's five o'clock class is canceled.'

Instead of relief, he feels uneasy. Jane has never canceled class before. He's sure it has something to do with him. Did the school find out about them? There's a pay phone in the lobby. He takes a 'Malcolm X' phone card from his wallet, inserts it, and Denzel Washington's face is sucked into the slot. Ten units left. He punches in Jane's number. After the third ring, she answers in a sleepy voice.

'Hello. This is Toshi calling,' he says in English.

'Oh,' she says. Then, 'I was hoping you'd call.'

'Yes.' What should he say to her?

'I've been waiting for you.'

'Are you sick?'

'Am I sick?'

'Our class is canceled, it says on the blackboard.' He's sweating. Why is he explaining this to her? Doesn't she know?

'Please come over. Right away. I need to see you,' she whispers, then hangs up before he can reply. Nine units left. He replaces the receiver. Denzel Washington pops out into his hand.

Opening a box of Domino's pizza, Jane kneels by the table and points out the toppings one by one, as if giving Toshi a pronunciation lesson: 'Grilled eel. Mayonnaise. Pineapple. Chopped lettuce.' She wipes her finger through a curl of mayonnaise and brings it to his lips. He isn't sure what to do; her finger waits poised outside his mouth. He sticks out his tongue and licks it. She giggles, then puts her finger in her own mouth, pulls it out with a popping sound.

She turns on the TV while they eat. A man carries a cat up a flight of stairs. The cat curls up into a ball and rolls down the stairs. The man carries the cat up the stairs again.

'I couldn't teach today. I was afraid you might be in class and I knew I wouldn't be able to look at you in front of the other students. Especially those awful Ishikawa sisters.'

'Why?'

'God, Toshi, don't you know?'

'No,' he says, telling the truth. He didn't want to come, and now he wishes he wasn't here. He's made a mistake with Jane. He notices for the first time: A broken fingernail. Light hair growing on her arms. Specks of food and dust balls on the kitchen floor. Toshi is allergic to dust, and his nose is stuffed up.

On the night of his birthday dinner, Jane had said as she opened her front door, 'I have to warn you, I never clean.' She said this with a finality that suggested a disability, or doctor's orders. His friend Paul often did this too, eagerly told him things he couldn't or wouldn't do – iron his own shirts, learn to program his video recorder – as if laziness or ineptitude was something to boast about.

'Toshi, look at me.'

He does, reluctantly, and he sneezes.

'God bless you,' she says, pushing up the sleeves of her red dress, as if she is getting ready for a fight. Except for shrimp-shaped silver earrings, she isn't wearing any jewelry. Or makeup. She looks tired.

'Are we going to argue?' he asks.

'Everybody argues. It's normal. Confrontation can be a good thing.'

He doesn't know what *confrontation* means, but he nods.

'I wasn't a virgin before the other night.' She giggles again, and for just a moment she looks girlish and vulnerable. But then she shakes her head vigorously, as if to dismiss that part of herself. 'You can't fool me. I'm not wrong about what happened between us.'

'What happened?' he asks, wishing she would tell him what she wants. He could stop on the way home for a long bath, then pick up a movie at the video store. Audrey Hepburn sitting on the veranda of a ski resort.

Instead of answering him, she stands abruptly and whirls around the tiny room. 'Once a man loved me so much he wanted to kill me. I thought he would strangle me, or set me on fire.' She stops and stares at him, staggering slightly. Could she be drunk already, on only one glass of wine? She was drinking before he came over, he guesses.

'See those bars on the windows?'

There are metal bars he hadn't noticed before. Seeing them, he feels trapped.

She drops to her knees and reaches for her cigarettes. 'I had them put on. I was afraid for my life. But when he came to my door, I always let him in.'

'Why?' Is she making up this story? He doesn't believe anything she says anymore.

'He was so beautiful. He was the most beautiful Japanese man I've ever seen.' She shivers. 'I ached when I looked at him. I couldn't refuse him.'

She lights a cigarette, takes a deep drag, then immediately grinds it out on the lid of the pizza box. As smoke trickles from the corners of her mouth, she plucks a piece of eel off the pizza and eats it.

He sneezes again. She hands him a box of tissues.

'You know that feeling, don't you? The night of your birthday? The sex was incredible. I can't stop thinking about it, it's like I'm going crazy.'

He doesn't know what to say. He wishes she would sit still. She keeps moving, changing direction and subjects. All of the pictures on her walls – not just the woodblock prints, but the photographs and postcards – are of naked men and women. Over her desk, there's a drawing of a man with a penis so big he holds it up with both hands, the head fanning out over him like an umbrella. What kind of woman would have a picture like that on her wall for everybody to see?

'You felt it too, I know you did. It couldn't have been just me.'

'Yes. I felt it.' Felt what? His nipples still chafe under his clothes. He's chafing too, in her small apartment – the dust and cigarette smoke, and she has so many things, too many things. There are piles of clothes and books everywhere, and boxes stacked against the walls. Boxes filled with letters, he imagines. Letters to men. Years of letters – although he realizes that this is illogical. If she'd sent the letters, they wouldn't be here. But then, Jane isn't logical. And Jane might make copies. She is someone who would copy every letter she writes.

'Don't lie to me,' she cries suddenly. 'You think I'm awful, don't you? I am, I'm dreadful, and I'm not pretty. You should leave now, just go home.'

'No. You're pretty,' he says as she starts to sob.

'Do you mean that? You're not just saying it?'

'Yes. Yes, I do,' he says, feeling himself being drawn in against his will.

'Oh God, I'm sorry. I'm so, so sorry.'

She is on top of him so fast he falls over backward, a slice of pizza crushed between them. He struggles to free himself, but she wraps her arms tightly around him, and he feels the pizza soak through his shirt.

'Don't go away. Please, I don't know what I'd do. Just tonight, please stay, only for tonight, I swear.' She kisses him, her tongue pushing through his teeth. He tastes eel and pineapple. She fumbles with his zipper. Aroused, he gives in. He pulls up her dress and slips his hand under the waistband of her tights. 'Oh, Toshi, oh, God.' His fingertips graze her bare skin, and he feels her rising heat. Light from the TV flickers faster and faster on the insides of his eyelids until a moving image comes into focus. Audrey Hepburn dances around the rim of a magnificent fountain in Rome. Her tongue fills his mouth. His nose is blocked. He gasps for air.

The acupuncturist's clinic was above a furniture store just off Shari's main street. Toshi's father read a magazine in the waiting room, his stocking feet resting on an electric foot massager. Toshi could hear the *thump thump* of the motorized machine from inside the treatment room as he took off his clothes and folded them in a plastic basket at the foot of the treatment table. The acupuncturist covered him with a white sheet. Someone was snoring on the other side of the curtain.

'Another patient,' she said in a soothing voice. Mrs Suzuki was a plump, middle-aged woman in a white smock.

A month after his mother left them for the inn in Utoro, Toshi woke up in the middle of the night, startled to find himself sitting upright in the dark room, gasping for breath. Outside the window, snow fell steadily, and he imagined it piling up in his chest.

'Close your eyes now. The needles may hurt a bit, but it's a good pain,' she said. 'A boy as handsome as you surely must be brave, too, isn't that so?'

He felt the needles as she inserted them in his shoulders, in his arms and legs, in the crooks of his hands between his thumbs and fingers. They slid in easily, each one striking a forgotten fear: His mother leaps into the heaving winter sea. She will disappear in a snowstorm.

She jiggled the needles in his forehead, and a liquid heat sprang from his hips and rushed to the tips of his feet.

A memory welled up: Toshi wakes up in the middle of the night to see his father kneeling next to his mother's mattress.

'Please,' his father whispers.

'I can't. Forgive me.' His mother rolls away, her back to him.

Toshi cried out in the dark, then opened his eyes. Mrs Suzuki was leaning over him.

'Are you all right? I didn't hurt you, did I?'

'Yes, I'm all right. I'm sorry,' he said, ashamed that somehow she knew what he'd seen. What had his father asked for that his mother had refused him?

She burned *moxa* on either side of the bridge of his nose, and he felt the heat on his eyelids. Could she burn his eyes and blind him? Did his father know she was lighting fires on his face?

When she lit *moxa* on the crown of his head he felt a sharp, quick burn, like when he touched the metal handle of the *ramen* broth pot, and inside his narrow chest, thin spring ice cracked over a rushing stream. Clear water gushed out, and the vision of his parents disappeared.

Toshi could breathe again.

Afterward, in the waiting room, the acupuncturist said to his father, 'He may be allergic to dust. Please tell his mother that she should keep his room very clean.'

'I see,' his father said. Toshi was afraid he would tell her about his mother, and about how they were alone now. It was Toshi who vacuumed and dusted the rooms. His father did the laundry.

'Can you bring him back once a week? He needs three or four more treatments.'

'Hmmm' is all he said.

'Just look at his face. He has much more color already.

He looked so tired when he came in. Such a handsome boy shouldn't look tired.'

His father stared at him, as if for the first time. Toshi blushed.

They left the coast road and drove across the peninsula inside a plowed white tunnel of snow, a strip of brilliant blue sky over their heads. His father lit a cigarette.

'Did it hurt?'

'A little.' Toshi couldn't look at his father's face. The memory her needle had inflamed had faded, but the place where the memory had been was tender as a wound.

'Do you think it helped?'

'She said it would take time.'

Then they were quiet until they drove up to the end of the road and parked the car next to the noodle shop. The heavy winter sea groaned.

'Why don't you ask your mother. See what she thinks,' his father said.

That evening, he called his mother. Her voice sounded tired.

'Mother, are you well?'

'To tell the truth, I haven't been sleeping. But I'm okay. And what about you? Are you and your father fine?'

He told her about his allergy and the visit to the acupuncturist.

'Do you think I should go back to see her again?' he asked. 'Father said I should ask you.'

She was silent.

'Mother?'

He could hear her labored breathing.

'Forgive me,' she said.

And the memory welled up again.

The first time I wanted to make love to a Japanese man was when I was fifteen years old and I saw Toshiro Mifune in Rashomon.

Two days later, Jane's second letter arrives, by ordinary mail, in a red-tinted rice paper envelope. She must have written and sent it right after he left her apartment, he realizes.

Jane wrote in black ink, the dark words moving restlessly across the soft paper.

> *He had the most beautiful thighs. Thick, sweaty thighs. I used to masturbate imagining Toshiro Mifune naked, lying on top of me, raping me instead of that silly woman in the film, his smooth thighs shiny with sweat.*

He calls his friend Paul.

'Why did you wait so long to tell me?'

'I don't know.'

'Meet me for dinner tonight,' Paul says.

'I'm too tired.'

'Of course you are after so much sex. It's a wonder you're alive. But I'll pay.'

'Are you sure?'

'I live to get you out of woman trouble. Come on, I can't wait to hear all the gory details. We'll go someplace nice, and I'll give you lots of sympathy.'

'Okay.'

'Meet me at Harajuku Station at six. We'll take a walk in the park before dinner. Fresh air will do you good.'

* * *

After the first time they met, Toshi returned to Rausu and wrote Paul a letter. Paul's being gay puzzled him more than it concerned him. And he admired Paul. 'I would like to be your good friend,' he wrote in careful English. Paul replied by express mail. 'I would like to be your good friend too.' Toshi still has that letter.

They corresponded regularly in English and in Japanese, by letter and postcard and, occasionally, by phone. Toshi drew pictures and sent them to Paul, explanations and questions printed neatly on the back. 'My mother shoveling snow.' 'My father watching TV.' 'Granny sweeping the street.' 'This is my father's noodle shop. Do you like noodles?' Once he drew two grinning fishermen holding up an octopus.

To his delight, Paul replied in kind – not with sketches, but with snapshots that made Toshi laugh. 'My foot.' 'My other foot.' 'A dead plant that I forgot to water.' 'The crowded train I take to work every morning' showed only the tops of heads lit up by a camera flash.

Toshi ended up going to college in Sapporo. Paul came to visit twice, both times in the winter, and took Toshi skiing. Toshi's college friends were surprised to see him with a foreigner, and they began to treat him with a mixture of caution and respect. Toshi studied English. Before spring vacation his third year, Paul sent him a round-trip plane ticket to Tokyo, along with a note: 'Don't worry. You can sleep in the extra bedroom.' After he graduated, he lived with Paul until he found a job and his own apartment.

Paul is his best friend, and the Tokyo Toshi knows is the one Paul introduced him to, the Tokyo of expatriates: Mexican and Italian restaurants. Luxurious apartments he could never afford to live in. Western-style supermarkets that stock their shelves with expensive products he's never heard of, where Paul fills his shopping cart with jars of Spanish olives and cheeses from France. Bars, gay and straight, that cater to Westerners and Japanese who are looking for one another. In this world, Toshi was pleased to discover, Paul's sexuality was not a problem. His friends and acquaintances knew but didn't care. By then, Toshi didn't care either.

The Tokyo Paul introduced him to keeps changing, though, faster than they can walk through it. Just a year ago, construction cranes crowded the skyline. Familiar buildings disappeared overnight and were replaced at a startling speed. But recently, the recession has been transforming the landscape: On the grassy lawns of Yoyogi Park, a tent city has blossomed. Dark-skinned foreign men gather around cooking fires and drink steaming cups of tea.

'Poor guys. They're just waiting to be caught and deported. I'll bet none of them have visas,' Paul says. 'Or jobs, now that the construction industry's gone belly up.'

'Belly up?'

'Bust.'

'Bust?'

'Collapsed.'

'Oh.' Collapse. Fall down. Buildings collapse. So do people. So, apparently, do industries.

He watches the foreigners pass food from hand to hand, hand to mouth, their swarthy faces illuminated by the flames, their backs turned to the quickening darkness. Toshi smells strong spices.

'Toshiro Mifune's thighs? Well, that's not an unusual reason for coming to Japan. Although I don't see the resemblance. I always thought your legs were too thin.'

'It's not a joke.'

'It wasn't supposed to be.' Paul stops walking. 'Look, I'm sorry you got yourself into trouble. But there's something you need to understand about people. We don't always do things for good, smart, logical reasons.'

'What do you mean?'

'I mean I ended up in Japan because I saw a picture of Yukio Mishima in a book when I was sixteen. I read his novels. Next thing I knew, I was studying karate. I learned Japanese from cassette tapes. My mother said my eyes were going to slant if I didn't stop. I went to college and majored in Japanese. Then I came here for my junior year.'

'I already know that. You already told me that.'

A man steps out from behind a tree, blocking their path and startling Toshi. But when he opens his outstretched hand, it is filled with rice.

'Jasmine. From Thailand,' he whispers.

'No, thank you,' Paul says politely. He grips Toshi's elbow and turns him toward the park exit. The cherry trees are almost in full flower, and their petals gather up what's left of the fading light.

'Look, there are lots of things that interest me about Japan. But let's be honest. What got me here? I mean, what was the pivotal event, the thing that changed the direction of my entire life, that carried me halfway around the world?'

'What?'

'A photograph of Yukio Mishima in a loincloth. That's what.'

He stops, still holding Toshi's elbow, and looks him in the eyes.

'And why am I still here? Why am I here in Japan, in Tokyo?'

'I don't know,' Toshi says, thinking that he really does know the answer.

'Yes, you do.'

'No.' He doesn't want to say it. But Paul does.

'I'm here for the men.'

'That's stupid,' Toshi says. He pulls his arm free and forces out a laugh. He doesn't like to hear these things from Paul.

'That's a stupid reason. You shouldn't say that. You're too smart.'

'No. I'm not. When it comes to love and sex, nobody is smart. That's what you haven't learned yet.' He pauses. 'Particularly about yourself.'

They walk out of the park in silence. Paul is always telling him things about himself that he doesn't want to hear. Is this what friends do in America? Criticize each other? Point out each other's weaknesses? For what reason?

Widened and planted with trees for the 1964 Olympics, Omotesando Street is Tokyo's most fashionable boulevard. Toshi is surprised to see how it's changed. Cafe Häagen-Dazs and Cafe Ropé have closed their doors. And the sidewalks are lined with foreigners selling wares spread out on blankets. Jewelry. Pottery. Framed oil seascapes, and sand paintings.

'Terrible,' he says.

'Well. More like inevitable,' Paul says. 'What goes up must come down.'

Up, down. In, out. In high school English class, Toshi had to memorize lists of opposites. Cold, hot. Light, dark. Happy, sad. Safe, dangerous.

'Will you help me with Jane?'

'You should learn to handle these things yourself.'

'Please. She's too strong.'

'She's American. She'll eat you alive.'

Toshi felt for Jane's teeth marks, hidden by his shirt. He couldn't show them to Paul. Could she really eat him?

'Please. You always know what to do.'

'I suppose we can write her a letter. That way you can say what you want without having to see her and endanger your poor, overworked penis. We'll write it during dinner.'

They stroll past SALE signs plastered in the windows of

Kiddy Land, Vivre 21 Fashion Building, and Shu Uemura. The Hanae Mori Building is dark. Outside on the plaza, where Toshi once sat on a Sunday afternoon and drank iced tea with Wanda Williford, a flea market has sprung up. Young Japanese women selling their Louis Vuitton bags and Hermès scarves. Men, their Rolex watches, Italian neckties, and leather briefcases.

'I'm starving. Korean barbecue, Indian, or Thai?'

'Thai.'

A Mercedes-Benz is parked at the curb with a FOR SALE sign in the window. A woman in black leather has spread a blanket on the hood, and on top of it, a crystal ball and a deck of tarot cards. She hands Toshi a business card as he walks by.

LEARN YOUR FUTURE. BUSINESS MATTERS. ROMANCE.

'Maybe we should try her.' He hands the card to Paul.

'She's selling her car. How good can she be?'

'Not for business. For romance.'

Paul drops the card into a trash can. 'There's no future in romance. It never lasts long enough.'

This is the letter that Paul writes for Toshi.

Dear Jane,

I'm sorry it's taken me so long to respond to your letters. I didn't want to reply without taking the time to think carefully about our relationship. I think we should no longer see each other. It's not because I don't want to be with you. I do. I want to be with you too much. I'm sure you understand what I'm trying to say. I'm in awe of you. You're such an extraordinary woman that you've overwhelmed me, and my life. I'm afraid I'm not ready for such an intense relationship. I hope you'll agree that this is for the best.

I will see you in class next week.

Toshi

'Literate yet firm. This should do the trick.' Paul folds the letter up and sticks it in Toshi's shirt pocket.

'Do you think she'll believe I wrote it?'

'She'll believe it because it says what she wants to hear.'

A young, handsome Thai waiter brings their bowls of coconut ice cream.

'Thank you.' Paul runs his hand through his bright red hair. 'Do you come from Bangkok? I've been to Bangkok many times. It's my favorite city.' He gives him his most charming smile. 'I'm very interested in Thai culture.'

The next morning, Toshi sits at his *kotatsu* and prepares to copy the letter in his own handwriting. He sits facing the balcony, his futon still laid out on the floor next to him. Outside, the sky is busy with helicopters and blimps. He looks down at the white sheet of paper.

'When we Japanese write personal letters, we write vertically, from top to bottom, and from right to left, don't we?'

Toshi's ninth-grade English teacher, Mrs Hayashi, pointed with a stick to a demonstration letter already printed in neat, even columns on the blackboard. 'We follow a prescribed form, and we do not deviate, correct? First, a comment on the weather. Next, we inquire after our correspondent's health.'

She put down her stick and looked out the window at the frozen athletic field where the first snow of autumn was falling in thick, wet flakes. Boys in rugby shorts, their legs red from the cold, stood in a straight line and bowed in perfect unison to their coach.

'But in America, where, of course, they write horizontally, left to right, there is no form for writing personal letters. People write anything they please, anything that comes into their heads at all, and in any order.'

A murmur of disbelief ran through the class like a school of fish passing just below the water's surface. Heads swiveled and eyes widened. Toshi pictured an American letter: words running in every direction, in circles, upside down, crisscrossing on a sheet of red, white, and blue paper. In back of him, someone whispered, 'America sounds good, doesn't it? I want to go to America.'

Mrs Hayashi clapped her hands and the class was silent.

'In America, there is no order.'

Each student was to write a personal letter in English to someone in America. If they had no one to write to, their teacher, who had lived for two years in a place called Portland with her sister's family after her own husband's fishing boat capsized in a storm, would supply them with names and addresses of schoolchildren. After they handed in their letters and Mrs Hayashi corrected them, they would copy them over and then actually mail them.

The only person Toshi knew in America was Audrey Hepburn, so he wrote his letter to her. He worked on it every night after he finished his other homework. On the morning it was due, he woke up very early and, without disturbing his father, went downstairs and switched on the rice cooker for their breakfast. In the back room, he put on the water for tea. It was still dark when he turned on the heat lamp under the *kotatsu* and slid his legs under the padded quilt, so he saw only his own reflection in the window: a sleepy-faced boy with a crewcut, a white sweatshirt with a bold pink English inscription in reverse. STRAWBERRY BOY. LET'S PLAY VIOLENT SPORTS EVERY DAY. He began to write, horizontally, left to right.

When he looked up again, blue light was washing over the slope. It swirled around the birch trees, and woke up the red foxes and the antelope.

He wrote:

Dear Miss Audrey Hepburn,

It is almost winter here in Hokkaido, Japan, where I live. It is very cold, but I don't mind. How are you? Are you fine? Is your health well? I am hoping for you.

I and my mother saw your film Roman Holiday. *Yes. It was my birthday when I was nine years old. It was my first movie in English. I didn't understand the words. But you were the most beautiful woman, I think. After you take a haircut. Now I saw after that many movies you act.* Breakfast at Tiffany's, Funny Face, Sabrina, The Nun's Story. *These movies are videotapes. Your movies can be easy to see in Japan, did you know? All Japanese people likes you very much, I am happy to tell you. Because you are beautiful and a good actor. It's true.* The Nun's Story *is so, so sad story. I cried. Really. Just please ask my mother.*

Now I am fourteen year old boy. I like to draw pictures. I will send you some pictures. Maybe if you come to Japan I can meet you? Do you think so? I am learning English. You can come to Hokkaido and you can stay at Hiraiwa, it is like a hotel where my mother is. You don't have to pay money. We are so happy if you can visit. Do you know about Japanese bath and bed? We don't have bed. Don't worry. I will explain to you. It is a problem?

When do you make the next movie? Do you like Japanese food? I hope you will read my letter. Can you answer it? I will wait. If it takes many time, don't worry.

Your friend,
Toshiyuki Okamoto (let's call me Toshi!)

He put his letter in a big envelope along with two sketches

– one of his mother, and the other of Audrey Hepburn from the cover of the *Breakfast at Tiffany's* videotape. He addressed the envelope to: Miss Audrey Hepburn, Hollywood, California, USA.

Three months later, he received a manila envelope with an autographed black-and-white photograph of Audrey Hepburn and a letter.

Dear Toshiyuki Okamoto:

Thank you so much for your kind letter. I'm so glad you enjoy my films. Hearing from fans is such a pleasure. It's what makes my work worthwhile. As you may know, I no longer make films very often. Instead, I am fortunate to be involved with UNICEF, and am busy traveling the world, trying very hard to make sure that children everywhere are well fed and healthy. It's difficult but rewarding work.

Good luck in all your endeavors.
My very best wishes,
Audrey Hepburn

The letter was typed, but Audrey Hepburn had signed her own name. Toshi framed the letter and the photograph and gave them to his mother to keep in her room at the inn. Granny often brought them out to show to guests, and, eventually, she asked Taro to hang them on the dining room wall. Over the years, almost everyone in town stopped by to have their own photographs taken standing next to Audrey Hepburn's letter and autographed picture.

45

Of course we must stop seeing each other. I was about to write to you and tell you just that when I received your letter. Did you really think I wanted to continue this foolish relationship? No! Never!

An errant gust of spring wind blows in through the open balcony doors to lift the single page of Jane's third letter off the table.

> *The sexual attraction is too powerful, it controls us. It possesses us. We are wild animals. A nasty monkey and a dangerous tiger. The monkey riding on the tiger's back.*

The letter rises up into the air, pauses for a moment, then floats back down to the tabletop.

> *The tiger's back. Your back, smooth as silk. The silk lining of her mother's mink coat. She hid in the closet, wrapped herself in her mother's coat, the silk rubbed against her bare arms, covered her face like a hot rush of blood, a wonderful dark death.*

The letter arrived during the night while he slept, dropped through the front-door mail slot. The red envelope bore neither postmark nor stamp. Toshi checked the lock on the door.

The cherry trees are in bloom. We'll say good-bye tonight at Aoyama Cemetery. Under a blossoming cherry tree. Surrounded by those sad gravestones. Our farewell. Six o'clock. The north entrance.

I'll go. If I don't, she'll never stop writing to me, he thinks as he neatly folds the letter back into the envelope and puts it in the drawer with the others. If I don't go tonight, her letters will never stop arriving. He imagines the envelopes piling up by the front door like a red snowdrift, waiting for him each morning when he wakes up. And Jane writes like a crazy person. Like there are no rules at all.

'I wasn't sure you were going to come,' she says shyly, then she lifts the hem of her white dress and curtsies. In the soft fading light, she looks so pretty and innocent, her hair tied back with a white scarf. Is this really the same woman who wrote those letters?

'I was looking forward to it,' he says impulsively as, against his will, he feels himself being charmed by her.

She smiles. A shopping bag in one hand, she takes his arm with the other and leads him down the crowded path. Soon, they enter a grove of cherry trees.

'Oh, look!'

She drops her bag and runs to the center of the grove. Petals settle on her dark hair like snowflakes. Enclosed in a circle of gravestones, she spreads her arms wide.

'Look at me, Toshi!' she shouts. Everyone around them turns. What is she doing?

She whirls round and round, making herself dizzy, until she falls back onto the petal-covered lawn. She flaps her arms up and down like a bird.

Someone in the crowd says, 'She's having a seizure!'

'No, just a weird foreigner.'

Toshi runs to her.

Digital Hollywood The MultimediaSchool presents

OTO 2ND ANNIVERSARY PARTY

小さい箱ながらも、いろいろな方々に支えられてきたお陰で、我らがOTOも二周年を迎えることになりました。これまで応援していただいた皆さまがた、本当にありがとうございました。これからもより一層頑張っていくので、よろしくお願いします。そこで、そんな皆さまに感謝の意を込めて今年も、二周年記念のパーティーを開催したいと思います。ということで、とにかく豪華なんです。なにがって、まず参加していただくDJ＆アーティストが、総勢6名＋1組と盛り沢山。それも今、一番美味しいメンツばかりが勢揃い。

それでは、まず最初に紹介するのは"Drum'n'bassのカリスマ"DJ FORCE。豊富な経験から生み出されるそのプレイは、鳥肌が立つほどにCool。男気がひしひしと伝わってきます。二人目はご存じ"100万ドルの笑顔を持つ男"Yo*c。彼の光り輝くスマイルはまさに、テクノ界に降臨した天使のよう。プレイもまた然り。みんなで幸福な時間を過ごしましょう。三人目は最近、爆発的に信者が増加中のSHINKAWA。その絶好調のイケイケぶりはプレイにもそのまま表われ、クラウドを次々と「秒殺」。いま一番危険な男です（笑）。そしてTASAKA。LOOPAでは卓球のかげに隠れがちだが、その確かな技術に裏打ちされたプレイは本物。レコードというのはここまで「使える」モノなのか？テクノDJという枠では収まりきらない、その衝撃のスタイルはまさに「革命」です。そしてOTOからは、今回のOrganizerでもあるI-WAXとPooAH！のNAΣTOOが参加。I-WAXは現在、新レーベル発足に向けての準備を、着々と進行中。その名も「HEAVEN UP HERE」。一方NAΣTOOは、Delightの「Fiesta!」でもスピン。この二人の今後にも期待して下さいね！

そしてイベント唯一のLiveをつとめるのが、いま売り出し中のバンド、BOOM BOOM SATELLITES。97年6月末、R＆Sよりヨーロッパデビュー（12inch）を果たし、9月末にも2ndリリースを予定。田中フミヤのレーベル「アンタイトル」からもハイクオリティーなサウンドを世に送り出している。普段は見られない彼等のLiveを今回yellowで実現。必見です。

そして、今回のイベントでは、日本初の実践的マルチメディアスクールとして有名なデジタル・ハリワッド がビジュアル面を全面バックアップ。B1ラウンジスペースを中心に、最新鋭の技術を生かしたCGワールドを展開。また、カッコいい企画も多数アリ。次世代のデジタルクリエイターを発信します。

I-WAX　　NAΣTTO

FORCE

YO*C

SHINKAWA

TASAKA

Date:	1997/10/06 MONDAY
Open:	9PM
Place:	YELLOW
Fee:	ADV 2,500yen/DOOR 3,500yen(w/1d)

Djs:FORCE/YO*C/SHINKAWA/TASAKA/I-WAX/NAΣTTO
Live:BOOM BOOM SATELLITES
Vj:MORRY

BOOM BOOM SATELLITES

supported by:

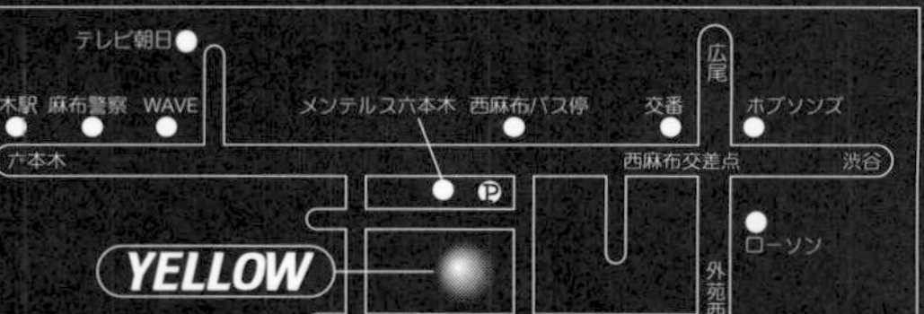

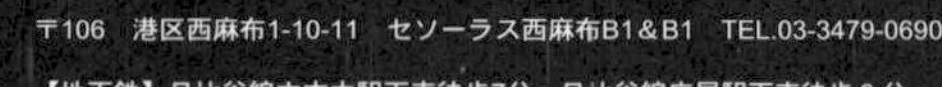

〒106　港区西麻布1-10-11　セソーラス西麻布B1＆B1　TEL.03-3479-0690

【地下鉄】日比谷線六本木駅下車徒歩7分・日比谷線広尾駅下車徒歩８分
・千代田線乃木坂駅下車徒歩６分
【都営バス】渋谷駅発都01系統-西麻布下車徒歩３分

OTO：新宿区歌舞伎町1-17-5-2F　TEL 03-5273-8264　リジョイス　プランニングオフィス：新宿区歌舞伎町2-45-5-402号　TEL&FAX 03-3204-7225

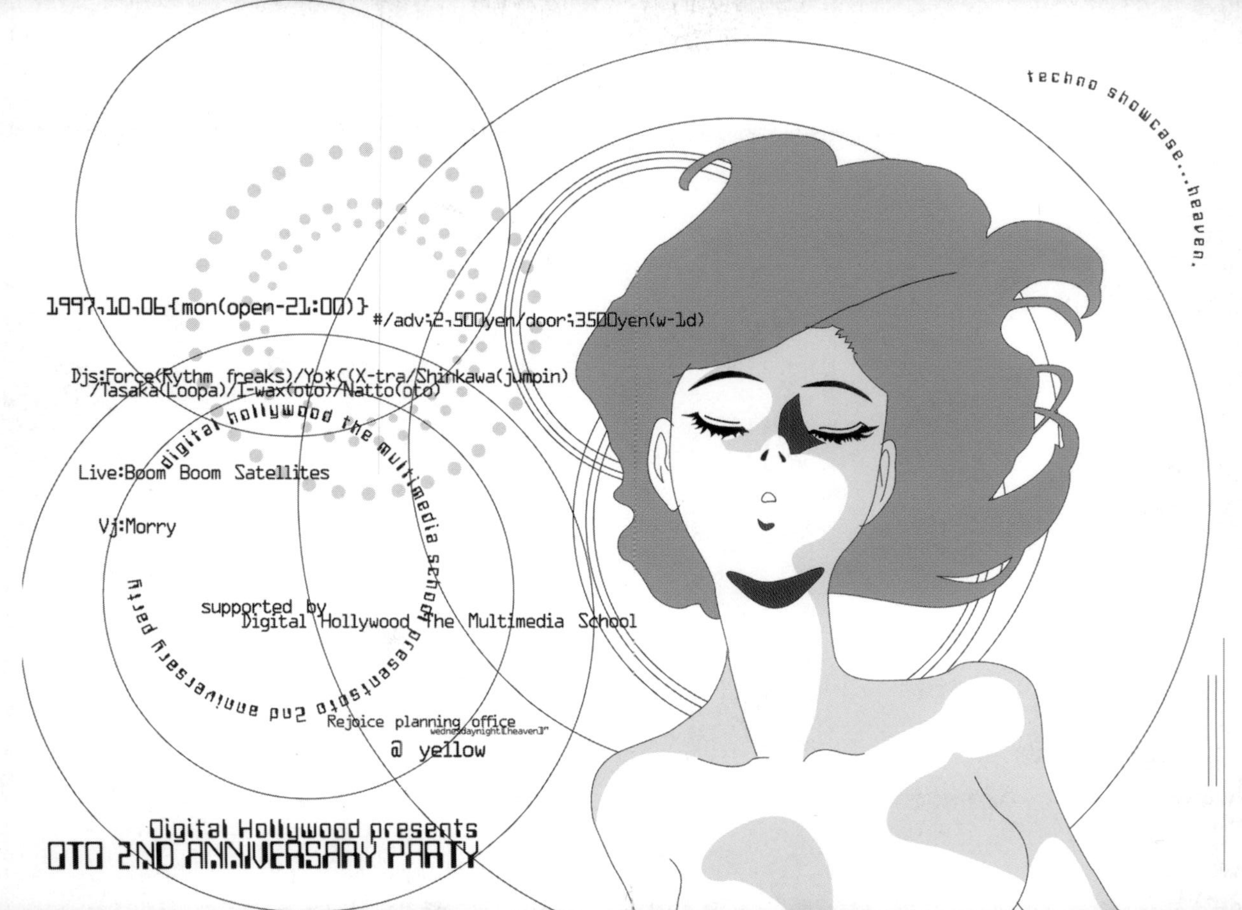
techno showcase...heaven.
1997,10,06{mon(open-21:00)}
#/adv;2,500yen/door;3500yen(w-1d)
Djs:Force(Rythm freaks)/Yo*C(X-tra/Shinkawa(jumpin)
/Tasaka(Loopa)/I-wax(oto)/Natto(oto)
digital hollywood the multimedia school presentsoto 2nd anniversary party
Live:Boom Boom Satellites
Vj:Morry
supported by
Digital Hollywood The Multimedia School
Rejoice planning office
@ yellow
Digital Hollywood presents
OTO 2ND ANNIVERSARY PARTY

But Jane's laughing. 'Look, Toshi! Look! I'm a snow angel!'

Under the bursting trees, families and young couples and groups of office workers sit – men cross-legged; women, their legs tucked under them – their shoes lined up in neat rows, toes pointing out, at the edges of their plastic mats. The soy-and-sugar smoke of basted meat and shellfish grilling on hibachis mixes with cigarette smoke in the cool air. Bottles of sake and beer and wine are opened. Wooden chopsticks click like cicada legs, their sound filling the darkening night.

Toshi and Jane sit facing each other on a bedsheet.

'This is good wine,' he says, sipping out of a plastic cup. He's not just being polite. It is good.

'Some guy was selling it in front of the Hanae Mori Building. It was too expensive, but I put a spell on him. I used my powers to charm him into selling it to me for almost nothing.'

She stares into his eyes as if she is trying to put a spell on him too. Petals float down out of the darkness and settle on the food as she spreads it out between them. 'A multicultural dinner,' she says, arranging cheese and crackers, then sushi, on paper plates. She produces a pocketknife from the shopping bag and slices a red apple into wedges. The apple is perfectly round, the flesh pale. Somewhere a switch is pulled, and the paper lanterns strung from the trees flicker, then glow, casting a warm light on the white blossoms.

'Oh, how wonderful. It's like we're in a snow cave, an enchanted tunnel of light,' Jane whispers. She closes her eyes and lets her head roll back, exposing her neck and the shadowy outline of her breasts. He feels himself getting hard.

'There are spirits in the air,' she whispers.

A man strums a guitar. A woman sings.

Jane opens her eyes and smiles. She looks sweet and eager, not at all like a person who could have written those letters. Maybe he's been wrong about her.

She puts a slice of cheese on a wedge of apple and holds it up. He opens his mouth, and she slides the cheese and apple in, leaving her fingers to rest lightly on his tongue. He closes his eyes, and she slowly withdraws her fingers across his teeth and lips. He imagines her tongue in his mouth. He chews and swallows, tasting the sharp cheese, his eyes still closed.

The guitar player strums an old folk song, and more people join in the singing.

The rim of a plastic cup touches his lips. Jane pours wine into his mouth. He is getting drunk.

'Drink. Drink,' she says, emptying the cup, then taking it away. His mouth opens and he waits for more. The music. The barbecue smoke. He's happy.

He feels something, a startling sharpness, then a shiver of alarm.

He opens his eyes.

The gleaming blade of the pocketknife runs across his thumb.

Blood.

She grabs his hand, jams his thumb in her mouth, and sucks on it.

'What!'

He pulls his hand away just as her teeth clamp down, scraping his skin. He stands up and backs away from her.

'I'm sorry. I didn't mean to,' she says.

Beneath his stocking feet, he is aware of the cold ground, twigs, and sharp stones. Jane sits calmly and looks up at him, a drop of blood on her lower lip. She's still holding the knife.

'What are you doing?' he asks, too loudly, suddenly afraid.

People turn to look.

'You see, I've never been without someone to love,' she says.

A red stain blossoms on her white dress.

He holds up his thumb, which starts to throb.

Beads of blood. Beads of sweat drip down his face.

'You cut me,' he says stupidly. He doesn't know what to say, what to do now. She has the knife. Should he try to take it away from her?

'You're just trying to make it interesting, aren't you?' she says softly, as if she is talking a child to sleep. 'I know that. You're not really leaving me. That's all right. I understand. I like it interesting too.'

She picks up the apple and continues to slice it as if nothing has happened, and his blood smears on the pulp.

A gust of wind stirs up the cherry blossoms and blows petals all over their plates of food.

'Oh!' Jane cries, as if she's been hurt. She jumps up. 'Look! Look! Now it's ruined!'

She bursts into tears.

The guitar player stops playing.

'It's okay. It's only petals,' he says, his voice now gentle. He needs to calm her down.

'You've ruined everything. You tricked me,' she yells.

What is she saying? She's not making any sense.

And then, in Japanese: 'I'm not a whore!'

Now everyone around them is quiet. Where did she learn that word? She's never spoken to him in Japanese before. Everyone is watching them.

'But you cut me,' he says, foolishly holding up his thumb to her, as if she might not remember.

'Leave me alone!' she yells. She picks up a cup of the red wine and throws it in his face.

Somebody gasps.

Jane backs away, stumbles over people and their dinners. She knocks over their bottles of beer and wine and overturns grills. Children cry. Careening backward, scattering glowing charcoal with her bare feet, she weaves through the gravestones and glowing trees like a ghost, and disappears into the dark night.

During the time it takes him to get back to his apartment, Jane has already left three messages on his answering machine. He washes and bandages his thumb, then strips off his wine-stained clothes and throws them into the washing machine on his balcony. Naked, he stands outside and listens to her voice. The night air is cool, but the lights of the city burn. Blazing banks of white illuminate the National Stadium. Tokyo Tower is outlined in red.

Her first message, her voice strangely calm, as if her words are weighed down by water. 'Are you there?' She waits. Then, 'You shouldn't have said all those nice things to me. Because you didn't mean them, did you?' She sighs. 'Maybe it was the wine. The wine was a mistake. We shouldn't have gotten drunk. I haven't been sleeping well. I'm up all night, then I'm too tired to get anything done during the day. I just wander around my apartment, my two little rooms, totally exhausted but too restless to sleep. I cancel my classes and I don't go out.'

She strikes a match and lights a cigarette.

'I have this antique kimono. It's silk and very, very old. Ancient. I stay at home all day and wrap myself up in it. You'd like it. I wear nothing else, I'm naked underneath. The kimono is green, the color of the seaweed you wrap around rice.'

She blows smoke into the mouthpiece.

'I'll probably be fired. What do you think about that? No, the kimono is not green. I didn't lie to you, I imagined the color. It's the color of a sliced pomegranate, pale, and so fragile it would crumble if you touched it. Sunlight turns it to dust.'

She pauses, and he listens to her breath. Water running. Jane has a cordless phone. He can see her. She exhales smoke, paces in front of her woodblock prints. Geishas unfold their kimonos and reveal themselves to their samurai lovers. Does Jane really have a kimono? Or is it a lie?

'Please call me right away. I need to talk to you. It doesn't matter what time. I don't sleep anymore.'

She hangs up.

Ten stories below his balcony, huge arc lamps light up a road repair crew as they shatter the pavement with jackhammers. Salarymen and taxi drivers drift out of a *ramen* shop like daubs of blue smoke. Toshi looks for Jane on the street, but there's no sign of her. Unless she's hiding in dark doorways. But she's not that crazy, is she? He looks at his thumb. He backs away from the railing.

The second message.

'You're not home yet? Where are you? Maybe you're still at the cemetery. You met someone else there, someone prettier, another American woman who won't give you trouble like I do.' Something shatters. 'Shit.' A bottle? 'Oh, God. Did I really say that? Another American woman. I am so pathetic. Erase this from your message tape.'

She takes a long drag on her cigarette.

'I never used to say things like that. I used to be a nice girl.' She coughs. 'Did I ever tell you about my Vietnamese boyfriend? When I was in high school? He was ten years older. He had tattoos on both arms, and a motorcycle. My father hated him.' He hears her open the refrigerator. 'But my father's an asshole.'

She sighs loudly, and he pictures this: She kneels down and stares, disappointed, at the refrigerator's bare shelves, its damp whiteness. A shriveled lemon. An empty, crusted bottle of soy sauce. A bottle of vodka.

'Are you angry at me? Don't be. I mean, I can understand how you could be, but I didn't mean to hurt you. I just wanted to, to get your attention.'

She suddenly shouts, startling him, 'I wanted you to notice me!'

She whispers, 'I'm sorry. Please call me.'

The third message.

She is angry.

'Oh, I know Japanese men think it's a big adventure sleeping with American women, you think all American women are sexually promiscuous, don't you, that we're whores and that you can treat us badly and it doesn't matter.'

She starts to cry. Toshi almost feels sorry for her, but he catches himself. This is a trick. Everything she does and says is a lie.

'But what you don't understand is that I'm in love with you and, oh God, I can't, Toshi listen to me.'

She's slurring her words. She's drunk. She's on drugs.

'I need to I need to touch you I need to touch the skin on the inside of your thighs, to let my head drop between your legs and to just fall asleep. To fall and fall and fall, do you know what I'm saying.'

He hears a muffled, hollow sound, as if she's bumped into the wall. She drops the phone on the floor. 'Oh.' Her voice is far away. Then, she's back. But her words come slowly, and there is an odd gap between them, such a long interval that Toshi is surprised each time she continues.

'I must make you understand this. I will do anything to touch you again I will stay in my room and wait for you. Are you listening? Do you hear me? I will wait for you I will be naked all the time touching myself imagining you. I'm imagining you.'

She hangs up.

A dial tone.

Toshi stays on the balcony. He's shivering from the cold, but he wants only the night air and the darkness, to think about nothing. His thumb is throbbing. It's still early, but he's exhausted. From the cemetery. From the phone messages. From the subway ride home, which was packed with drunken people out celebrating the cherry blossoms.

When he was a boy, they taught him about cherry blossoms in school. About the moon. Maple leaves in the autumn. These things are special to the Japanese people, his teachers told him. The cherry trees bloom very late on Shiretoko Peninsula. There were no drunken crowds. Granny brewed tea from the blossoms, which they drank with homemade sweets that were fashioned into pink-tinted petals and green leaves.

Here in Tokyo, though, extra people-pushers are employed on the subways during cherry blossom season. Tonight, he had to wait for five trains to go by before there was enough room on one for him to be shoved aboard.

He'll call Paul. Paul will know what to do. He goes back inside, but just as he reaches for the phone, it rings. He jumps back, startled, then lifts the receiver.

'Toshi? Toshi Okamoto?'

It's not Jane.

'Yes. This is Toshi Okamoto,' he says in English.

'Hi. You probably don't remember me. This is Lucy. We had dinner together on your birthday. With Jane and my husband, Hugh? Remember?'

'Yes. I remember you.'

Lucy. She was pretty. And charming. As she talks he recalls these things about her: Her long, bare arms. Her hands resting on the tablecloth, her strong fingers splayed. What was she? A composer?

'I hope you don't mind my calling you at home, but I

have something I'd like to talk to you about. It's business. If you're not too busy, I was wondering if we could get together sometime soon.'

Is this a trick? Did Jane ask her to call him? But then he remembers: When they were introduced in front of the restaurant, he handed her his name card, with his home address and phone number printed on it. She took it from him with both hands and flipped it over again and again, from the Japanese side to the English and back again.

'Yes. We can meet,' he says, deciding to take a chance.

'Great. Great.' She really sounds pleased.

Now he remembers more: Her short hair hooked behind her ears like window curtains pulled back to let in the sunlight. How she leaned over his birthday cake and puckered her lips.

'Yes,' he says. 'Great.'

The washing machine stops spinning. He takes out his clothes and hangs them on the laundry pole to dry, all the while repeating their names in his head: Jane. Lucy. Jane. Lucy. The two American women encircle him in an endless parade – Jane in her moldering kimono, Lucy with her long arms and clear skin. They advance and retreat, their faces pressing up against his, unyielding and insistent. And ten stories below him, a procession of trucks rolls down the street, loudspeakers blaring. The radical Rice Party.

'Foreign rice will destroy Japan. Japanese have different digestive systems, and foreign rice cannot be properly digested by our bodies. This is a world plot to destroy Japan.'

He goes back inside and slides the balcony door shut. He turns off his answering machine. He doesn't want any more messages. He unfolds his mattress, shuts off the light, and finds himself in a Paris hotel room with Audrey Hepburn. They are being pursued by ruthless killers, and there is a gash on his back. Audrey cleans the wound. Her hands caress his skin. Outside the hotel room window, he sees the bare, gnarly branches of a cherry tree, in silhouette, on a background of pure white.

When he was a small boy, Toshi thought saplings buried under the snow were drowning. That their thin, bare branches sticking up out of snowdrifts were flailing arms. He'd dig them out, to save them. But once it started snowing up on Shiretoko Peninsula, it didn't stop until spring. He'd uncover a young birch tree, and the next day it would be buried again.

His mother watched him from the back window one dark afternoon, the clouds full and still. She put on her blue hooded parka, and together they walked along the bottom of the slope. She walked ahead of him, and her green rubber boots made holes in the snow, shadows that he stepped into. He stayed close to her. Once she had walked off into the snow and hadn't returned for hours.

'What were you doing?' she asked him.

He told her.

'But they're not dying. They're sleeping. Some plants, just like some animals, sleep under the snow,' she said. 'The snow is a blanket. It protects them from the wind and keeps them warm until spring.'

The clouds broke open, spilling out snow so fast and thick he thought that they could drown in it.

She saw the doubt on his face. 'Bears sleep under the snow. You know that, don't you?'

He nodded, imagining the warmth of a bear curled up into a dark furry ball.

'Come here.' She knelt down by two bony branches. 'You're right. They do look like hands.' She began to dig around them. He helped her.

'Look. See these little knobs? These will bloom in the spring. New branches will grow, and green leaves. See how healthy and happy this little tree looks?'

She held the limb in her gloved hand. Toshi took off his mitten and touched it. It did look alive. Snowflakes settled on his bare wrist and briefly revealed their intricate patterns.

His mother took off her glove too and pressed the branch against his cheek. 'Feel how warm it is?'

He felt the unexpected heat from her hand. He wished she would leave her hand there. She put his mitten back on for him and tucked it into his jacket sleeve. She stood up, and wiped the snow off her pants.

'Lots of plants and animals live happily under the snow. Only people are weak, and need to put on heavy clothes and stay inside in the winter.'

'But being a person is better than being an animal or plant, isn't it?' He didn't want to live under the snow, alone all winter. As he looked up at her, snowflakes caught on his eyelashes. He wiped them away.

'I don't know if that's so,' she said.

It hadn't really been a question, but her answer didn't surprise him. He was already accustomed to his mother's abrupt and unexplained sadnesses. Without warning, a look of despair would sink into the skin of her face like a great weight. She seemed to be thinking of somewhere far away, someplace he'd never been and could never go.

Toshi suddenly felt cold.

'Mother?'

The snow fell in a thick curtain around them. He could

barely make out the yellow light from the noodle shop. But she stared hard at the slope, as if she could see something there other than the dim outlines of trees.

'Mother?' His mittens were wet. He wanted to go inside.

She put a finger to her lips, and pointed. He followed her gaze. A family of red foxes scampered across the top of the slope.

She smiled.

The yellow light from the noodle shop glowed brighter. The light rushed out to envelop him and warm him.

'Good doggy, good doggy. Do you want to play with Toshi for a while?' Mami coos at the tiny white dog sitting on her desk. The dog wags its fluffy tail.

'Toshi-chan, you want to play with Wan-chan?'

Toshi looks up from the storyboard on his desk. 'No, thank you. Not right now.' His bandaged thumb makes it difficult for him to draw. The characters before him look edgy, the flesh of their skin bleeding onto their clothes.

Akira comes in the door and removes his Walkman headphones. From across the room, Toshi can hear American rap music. 'What? Another dog?'

'Come meet Wan-chan,' Mami says.

'Just for an hour again?'

'No, Wan-chan is ours forever.'

Akira shakes his newly dreadlocked hair, and white grains of rice clatter to the floor.

'They're still at it?' Toshi asks.

'At what?' Nakamura turns away from the window and

the rainy sky, sweeping smoke from his face as if brushing hair out of his eyes.

'Those crazy farmers have set up barricades in front of Mitsukoshi department store,' Akira says. 'They've dumped truckloads of rice.'

The fluffy dog blinks his eyes faster and faster, and then his bark weakens. 'Yip, yip, yip, yip.' His tail stops wagging and he tips over, headfirst, onto the desk. Toshi smells something burning.

'Oh dear, he's died,' Mami says. 'Naughty dog.'

'What? Died?' Akira says.

'Smack him,' Nakamura says. 'Hard, on the head.'

Mami hits the dog. Wan-chan shudders violently, then wags his tail. 'Yip, yip, yip.'

'Why, he's only a silly toy.'

'He's not silly. He's cute. And he's much better than a real dog. Always friendly, aren't you.' She picks Wan-chan up and cuddles him.

'But you can't love a stuffed toy.'

'It's not stuffed. It's filled with computer chips,' Nakamura says. 'That dog cost me forty thousand yen. Still, less than a rental dog in the long run.'

'You need a boyfriend, not a toy dog,' Akira says. 'Maybe you should ask Toshi to take you out on a date. He's a nice, trustworthy guy. Not like me.'

'Mind your own business. Besides, Toshi only likes American women. He thinks they're more exciting than we Japanese girls. Isn't that so, Toshi-chan?'

'No. That's not true,' Toshi lies.

'Don't distract Toshi. He's working. Which is what you two should be doing,' Nakamura says. 'I don't know why I pay you.'

'Now, Sensei, you know you can't rush talent. We creative types need freedom.' Akira dons his headphones again and does an exaggerated, jerky dance across the room.

Grains of rice fly from his hair and roll across the storyboard on Toshi's desk, where panels of faceless characters wait to be filled in. A pair of high heels materializes on the white paper, runs across wet pavement. A woman's hand nervously clutches a metallic pistol. American women, Toshi thinks. Why do I like American women? They're only trouble. Today he wants to forget about them and concentrate on his work. But he can't. The white bandage on his thumb is unraveling. The running woman is Jane, and she pursues him across the page.

Toshi hurries through a maze of crowded underground passageways, past shoe stores and coffee shops, noodle stands, and travel agency kiosks plastered with sunny advertisements for vacations in Hawaii, Guam, and Saipan. In front of a poster of two bikinied girls tossing a beach ball, a homeless man grills rice balls over a fire he's built inside a hubcap. The smoke stings Toshi's eyes but makes him hungry too. The man feeds the fire with old magazines, tossing in a cover photo of the Crown Prince. 'Desperate Search for Bride Continues' goes up in flames.

Paul is standing in a long line outside the Texas Steak House, talking to a young Japanese man.

'Toshi, this is Ueda-san. Ueda-san, this is my good friend Okamoto-san,' Paul says.

Toshi bows. Ueda bows lower, giving Toshi a top view of his close-cropped athlete's haircut and broad shoulders. He looks about fifteen years old.

Paul says very quickly in English: 'He doesn't understand English so just speak fast if you don't want him to know what you're saying.'

Ueda smiles and takes out a pack of Happy cigarettes, lights up.

'High school?' Toshi asks.

'Don't be cruel. He's in his first year at the Physical Education University. He plays soccer. And he's very intelligent.'

A waitress, her uniform a pattern of buffalo heads and American flags, moves down the line with a clipboard and menus.

'No American steaks today. Only Kobe beef, fish, and the salad bar.' She smiles brightly. 'We're boycotting American beef. The rice thing, you know.' She hands Toshi a slip of paper. 'Three of you? Here's your number. You should be seated in about an hour.'

'You know, you could really be in danger.' Paul holds Toshi's bandaged thumb between his own smooth thumb and forefinger, and turns it back and forth. Ueda has gone back to the salad bar for his third refill. His place at the table is littered with crumpled napkins, prawn tails, shredded lettuce, squished packets of ketchup, mayonnaise, mustard, and soy sauce.

'I mean, she's obviously crazy. That whole thing at Aoyama Cemetery. And those last phone messages.'

'Maybe if I don't answer her, she'll forget about me.' He doesn't really believe this.

'You should move into my apartment for a while. She doesn't know where I live, does she?'

'No. I never told her about you.'

Paul frowns. Toshi changes the subject.

'I forgot to tell you. Lucy called me.'

'Who?'

'She's this really nice woman I met the night Jane took me out for my birthday.'

Paul leans back in his chair and shakes his head.

'When will you learn?'

'Learn what?'

'Learn that when you mess with American women you're in over your head.'

Toshi looks up. There's nothing over his head.

'Lucy isn't like Jane.'

'You met her through Jane. She's Jane's friend.'

'She's a composer.'

'Oh, God.'

'She wants to see me.'

'Go. But don't come complaining to me if you wake up with a knife in your back.'

A knife in his back? Could Lucy do that? Jane could. They're Americans, after all. Jane has a pocketknife. Does she have a gun too? Does it even matter? Toshi's seen it in the movies and on the news: Anything can be a murder weapon in the hands of an American. They kill one another frequently, nonchalantly, and with everyday objects – hammers and golf clubs. Plastic dry cleaning bags. He picks up his fork and examines the sharp prongs.

Ueda returns, his plate piled high with lettuce, and topped with scoops of red and yellow Jell-O, chocolate pudding, and whipped cream.

'American salads are amazing,' he says. And it does look delicious, until he mashes it all together with his fork and spoon.

'He's sweet, isn't he?'

'I guess so.'

'He is. His boyish enthusiasm is refreshing. And he's quite intelligent.'

'You already said that.'

'And you of all people have no right to judge. A composer. God. Let me guess. New Age. She mixes whale songs with Chinese harps and Balinese gamelan, or something like that.'

Toshi doesn't say anything. He doesn't like Paul when he's like this.

'I'm sorry. I was trying, but obviously failed, to be funny.

Look, at least come spend the night tonight. I seriously don't think you should go home.'

'What about him?'

They both look at Ueda, who grins as he lights up another Happy cigarette. His face is bright red from drinking beer.

'Oh, you know,' Paul says.

'Know what?' Toshi asks.

Toshi and Paul are in the kitchen, waiting for the tea water to boil. Ueda is in Paul's bedroom watching an American porn video, and the soundtrack, audible in the kitchen, makes Toshi uncomfortable. Heavy breathing. Moans and groans. Two men having sex sounds to him like a car accident.

Ueda yells from the bedroom, 'This is fantastic. Are all Americans so big?'

Paul sighs. 'Okay, so he's young. Weren't you like that when you were young?'

'No.'

Paul turns the gas off under the whistling kettle and opens a cabinet. 'Choose a cup.'

Ueda yells again, 'Is there more beer?'

'Oops. That's my cue.' He takes a beer can from the refrigerator. 'He should be sufficiently warmed up by now.'

'Good luck,' Toshi says. Then Paul is gone. The bedroom door slams shut. Toshi is left staring into an open cabinet filled with cups and mugs of all sizes and shapes.

When he's alone in Paul's kitchen, Toshi likes to open up all the cabinets and cupboards and drawers, the refrigerator and freezer, even the dishwasher. The surfaces in the kitchen are all white and immaculate, but inside, the colors and shapes, the variety and quantity of Paul's possessions, overwhelm him. Some of the appliances he'd never seen before he came to Tokyo, couldn't even guess their purpose when he saw them: The food processor, the pasta maker, the coffee grinder. The espresso machine. The juicer.

He chooses a white mug with a smiling cow face, then opens another cupboard. Tins and jars filled with teas. Herbal tea. Chinese tea. Green tea. Indian tea. Apple, peach, rose hip, Sleepytime, jasmine and oolong and Iron Buddha. English Breakfast. Passion Punch. He takes out a tin of Darjeeling and places it on the counter next to a tall glass jar filled with spaghetti. The toaster oven. The blender.

He pours his tea and takes it into the living room. The floor-to-ceiling shelves are filled with books, pottery, woven baskets, and antique Buddhas from Paul's travels through Asia. The walls are covered with woodblock prints and calligraphy scrolls. A Noh mask. Behind the dining room table, an old embroidered Chinese robe, black and red and gold silk, is stretched and hung on a bamboo pole like a piece of art. Toshi loves Paul's apartment, but sometimes he feels confused with so many things around him, so much to look at and admire. It makes him anxious, for he feels obligated to keep looking. His own small apartment is almost as empty as the rooms he grew up in above the noodle shop. There is nothing on the walls except for one woodblock print of a captive samurai, his wrists tied behind his back. By the nineteenth-century artist Yoshitoshi, it was a gift from Paul for his college graduation.

When he first met Paul, Toshi asked him why he had so many things.

'Spending money keeps me from being lonely,' he said. 'When I find a real boyfriend, then I'll throw out everything and live like a monk.'

He wondered at the time if Paul was joking. Now he wonders: If my father and I had had more things at home, would I have felt less lonely growing up?

Steam rose up past the second-floor window. Pale moths passed through it and into the room, their wings heavy with moisture. They cast whirling shadows, which fragmented, and then they flew back out into the black night. Sounds drifted up from the open bathroom window. Toshi heard the scrub brush scrape his father's pale skin, a splash of water, then the stool shift on the tile floor as his father stood, then lowered himself into the tub.

Before his mother left them, his father often took Toshi into the bath with him, sat him down outside the tub, and washed his back with a sea sponge. Since his mother left, his father always bathed alone.

Toshi was drawing a picture of the back room in a new sketchbook Granny had given him. With crayons, he drew the *kotatsu* table, its wooden surface scarred with dark rings, years of hot teacups. The fluorescent light hanging from the ceiling, and the moths circling it. The two blue floor cushions he and his father sat on every day.

His father stepped out of the tub, and his wet feet slapped the raised wooden planks. The bathwater dripped off his body to the tile floor. Toshi drew a vase on the table and filled it with branches of wolf willow. He colored the vase blue. On the wall next to the window, he added a framed drawing, one of his own. Against the opposite wall, the narrow *tansu* that had sat there for years. On top of it, his collection of seashells and rocks.

His father fit the cover on the tub, a dull *thump* of wet wood on metal. Now that his mother was gone they often used the same water for two or three days, reheating it each evening. He listened to his father walk from the bathroom into the shop and open the refrigerator, pictured the sudden cold air and white light on his face. Toshi added a wall calendar to his drawing. He shaved down the point of his black crayon and neatly drew in the character for the month of July. He heard the hiss of released air as his father opened a can of beer, then his slow steps on the stairs. He kept drawing as he came into the room and stood over him. Toshi wore only a pair of cotton shorts. He felt the heat of the bath radiate from his father's body.

'Here, for you.' His father bent down and placed a glass of cold barley tea on the table, away from the drawing.

'Thank you,' he said without looking up. He drew in the borders of the tatami mats, the color of moss. He put his crayon down and drank some tea. His father stood over him and sipped his beer.

'That's a good drawing.'

'Thank you.' His praise surprised Toshi. He wasn't a critical man, it was just that he rarely offered an opinion.

'But, well, that's not really what the room looks like, is it?' his father said.

Toshi looked at the picture he'd drawn, then at the room.

'No, it isn't.'

In the room where they lived, there was no vase filled with wolf willow. No calendar or framed picture on the wall. No *tansu*. There was only the bare fluorescent light, the *kotatsu*, and the two old floor cushions. Nothing else. After his mother left them, his father sent the *tansu* over to Utoro in a truck. It was in her room now at the inn. Toshi's framed drawing was hanging there too. Last year's calendar came down at the New Year and was never replaced. His father had slowly emptied the two upstairs rooms, and kept them bare. Toshi brought home seashells, bleached white as rice. After walks in the woods, he emptied his pockets of small and perfect pinecones, like bunched brown fists. His father put them all away in the closet.

They lived in silent, empty rooms. In the front room, they took their mattresses and quilts out of the closet at night, and then folded them up and put them back each morning. That was all. The rooms felt abandoned.

Outside the windows, the sea. The wind. Sunlight and moonlight. White birch. Seasons changed. Leaves fell. At dusk, the stars appeared. In the spring, bear cubs tumbled down the steep slope. The fishermen shouted to one another as they returned in their boats each afternoon. Toshi pushed open the front windows, and he could smell their catch. Dark holds filled with layers of fish gasping for air, the fish on top throwing themselves against the walls of the hold, trying to escape. Dying fish still caught in nets, the nets now faded the color of pickled radish.

5

There's an amusement park on the roof of Seibu department store. On a clear night, the twinkling complexity can be seen from as far away as the summit of Mount Fuji. Lucy waits in front of the Ferris wheel. It is the first hot night in May, and the Ferris wheel revolves languidly, its colored lights blinking and burning, vanishing into the low clouds that trap the day's heat and the smoke from hundreds of millions of cigarettes lit, inhaled, exhaled, then ground out on the streets of Tokyo. The night air is tobacco scented. Mercury rises. Neon light wraps itself around buildings to define both shape and distance.

Lucy looks cool, dressed in black, her long arms bare. Leaning on air. She smiles, then waves, even though he's up so close.

'Hi. It's so nice to see you.'

'Yes,' he says, nervous. She laughs, relaxing him.

'You're not supposed to say yes. You're supposed to say, "Nice to see you, too."' She takes his arm easily, a gesture she doesn't seem to think about. 'Come on. I'm starving. And thirsty.'

He's charmed by her straightforwardness. Americans can say, This is what I want, let's go get it now. She leads him across the roof, moving in and out of light and darkness. She's a quarter step ahead, so he can admire the shape of her head, the moment where her bare neck disappears into the wavering shadow her shirt casts.

The frosty floodlights on her skin.

A blond foreigner in a T-shirt and bathing suit seats them under a striped beach umbrella in the 'Let's California Beer Garden.' Painted ocean waves splash over the tables and chairs; on a giant wall mural, Madonna and Charlie Sheen hover on surfboards in front of a psychedelic sunset. The music is loud. To hear each other, they have to lean across their round table.

'The Beach Boys,' Lucy says. 'Do you know them?'

'Beach Boys?'

'The music. Never mind. It's not at all important. In fact, it's silly. All of this.' She opens her arms and looks around. 'I mean, look at this. Where are we? Tell me that. Where are we?'

Toshi thinks for a moment. 'Shibuya. Tokyo. Japan,' he tells her. And she laughs. She has nice teeth. Her thick eyebrows and short hair remind him of Audrey Hepburn in *Funny Face*. Audrey the former bookstore clerk being photographed by Fred Astaire in Paris.

Their waiter reappears with a pad and pen. They order impulsively, intrepidly, calling out items from the menu to each other like a word game. Salad. Pizza. Potato. A pitcher of beer. Toshi feels emboldened by her presence.

'You know, I tried calling your home number a few times, but you weren't in and your answering machine wasn't on,' she says.

'I've been staying with a friend.'

'What's wrong with your apartment?'

'Nothing.'

'Oh, well.' She drums her fingers on the table, smiles

at him. 'It's nice to stay somewhere else sometimes. I understand that. You must get sick of your own place.'

When is she going to talk to him about Jane? Isn't that why she asked to meet him? He's expecting her to tell him something, to give him a message.

The beer arrives, a big, sweating pitcher. Toshi pours.

'You want to talk about Jane?' he asks.

'About Jane? Well, okay.' She looks surprised. 'If you'd like. How is Jane?'

'Don't you know?'

'I haven't seen Jane since your birthday dinner. She was Hugh's friend, not mine. And he and I split up.'

'You and Hugh—'

'We're getting a divorce.' She says this cautiously, as if she isn't sure whether he'll consider it good or bad news.

'I'm sorry.'

'It's not a sorry thing. Really. We're still best friends. There was no fighting. We both wanted it to be over. We got married right out of college. We were way too young. And then we grew up, you know?'

He shakes his head. 'I don't know.' She makes it sound so effortless, and inconsequential. Is that what happened to his parents? Did they grow up? For the first time, it occurs to him that he might have been the reason they stayed together as long as they did. If Lucy and Hugh had children, then would it be a 'sorry thing'?

'I didn't mean to make it sound so trivial,' she says. 'It's a habit I have, not wanting to make people uncomfortable.'

'It's okay,' he says.

'Anyway, I'm studying aikido now. Have you ever studied aikido?'

'No, never.' He's confused. Lucy speaks slowly and clearly, so her words are easy to understand. But the connections are hard to make. She leaps blithely from idea to idea. Does aikido have something to do with divorce?

'Well, try it. It's amazing.'

'In what way?'

'In many ways. It's a kind of spiritual therapy. It teaches you to concentrate, to focus, to be calm.'

He learned *calm* in high school English class. They sat tensed at their desks, pencils in hand, and listened to taped news broadcasts and to weather reports. It was always calm after a battle, calm before a storm.

'Aren't you calm?' he asks.

She smiles. 'I'm often calm, but not always, no. I'm calm right now.'

He wants to ask her more. He inexplicably feels free to ask her anything, everything. But the food arrives, and the table is covered with platters. Lucy serves them both, moving her chopsticks over the potato salad, the tomato salad, the jellyfish salad, arranging the shapes and colors on their plates into pictures. Then he starts to tell her about Jane, and she puts down the chopsticks and listens. Before he is finished, she leans across the table to take his hand.

'You do know about Jane, don't you?' she asks so seriously it unnerves him.

'No. I don't know.'

'Oh, God.' She removes her hand from his and fans the air, as if waving away bad things.

'Listen to me,' she says, very slowly. 'Jane has had a terrible, terrible time.'

'A terrible time,' he repeats, and a shiver passes through him. He feels an unexpected thrill. He tries not to smile, but he can't help it. Lucy leaning across the table. What she is about to tell him.

'Her *ikebana* teacher? Remember, at dinner that night?'

'When she was crying?'

'It was a horrible experience for her. This guy was really psychotic.'

A word he doesn't know, but it sounds very bad, very American.

'He was into some bizarre sexual things. I think he hurt her.'

He blushes. Sex. He doesn't know what to say.

'I'm sorry. I know it sounds awful. I don't really know everything about it. Hugh told me. He's known Jane since high school. She's always been out of control, apparently. And she's always had this thing for Asian men.'

'Thing,' he repeats aloud. A dark object, something heavy, metallic, floating in the air. You can hold it in the palm of your hand.

'She only dates Asian men. I don't know why. To be honest, I think that American men catch on to her act right away. But Asian men seem to find her affected behavior attractive.'

Is Jane unattractive? Is that what Lucy's saying?

'Did she tell you she's an actress?' Lucy asks.

'Yes.'

'Hugh said that she's never had an acting job in all the years he's known her. But here she passes herself off as some big talent. Of course, so many foreigners come to Japan and do that.'

He's lost. What do foreigners do in Japan?

'But what happened? With her *ikebana* teacher?'

'I don't know exactly. Except that she fell apart. She drove Hugh and me crazy, calling a hundred times a day. Jane needs an audience for all of her dramas.'

Jane falling apart. Jane breaking.

'She may be taking drugs. Antidepressants. Tranquilizers. She's not in good shape. You should be careful. You're not still going out with her, are you?'

'No. I'm not.'

Just then the music stops, and they're suddenly aware of a rustling around them, a murmuring. Everyone has stopped eating and is staring up at the sky. Lucy and Toshi lean back in their chairs. A blimp sails silently over the rooftop of Seibu department store – a whale, a shadow, a dream – so low that a boy on the Ferris wheel reaches out to touch its shimmering surface. A blinking dispatch lights up their faces like heat lightning: INTERESTED IN MARRYING THE CROWN PRINCE? QUALIFIED? CALL THE IMPERIAL HOUSEHOLD AGENCY AT 1111–1111.

The dishes have been cleared away.

'Why did you call and ask to meet me?' he asks her.

She smiles. 'Thank you. I'm having such a good time, I almost forgot that this is business.'

'What kind of business?'

'I'm recording a CD. It's all my own music, and I'm producing it myself. I thought you might be interested in doing the cover. It's contemporary, a mix of Japanese and Western instruments. Piano. Koto. Shamisen. I thought that something in a *manga* style would be appropriate.'

'You want me to draw the cover for your CD?'

'I'd pay you. This is a job, not a favor. Of course, I'd have to see your work first.'

'But why did you ask me if you haven't seen my work?' After Jane, he can't help being suspicious.

'I don't know any other *manga* artists. You're it.' She smiles. 'And I like you.'

He smiles too, feeling seduced in a pleasant, relaxed way.

'I'd like to play you my music. You should hear it before you decide.'

'Yes, I'd like to hear your music.'

'Good.' She hands a pink business card across the table, English on one side, Japanese on the other. LUCY PINK. COMPOSER/MUSICIAN. Her address, phone and fax numbers.

'Pink? Like the color?'

'Like the color. People think I made it up. But I was born with it. It used to be much longer, but my grandfather changed it a long time ago.'

'He changed it?' He couldn't imagine changing his name. Why? And to what?

She laughs. 'You know Americans.'

'No, I don't,' he says. And he really doesn't, he's beginning to realize.

'Self-improvement. No matter who or what we are, we're always working on ways to become somebody else.'

The school bus dropped him off, turned around in the gravel, and rumbled back down the coast road. Toshi dropped his leather book bag on a patch of dirt by the back door. The aroma of simmering broth and the gunfire of a TV detective show floated out the open window. He started up the slope.

He climbed uphill into the comforting smells of the forest. It was late September. The slope was dense with faded scrub bamboo, and with wild grasses that grew past his waist. He climbed above the drab concrete walls and blue tile roof of the noodle shop to a view of the dark sea. The Russian islands were ringed by clouds. He climbed above the screeching tires of a car chase. A woman's scream sailed up the slope on a gust of wind, then the sounds of the TV faded into the tangled brush. Stopping in the shadow of a white birch, he pulled his shirt over his head, and wiped the sweat from his face and chest. He sat down and watched the upstairs window. The leaves of the bear berry were beginning to redden. A dragonfly alighted on a wildflower, and the stem bowed.

An hour passed. Above his head, there were three colors in the world. Green leaves. White clouds. Blue sky. His mother's face appeared at the back window. It was a face he thought he knew, but now it seemed more distant than the cloud-covered islands. She leaned out, her arms on the ledge, her hair loose. She was crying.

Look up! Please look up! he called out silently through the wild grasses and the air busy with insects. Swarming mosquitoes were a dark smudge against the sky. But his mother just stared at the slope, which rose up at such a steep angle behind the shop that she often called it the 'wall.' 'Trapped between the wall and the sea,' she'd sigh.

He saw her lips move, but the angry sounds that carried up to him were the nonsensical language she spoke in her sleep. She turned abruptly, and he heard his father shout. His mother moved away from the window.

'What are you doing? He'll be home soon. Do you want him to see you like this?'

He'd never heard his father yell before, not at his mother, not at anyone. The words struck his bare chest like pitched stones, and he lost his breath. His father leaned out the window and looked up the slope, right at him. Toshi watched the anger drain from his face and saw the sadness that replaced it. He pulled the window shut, and he was gone.

Every afternoon when the school bus dropped Toshi off at the end of the road, his mother would be waiting at the front door. In the winter, the teakettle whistled on the stove top. In the summer, a glass of cold barley tea in the refrigerator. Yesterday, the front door had been closed. He'd rushed inside, his stiff leather book bag bouncing on his back. His father was chopping green onions. One hand pushed the long stems forward, the other gripped the broad knife, its wooden handle as veined as his father's arm.

'She's sick. You shouldn't bother her.'

'What's wrong? What kind of sickness?' His mother's illnesses frightened him.

'Don't ask questions. Just stay down here and don't make noise.'

He did his homework at the counter, listening for sounds from upstairs. But he heard nothing. Later, he had his dinner with the fishermen, who teased him about his growing boy's body.

'If you keep on like this, you're going to be as tall as a foreigner.'

'It must be his father's cooking.'

They all laughed, their sweat dripping into their bowls, hot food on a warm night. His father turned away to lift the lid off a pan of *gyoza*, releasing a cloud of steam, and someone gave Toshi a sip of beer. It tasted bitter, smooth as glass.

They closed up the shop. He wiped the tables while his father poured green tea over rice and carried it upstairs. He couldn't hear them talking. Whatever words passed between them were whispered.

He waited.

His father came down.

'She's feeling better now. You can go up.'

His mother sat in the back room, her chopsticks hovering over her bowl of tea and rice, which had cooled uneaten. When he saw her futon laid out next to her, he stopped in the doorway, afraid to go farther.

'I'm sorry, Toshi-chan. I'm not being a good mother, am I?'

'You're a good mother,' he said, terrified she would stay sick and stop taking care of him. 'Really, you're a good mother.'

'I'll be better tomorrow.'

But that night she slept alone in the back room.

And this afternoon, when the school bus drove up to the noodle shop, the front door was closed again.

The sun set, and three planets appeared in the September sky, bright as new ten-yen coins. Fireflies weaved through the dark forest like a procession of paper lanterns carried by invisible hands. The air cooled down, and he put on his shirt. His mother came up the hill, humming 'Red Dragonfly,' a song she had sung to him the Sunday before when they'd gone into the forest to gather spoon ferns. Later, she'd coated them with tempura batter and fried them for dinner. Her deep and pretty voice made him want to cry.

She sat down next to him and leaned back against the tree trunk. Her hair was neatly tied behind her head again.

'Aren't you hungry?'

He didn't answer her.

'It's so pretty up here at night. And cool. Funny we never think to walk up here after dinner. Well, from now on, let's see if we can do it.'

He wanted to talk to her, but he was angry, and afraid. He'd always known that he had to be careful with her. Only recently was he beginning to understand that he could lose her.

They both waited, listened to the shuffling behind them, the sounds of the forest accommodating the night. The sky grew black. Suddenly, far out at sea, there was a burst of bright orange light. The light bloomed silently, dancing wildly in the darkness.

'Mother . . .'

'A fire on one of the islands,' she whispered, as if they might be overheard. Her voice was a comforting rustle of leaves.

The fire spread, its preternatural glow reflected on the gathering rain clouds.

'Will someone put it out?' he asked.

'It doesn't matter,' she said.

'But people live there, don't they?'

'I don't want to talk about the islands,' she said, her voice far away.

Now what had he said? Lately, she drifted away from him so easily. There was nothing he could do to bring her back except wait.

They sat a while longer, saying nothing, watching. Finally, his mother said, 'I made dinner for you. It's waiting. Shall we go down now?'

'Okay.' He was too hungry to stay angry at her.

They started down the slope. The shop rose up and blotted out the flickering red sky, and they were plunged into darkness, as if into sleep. Then he remembered.

'Mother?'

'What is it?'

'Are you sick?'

He listened to her breathing. Was she afraid to tell him?

'No, I'm not sick. I was sick, a long, long time ago. Way before you were born. But having you made me better.'

'But yesterday. And today . . .'

'It was nothing. Only a little cold.'

They reached the back door, and they both hesitated. On the other side of the door, his father sat alone in the dark, watching TV. He must be afraid of losing her too, Toshi realized. His father knew all about her sickness but told him nothing. Shouldn't they be doing something to help her?

On the TV, the Emperor, in hip-high rubber boots, waded through a rice paddy.

'Toshi-chan,' she whispered.

'Yes?'

'Please be nice to your father. You should always be very nice to your father.'

Do you think you can just throw me away, DISCARD ME? Forget about me like you would a whore? GARBAGE? I'm not a whore. Is that what you think of American women?

The phone starts to ring the moment he unlocks his front door. He doesn't know why, but he counts the rings. Twenty, and then it stops. He locks the door, steps out of his sneakers into his slippers. There are three red envelopes on the floor by the mail slot, like red stains in the snow.

Jane.

Did I tell you? I bought this exquisite antique birdcage at the flea market at Togo Shrine. On a cloudy Sunday morning. It's delicate, it's carved wood. Don't breathe on it. Careful.

He opens all three envelopes at once, fans the pages out, and studies them like pictures, like a collage.

I bought two lovebirds. They're my only friends now. At night I cover their cage with a silk cloth, it floats down over the cage, ancient darkness. They sleep.

These pages, Jane's handwriting, the English words, shock and seduce him.

Please, please, please, I need to see you. I need to hear your voice or I'll go crazy. Oh, yes, I could, I would, I swear.

He touches the paper gently, and he bruises her flesh.

She stays at home, in bed, and imagines you. Your chest and your stomach, your thighs. Your skin. She has you memorized. She thinks she would die if she couldn't ever touch your skin again. Does that please you?

The sheets of paper tremble.

Are you the devil sent to torture me? I can't sleep nights. I lie in bed and I imagine your body pressing against mine and I have an orgasm.

The doorbell rings.

Sometimes she imagines that she will die in flames, that someone will set her on fire.

The knob turns and he panics. Did he lock it? Jane – could it be someone else? – pounds on the door with a fury that frightens him. Then, silence. He is barely breathing. He waits, stays still, for five minutes, ten minutes. The curtains are open. The building across the street. Is she watching him? He quietly pulls the curtains closed, tiptoes to the front door. He checks the lock, lifts the rusty chain, and slides that into place, too.

The phone rings again.

His heart pounding.

Thirty rings, it stops, then begins again. Twenty rings. Why is he counting? Is she counting too? In the silence, he pulls out his old school duffel bag and throws in underpants, T-shirts, jeans.

The doorbell rings again. Of course: She's been calling from the pay phone on the corner. He goes to the door, looks through the peephole. Jane. Her face, distorted by the lens, is grotesque, her red lips swollen. She seems to look right at him, and he backs away. She pounds on the door. Can she see him standing here?

He sinks down to the tatami, exhausted by her assault. She rings again, then drops a red envelope through the mail slot. He hears footsteps, the elevator door opens and closes. He waits, suspecting a trick. She didn't go down in the elevator, she's hiding outside.

Suddenly drowsy, he picks up the envelope and puts it in his pocket. He lays down right on the tatami by the front door, and he falls asleep so fast it is as if he is falling down into blackness.

Audrey Hepburn is being stalked in a dark apartment by a sadistic killer. She is blind. She stumbles. She trembles. She cries out. The killer strikes a match and illuminates her terror-stricken, yet still lovely face. The light of the flame flickers on her long, pale neck, then is snuffed out. Darkness.

He doesn't wake up until early the next morning, when an earthquake rattles the building and knocks a ceramic teacup filled with colored pencils off his desk. The teacup, a childhood gift from a potter, shatters, and the pencils scatter, arrange themselves into muddled ideographs. A reproach, Toshi imagines: Stay away from foreigners.

6

A few years after Toshi was born, Granny's son, Taro, built her a one-room pottery shop across the street from his inn. The shop had driftwood walls and a peaked roof of corrugated tin, and one wide front window, framed in blue, that looked out onto the street. Every weekend, when he crossed the peninsula to stay with his mother, Toshi visited with Granny in her shop. In the winter, he carried firewood over from the inn for her stove, his small arms filled with powdery logs, his boots crunching on the snow and ice. Inside the door, he stepped out of his boots and into slippers. While he drew pictures with the paper and crayons she kept there for him, Granny swept the floor and dusted her pottery. She made them strong tea – dark and smoky, or pale green with emerald specks floating on the surface like seaweed. When the warm weather came, he walked with her in the meadows above town to gather wild blue irises and peach-colored lilies. They filled the big urns she displayed on the shop's small porch to attract the tourists. The urns were dark as mud, the glaze mottled with ash and the thick green drippings of pine tree resin.

Three or four times each year, when the local potters who lived in the hills fired their wares, Granny drove Taro's pickup truck up to visit them and choose pieces for her shop. One Sunday, when Toshi was eleven, she asked him to come along. His mother was sick that weekend, and she didn't come out of her room. When Toshi knocked on her door, she wouldn't answer.

'It's better not to disturb your mother. She needs her rest,' Granny said. 'Come with me. I can use your help, now that you're so big and strong.'

It was early May, and patches of snow still shimmered high in the mountains. They followed the paved road up behind the middle school and over a series of low, indistinct ridges until first the town, then the sea dropped from view. The asphalt ended. The dirt road was dry and hardened to the color of flesh. On the floor at Toshi's feet, a crate of apples and dried fish.

'Your mother doesn't mean to upset you,' Granny said.

'I know,' he said. It made him uncomfortable to talk about his mother with Granny. Besides, she was rarely sick since she'd moved to the inn. 'Where does this road go?' he asked, anxious to change the subject. He'd never been up here before. The road didn't seem to have a destination. It moved through the mostly uninhabited land between the two coasts, between his two homes. Riding on it excited him; it was like thinking about a new idea for the first time: an expanse of land like the sea. Around every curve, another curve. The pickup truck was their boat. On one side, dark forest. Out the other window, sawed-off tree stumps, pale earth, and sky.

'I don't know where it goes. I've been driving on it for years, but I just follow it, and it takes me where I'm going.' She laughed. 'Like life, isn't it?'

'What do you mean?' His attention shifted to the treeline. A red fox stretched out in the sunlight.

'Someday you'll understand,' she said.

Soon, puffs of smoke. A tin chimney.

They rounded a curve and saw a log cabin set far back from the road, chopped firewood stacked up one side all the way to the sharply sloped roof. He opened the window and leaned his head out, as if the air might solve this mystery: Could someone really live out here, in the middle of emptiness?

The potter's wife bowed when they came in. She took the apples and fish from Granny without speaking, and then she brought them cups of tea and a bowl of mandarin oranges.

The house was one big room. A ladder led to a sleeping loft. Outside the wide front window, white clouds moved quickly across the peninsula, stretching themselves thin. Trembling light poured in and lit up the wooden table and the rough teacups so dramatically that Granny remarked on the changing colors in the clay. But behind the kitchen counter, the potter's wife was in shadow. She seemed separated from them by a great distance. While they drank their tea, she stood at the counter and rolled out dark, speckled *soba* dough. Toshi watched her cut the dough into noodles, which she hung on the dish-drying rack and from the backs of chairs. The flour dusted her hands like gloves. It's quieter than the sea in here, he thought.

Iino, the potter, took them out to his workship and kiln behind the house. Two pairs each of snowshoes and skis were propped up against the thick earthen walls. Toshi wondered about children, but didn't ask. Everything here was unfinished, the shelves that held the pottery, the stools they sat on while Iino brought out pieces for Granny to look at. Iino was almost as silent as his wife. They both had long, braided ponytails that hung down their backs over faded blue overalls. Granny kept up a stream of friendly chatter as she chose teapots and cups, sake flasks, and bowls. The three of them wrapped everything in newspaper. When they were almost finished, Granny spoke to Toshi.

'Why don't you get your sketch pad from the truck and show Iino-san some of your drawings?' She turned to the potter. 'This boy is going to be a fine artist someday.'

Toshi ran to the truck and brought back his pad. Would Iino like his drawings? He'd never shown them to a stranger before. He handed the sketch pad to the potter, who wiped his rough hands on his overalls, then opened to the first page. Toshi nervously watched him as he slowly turned the pages, taking his time with each drawing. They heard the back door of the house open and shut, then the potter's wife's shuffling footsteps on the dirt path. She carried in a blue glass bowl filled with peeled apple slices, placed it on the table without a word, and turned to leave. But at the door she paused. Without looking up she said in a voice almost too faint to hear, 'What a handsome young boy.' And then she hurried out the door.

Iino grunted but didn't look up from the sketch pad.

Granny laughed and called out, 'Thank you.'

Toshi stared down at the table, aware of the blood coloring his cheeks. He was pleased. Was he really handsome?

'This one,' Iino said finally, laying the pad down.

It was a picture of the sea seen from the rooftop of the inn. Toshi had drawn it one Sunday morning while his mother hung out the laundry: the border between the sea and the town delineated by roofs, by windows opened to a spring day. Damp sheets and socks clipped onto laundry poles. A pair of pants fluttered like a flag. Between two houses, a glimpse of a fishing boat's mast. The white page and crayon-blue sea looked like a faraway, wet country on the dry, clay-covered tabletop.

'This is a beautiful picture. Really it is,' Iino said, speaking directly to Toshi for the first time. 'I'd like to frame it and hang it in my house so I can see the sea every day. Would you trade it for one of my works?'

Granny clapped her hands. 'That's wonderful. Isn't it good that you came along, Toshi-chan.'

Iino, a real artist, had praised one of his drawings, wanted to hang it in his own house. For the first time, Toshi felt desired. He experienced the potency of talent, and it made him dizzy. But he remembered his manners. He bowed and said, 'I'm very happy. Thank you very much.'

Iino bowed too. 'It's an honor to meet another artist.'

He took his time choosing a piece of pottery while Iino and Granny finished the packing. He picked up a tall, cylindrical teacup and carried it over to the open door. In the transparent light, the brown clay surface revealed itself: moss-covered riverbanks seen from above. The base was gray and speckled, a gravel riverbed. Toshi's drawing would remind him of the sea, Iino had said. This cup reminded Toshi of mountain streams. He held the cup out to Iino. 'Is this one all right?'

At the potter's request, he signed his own drawing.

'When you become a famous artist someday, it will be worth lots of money. Mr Iino can sell it and retire,' Granny said, and she and Iino laughed.

In the truck on the way home, he held the teacup in his hands and turned it around and around, following the course of its river. Granny had said that the road they were on was like life. When Iino had called him an artist, he gave Toshi a map. Now he knew where he was going.

It was dusk in the hills. When they crossed the last ridge in Taro's truck, he was astonished by the radiance of the sunlight spilling off the spring sea.

'Toshi-chan, are you sick? You look terrible.'

Mami shuffles across the studio in a bright orange kimono, an embroidered pattern of cranes circling the Empire State Building and the Eiffel Tower. Her face is powdered white as sugar, and her hair, adorned with daisies, swirls above it. She cocks her head and gazes intently into Toshi's eyes. She looks like something sweet to eat, something that would leave his fingers sticky.

'Yes, you are sick. You should rest.' Taking his arm, she leads him like a child over to his desk. Toshi follows passively. What does she see in his eyes? Can she see Jane on the other side, her face distorted, banging on his door? He could never tell Mami. He knows what she would say. Foreigners. It's his fault.

He puts his duffel bag down. 'Mami-chan, why are you so dressed up? Are you off to a party?'

She spreads her arms and turns in a circle for him. 'Do I look pretty? Please tell me the truth.'

Akira comes out of the toilet, zips up the fly on his baggy shorts. He's had his nose pierced, and today a gold ring protrudes, matching the half dozen rings in his ears. 'You didn't know? Mami-chan's going to marry the Crown Prince. She's going to be the Empress of Japan someday. Better be nice to her.' He lights a cigarette. On his computer screen, Japanese fighter planes buzz a cartoon Hawaii. Bare-breasted, grass-skirted girls dance the hula.

'Is it true?'

'Don't listen to Akira. He likes to tease. I'm going to the audition at Tokyo Dome, but just for fun. I know they won't choose me.' She pets the toy dog on her desk. 'Wan-chan, would you like to live in the Imperial Palace?'

The dog doesn't move. A tangle of wires juts out of an open panel under its tail.

'I'll bet you could make the finals. Then you'll at least get to meet the Prince,' Toshi says. 'Don't be discouraged so early.'

'You'd better spit out that chewing gum before you go,' Akira says, clicking his computer mouse. A bomb falls on Pearl Harbor, but misses its target. The computer groans.

'The TV news said they're expecting more than twenty thousand girls. I don't have a chance. I just thought I'd go and see.'

'Why would you want to be princess?' Nakamura looks up from the storyboards on his desk. 'That Crown Prince seems like a very dull man. Your life will be better if you stay here and work hard.'

'That's right. I read that he studies catfish or something dumb like that,' Akira says.

'At least you'll wish me luck, won't you, Wan-chan.' She kisses the lifeless dog. 'Bye-bye, everyone.'

'Good luck,' Toshi says.

She walks out the door.

Akira shuts off his computer, and the Hawaiian Islands dissolve into darkness.

'Her father lost his job. That's why she wants to marry the Crown Prince. She's afraid her family will end up out on the street.'

'Really? I didn't know. That's terrible,' Toshi says.

'Yes. He worked for Sony for thirty years. But they're laying off thousands of people. It was on the morning news.'

'Japan is becoming like America,' Toshi says.

'Don't worry. If people don't have jobs to keep them busy,

they'll just buy more *manga*. That's good for us. Isn't that right, Sensei?' Akira says.

Nakamura takes his cigarette out of his mouth, balances it on the rim of the ashtray, and lights another. He holds out his pack to Akira.

'Fresh Air. New brand. Try one.'

Akira takes a pack out of his shirt pocket, holds it up. 'Happy,' he says, smiling.

Nakamura gets up and puts his arm around the cardboard cutout Chocolate Girl. 'Only you can save Japan, my dear. The country is collapsing like a brick house in an earthquake. We've lost our spirit. Our Japanese soul.'

'Sensei, don't start on that again.' Akira puts on his Walkman earphones.

Toshi remembers Jane's letter, still unopened in his pants pocket. He left the house so quickly this morning, he didn't even change his clothes. He reaches into his pocket, feels his handkerchief damp with sweat, and his own warm skin through the thin cloth.

'There are dark forces at work in Japan, and I am still trying to understand them. I must capture them on paper.' Nakamura takes Chocolate Girl into his arms and dances her around the room. 'We've become a country of hamburger eaters. Golf course pesticides poison our water supply and destroy our rice fields. Our military budget grows. Our corporations ravage the sacred rain forests of Borneo and pollute the rivers of Southeast Asia. Young Thai farm girls are enslaved in our hostess bars.'

Toshi takes out the envelope and opens it.

'The demons of Japan's past continue to haunt us,' Nakamura shouts.

Only a single sheet of paper. He unfolds it, and waves the smoke away.

He stares at the message for a long time, reading it over and over again.

This is what she's going to do.

She's going to cut the skin off your thighs and line her coat with it, so she can feel you against her always.

'Beware, beware!' Nakamura and Chocolate Girl spin past Toshi's desk in a cloud of smoke. 'We will pay for our mistakes.'

'Paul?'

'In here.'

Paul is sitting at the kitchen table in the dark. Toshi turns on the light, sits down, and watches him finish a box of cookies.

'You're going to get sick.'

'Probably. It's all part of the pattern.'

'What?'

Paul still has on his suit and tie. His briefcase, the brown leather water stained, is lying on the gray linoleum by his chair.

'Ueda is gone?' He doesn't really have to ask this question. Paul's boyfriends always leave.

'Gone. Along with about twenty CD's, two videos, and my Issey Miyake sports coat.' Paul stuffs the last cookie in his mouth. 'Not that I care about material things.'

Toshi gets him a glass of water.

'Please don't eat so fast.'

'At least he didn't steal any of the art. Remember Adachi?'

'Which one was he?' Paul has had so many boyfriends.

'He took the woodblock print.' Paul gets up and searches the cupboards, opening one door after another. 'Or was that Morioka? Maybe Adachi is the one who took my leather jacket. No, that was that Doi. I think Adachi is the one who stole my Rolex.' He slams the cupboard doors in sequence.

'I don't understand it. I'm so nice to them. I take them out to expensive restaurants. I buy them presents. I let them wear my clothes.'

'College boys are too young, don't you think? They're not trustworthy.'

'You were trustworthy when you were in college.'

Paul gets up and walks into the living room. Toshi follows.

'Maybe you should try to meet older men?'

'Older than what?'

'Maybe you should try to meet nicer men?'

'I met you. You're nice.' He lies down on his side on the carpet, pulls his knees up to his chest, as if he is cold. He reminds Toshi of the homeless people who sleep in Shinjuku Station. He stands behind Paul and waits, listens to him breathe. Then, as Toshi knew he would, Paul reaches behind his back and pats the carpet. 'Please,' he says quietly.

The word rises up from him, a wisp broken off from the larger cloud of his body, which floats on the sky of gray carpet. 'Please' hangs in the air, waiting for Toshi's reaction. And so he lies down behind Paul, puts his arm around his waist, and hugs him.

'Thank you,' Paul whispers.

When he starts to cry, Toshi tightens his hold and says over and over again, 'It's okay. It's okay.' He tries to think about Paul but finds himself thinking instead about the feel of the carpet against his cheek. About his rain-soaked pants clinging to his skin. About the letter from Jane in his pocket. He watches the minutes pass on the VCR clock. He listens to the traffic and to the rain.

Paul stops crying. He says, 'Well, why don't I wash my face and we'll go out and get very drunk?'

* * *

A pale man with wispy blond hair stops Toshi as they walk into the bar, holds him at arm's length, and looks him up and down.

'You are gorgeous. Would you go home with me tonight?'

'No, thank you,' Toshi says. These things happen to him when he goes to bars with Paul. He doesn't mind. He enjoys being considered attractive, even by men.

'My, and polite, too. Well, give me a call sometime. You won't be sorry. I make lots of money.'

He hands him his business card and goes out the door.

Paul grabs the card from him.

'Morgan Stanley. I could have guessed. What an asshole.' He tears up the card and drops it on the floor. 'What do you want to drink? I'm having vodka.'

They take two seats at the end of the bar so Paul can watch the door, check out who's coming in. It is only ten o'clock. It won't start getting crowded for another hour. Toshi takes Jane's letter out of his pocket, unfolds it on the bar. Paul stares at the sheet of paper.

'Whoa. This is incredible. This is not funny. Voodoo weird. Were her other letters this spooky?'

He repeats what Lucy told him, about Jane's affair with her *ikebana* teacher.

'Why didn't you tell me before?'

He looks hurt. He never likes to be left out of anything in Toshi's life.

'I don't know. I guess I should have.' But he does know. He didn't tell Paul because he didn't want to admit that the letters excited him as well as frightened him. How could he tell him that?

'Look, this woman is obviously nuts.'

'Nuts?' Peanuts. Walnuts. Mami once brought Toshi a box of chocolate-covered macadamia nuts from Hawaii.

'Certifiable. Wacko. Crazy. And she may be taking drugs. Which means that she also may be dangerous.'

They finish their vodkas and order another round.

'I have to go see her.'

'You have to what?'

'I have to go see her.' Paul often asks him to repeat things. When they first met, Toshi mistook this for bad hearing, not emphasis. Now he knows: A request for repetition means Paul is either annoyed or delighted.

'I have to find out what she wants.'

'You're not going to find out because you're not going to contact her. She's too, too crazy. Even for me.'

He leans in toward Toshi and lowers his voice. 'Which brings me to a question I've been meaning to ask you.'

'What?'

'What kind of sex did you two have? I mean, she sounds very bizarre.'

Toshi feels the blood rush to his face.

'Oh, my God. I can't believe I'm embarrassing you. Was it that wild? Was there apparatus involved? Blood rituals? Sacrificial animals? What? Tell me. I want details.'

'It was normal sex,' he says. And it's almost true.

Paul looks disappointed. The bartender brings over their drinks, and he pays for them, then drinks his down fast like medicine. He raises two fingers. The bartender nods.

'One more question.'

'Yes?'

Paul turns and stares at him, frowning slightly. 'Was it safe sex?'

'Yes, it was safe,' Toshi says, relieved that he can answer him truthfully. He knows what Paul means by 'safe,' for Paul constantly lectures him, passes along articles and pamphlets on AIDS in both English and Japanese. And as crazy as Jane is, even she had been cautious.

'Well, thank goodness for that. At least I've taught you something. Excuse me, it's pee time.' Paul gets up and walks across the room to the toilet, closes the door behind him, leaving Toshi alone with two full glasses on white square napkins.

Vodka on ice.

He picks up one of the glasses, swirls the ice cubes around. And he waits: For Paul to return. For Jane to hurt him or not to hurt him. He watches the ice cubes rearrange themselves in the glass, as if he might read them like tea leaves. He waits for a future he can't imagine.

'You must be an actor. Am I right? Tell me I'm right.'

'I beg your pardon?'

He turns and tries to focus on the man sitting next to him. Paul still hasn't returned from the toilet, and the bar is filling up. How long has it been? There's a line now outside the bathroom door. Madonna is singing. In the center of the room, a gigantic flower arrangement, long, prickly limbs around which everyone moves cautiously, cigarettes and sweaty drinks held close to their chests like fragile objects.

'I said, You must be an actor. I've seen you, haven't I? In that ashtray commercial, the one that sucks up smoke? You're the husband, right? Wait. No, it's the one for breath mints. That's it.'

The man has a face like a frog. Toshi, drunk, imagines that he's a tree frog, escaped from the branches in the center of the room.

'No. Not an actor.'

He doesn't want to talk to anybody. He finishes his drink, then picks up Paul's glass. Cubes of ice almost gone, water into vodka. The frog turns away. Toshi thinks he is rid of him, but it is not that easy. A moment later he is back.

'Do you like movies?'

Toshi nods. 'Yes. I like movies very much.' He is having a hard time speaking in English. Too much to drink. Maybe it would be nice to talk about movies though, about something simple, something that has nothing to do with his life.

'I knew it. I adore movies. I spent my entire childhood in movie theaters.'

The frog waits, but Toshi doesn't respond. So he continues.

'Ozu is my absolute favorite director. So pure, don't you think?'

'I've never seen an Ozu film,' he says. He's had this conversation before with other foreigners. Everything foreigners like about Japan was already over before Toshi was born.

'Never seen Ozu?' The frog is incredulous. 'You mean to tell me you've never seen *Tokyo Story*?'

He nods, then shakes his head. He always forgets: Yes sometimes means no in English.

Across the room, the bathroom door opens. Paul steps out and smiles at him. Making his way back, he ducks thorny branches, nods to acquaintances, absently brushes away cigarette smoke, and searches every face. Paul is always looking – for a boyfriend, for other things.

'Well, if you haven't, you should,' the frog says. 'After all, you're Japanese. And it's one of the ten greatest movies ever made.'

Toshi is about to ask him what the other nine are when Paul sits down and looks at the two empty glasses. 'I should have known I couldn't trust you alone with my drink.'

'Are you two together?' The frog leans forward, speaks across him to Paul. 'I wasn't trying to pick up your boyfriend.'

'That's okay. He's not my boyfriend.' Paul signals the bartender for two more drinks.

'Really?' The frog looks Toshi over. 'Well. Then, maybe I was trying to pick him up.'

'I'm not gay,' Toshi says.

'No, no, of course you're not. Heaven forbid. Neither am I. Nobody here is,' the frog says. The drinks arrive. 'Please, let me get these,' he says, leaning back to take his wallet from his pocket. But he leans back too far, and his stool tips over.

'Look out!' Paul yells.

Toshi watches the frog fall in a slow, surprised descent, right into the arms of two women – one blond, one brunette – in rugby shirts.

'Gotcha.' The blond laughs. And they raise his chair, with him still in it, as if they are lifting a piece of furniture into place.

'Why, thank you. Thank you,' he says. His face is scarlet. His hand goes to his chest and flutters there, illustrating, perhaps, the movement of his heart. 'You two girls are wonders. I believe you just saved my life!'

The blond laughs again. 'Don't mention it.'

'Well, let me at least buy you a round of drinks. I insist.' He turns to Toshi. 'And another round for you and your friend?'

'Actually, we were about to leave. I haven't had my dinner yet.' Paul stands up. 'Ready?' he says to Toshi, who is still replaying the frog's fall in his head: The slow-motion descent, as if he were moving through water. Toshi saw the confusion in his eyes as the polished surface of the bar, the rows of liquor bottles, the mirrored wall, all passed by.

And the way he rose effortlessly back up, like a film run in reverse. Could Toshi move backward through time like that, and wipe out his mistakes?

The rainy season. On the TV weather maps, heavy clouds cover the Japanese archipelago from Okinawa all the way up to northern Honshu. Only Hokkaido is clear. On Shiretoko Peninsula, laundry is carelessly left out overnight, clean sheets snapping in the dark wind. Here in Tokyo's gay bar district, though, neon signs are stacked one on top of another four stories high, and their bright colors bleed together in the rain like watercolors. Toshi and Paul walk past Marine Club, Kings of College, 69, Zip, Morning Tissue, Idol Host Snack Bar. Rain swirls around them like vapor. An umbrella, even if they had one, would offer no protection.

Paul is ahead of him, walking quickly.

'Thanks,' he says to Paul's wet back. 'I didn't want to talk to him.'

'I didn't do it just for you. I really am hungry.' He stops and turns around. They are both drunk.

'Promise me,' Paul says.

'Promise you?'

'That you'll be careful.'

'I'll be careful.' He doesn't know what Paul means, but he's happy to repeat whatever he says.

'I mean about Jane.'

'Oh.'

'That was a truly scary note she wrote. I mean, who knows what she might do.' Paul glances quickly behind him. 'She could be stalking you. She might be watching us right now.'

'Watching us?' Toshi freezes. Is she really here? Around them, everything is wet and moves in bursts, the speed of objects described by the rain.

Sounds: hissing, snapping, splashing.

Taxis, bicycles, clusters of umbrellas.

A red paper lantern sways in front of a food vendor's stall.

'Hey, don't worry. If you were born to be shot, you won't be hung.' Paul smiles and slaps him on the shoulder.

'What?' Is Paul not making any sense, or is Toshi just too drunk to understand him?

'Let's go eat.' Paul crosses the street, his expensive loafers splashing through puddles. Toshi follows him, grateful to Paul for caring about him.

A taxi comes between them, and stops.

A shiny yellow surface.

A woman in a tight black dress steps out and opens a Snoopy umbrella.

Toshi recognizes her.

'Lucy!'

The taxi door swings shut. She looks up, startled.

The taxi pulls away, and they're both left standing in the middle of the street. Paul is on the opposite curb.

'Toshi! Oh my God, I wasn't supposed to see anyone I know with this umbrella. It's not mine. You mustn't think that it's mine.'

She laughs, closes up the umbrella, and hides it behind her back, then opens it again. She takes a step forward, so that it covers Toshi too.

'This isn't doing a bit of good, is it? Look, it's raining from the ground up.' She laughs, and closes the umbrella for a second time. 'I can't believe I'm carrying a Snoopy umbrella and I run into you. I never, ever, run into anybody in Tokyo. What are you doing here?'

He is drunk, and she's talking fast. She looks so beautiful. He's never imagined her in a black dress. But he has imagined her, many times. Tonight the rain settles on her bare skin like drops of fresh cooking oil.

'I'm on my way to hear some jazz. The club is somewhere around here. I have a map. Would you like to come along?' She looks at him suspiciously. 'Are you drunk? Oh, God, you're drunk, aren't you.'

He grins. 'I'm with my friend. He's right there.' He points to Paul, who waves, then crosses the street to them. The three of them stand in the rain. Cars swerve around them.

'This is my friend Paul. This is my friend Lucy.'

Seeing the two of them together, these two separate parts of his life, sobers him up slightly.

'So, you're the famous Lucy.'

'I'm famous?' She looks at Toshi, amused.

'I love your umbrella,' Paul says. Charming.

'God, I knew this would happen. You must think I'm a complete dork. I swear, it's not mine,' she says, flirting with Paul. He's handsome, the red hair.

'Of course it isn't. But your fashion sense is none of my business,' Paul says. They step up onto the sidewalk and start walking, forgetting Toshi. He doesn't mind. He's relieved. They like each other.

'We were just going to get something to eat. Why don't you come with us?' Paul asks.

'Sure. I'd love to.' She looks back over her shoulder without slowing down. 'Is this the friend you've been staying with? He's nice.'

'Yes,' he says, hurrying to catch up.

But can he ever catch up? They walk too fast, they talk too fast. The way Americans immediately relax with each other the first time they meet, are able to just start talking, amazes and discourages him. Will he ever be that sure of himself?

They duck into a small *ramen* shop, the first open doorway they come upon in the rain. An orange Formica counter with five stools, bare fluorescent tubes, a worn concrete floor. Toshi sits down and, out of habit, lines up the sticky jars of rice vinegar, chili oil, and soy sauce on the counter in front of him.

Toshi was born into an atmosphere heavy with molecules of *ramen* broth. In his earliest memories, his father stirs the broth in a huge pot on the stove. He throws in fatty chunks of pork. Before she left them, his mother made noodles by hand, by window light, lifting the dough over and over again like the hem of her apron.

A tired-looking man behind the counter watches TV and waits for customers. Like Toshi's father. He pours glasses of water, then takes their orders. Toshi watches as he weighs each portion of noodles in the palm of his hand before dropping it into the boiling water. The hiss of the rain is on Toshi's right, Lucy and Paul on his left. He only half-listens to their conversation as the cook takes three white bowls from a tall stack, lines them up, and spoons in the sauce. He's heard it before: Where they're from. When they came to Tokyo. Why.

But then there are details, events from Lucy's past he hasn't heard. She is twenty-eight years old. She spent three months living in a Zen temple in Kamakura when she first came to Japan. She swept the floors, practiced zazen, and learned to play the shakuhachi flute.

She laughs. 'I was awful at all of it, except the shakuhachi. I almost ruined my back and knees meditating. I was practically crippled.'

The cook shakes out the noodles, runs them under tap water.

'But why did you come back to Japan?' Lucy asks Paul.

He tosses the noodles into each bowl with a smooth, practiced motion of his arm.

'Back in America, I fell in love. My lover and I moved in together. We were in love, then my lover died.'

'Oh, God,' Lucy says.

Toshi is startled. This is a story Paul never told him.

The cook ladles in the broth. Working fast with chopsticks, he adds thin slices of pork and chopped green onions.

'Yes. My lover got sick. Every day for a year I watched him die. Then he died. And I fled. Back to Japan.'

On top of each bowl, the cook floats a crisp square of nori. The seaweed darkens, green to black, as it absorbs the broth.

'I'm so, so sorry,' Lucy says, and she takes Paul's hand.

Toshi is numb. He can feel that he has stopped breathing, but he doesn't know how to start again.

The cook reaches over the counter to hand them the steaming bowls. 'Be careful. They're hot.'

'Well,' Paul says, taking his bowl. 'You know. These days, it's become an old story, hasn't it?'

'No. No, it hasn't. Don't say that. It will never be an old story.'

Toshi is humiliated. Paul just met Lucy ten minutes before. Why didn't Paul ever tell him? He doesn't want to listen anymore. He concentrates on the white bowl in front of him. As the fragrant and familiar steam wets his face, his eyes fill with tears of anger, clouding his vision. In one hand he finds his chopsticks, in the other a plastic spoon. How did they get there? In the bowl, the white sky over Shiretoko Peninsula. Heavy clouds blow in from the sea and collide. He is hurt and angry and can't distinguish between longing and memory. Who is he angry at? he wonders, panicking. Paul? Lucy? A mother who left him? A father who chopped vegetables, fried up rice, weighed out servings of noodles in the palm of his hand day after day without ever speaking, without revealing anything? Why doesn't anyone ever tell him the most important things? Is it his fault?

He lowers his chopsticks, and his hand grazes the rim of the bowl, tipping it over. He watches as the scalding broth and noodles spill in slow motion into his lap. Lucy and Paul and the cook all look up when he cries out. For a moment, even he confuses the source of the pain.

They're standing in the rain. Lucy opens her Snoopy umbrella.

'Thank you. This was so great,' she says to Paul.

'Listen, you saved our evening,' he says. 'You and your wonderful umbrella.'

They kiss like old friends, like Americans. She turns to Toshi, hesitates, then smiles.

'Are you all right? Are you sure you're not burned?'

'I'm fine,' he says, and he looks down at his pants, wet from the waist all the way to the cuffs. Paul poured glasses of water over him.

'Well, I'll call you as soon as I have a finished tape for you to listen to. But send me your drawings, okay?'

Angry, he only nods.

She waves, disappears around a corner.

'We'll never get a taxi now. We'll have to take the train,' Paul says, maybe noticing Toshi's sullenness, maybe not. He's drunk too.

Inside the subway station, the homeless, in their government-issue blue uniforms, bed down for the night on rows of identical mats. He considers joining them. He doesn't have a home now, he realizes. Paul's home is not his.

Paul walks up to a ticket machine. 'Two tickets to Aoyama Icchome,' he says in Japanese.

'Welcome. Please deposit two hundred and eighty yen,' the machine instructs him.

He feeds in coins.

'That was the exact amount needed. You will change trains at Akasaka Mitsuke Station. Thank you,' the machine says, churning out two tickets.

'You're welcome,' Toshi says, feeling that he has more in common with the ticket dispenser, which is, after all, Japanese. He slides his ticket into the turnstile slot, then sticks his arms into the blood pressure checker. The rubber cylinder tightens, grips him, then releases with a hiss.

'One-ten over seventy. Work hard tomorrow,' the machine says in a pleasant voice.

'If I were straight, your friend Lucy is exactly the kind of woman I'd go for.' Paul comes into the room, carrying a glass of water.

It's morning. Toshi sits up in bed. He has a terrible hangover.

Paul drops two white tablets into the glass and hands it to him. 'Wait until it stops fizzing, then drink it. An American cure. It works wonders.'

'How come you never told me about your boyfriend who died?'

Toshi has been thinking about this since he woke up. Last night, he fell into a restless sleep thinking about it, imagining the boyfriend. Who was he? What did he look like? Imagining Paul sad, alone on an airplane to Japan.

Paul ignores him, seats himself on the edge of the bed, and arranges the hem of his bathrobe around himself like a skirt.

'You think I'd make a good princess? Perhaps I should have gone to the audition.'

Toshi doesn't laugh. 'You just met her. You don't even know her.'

'She's American,' Paul says. 'Drink your Alka-Seltzer like a good boy. It's stopped fizzing.'

He drinks it. It tastes terrible. Paul takes the glass from him.

'I don't know why I always listen to you,' Toshi says. He waits for the drink to take effect, to soothe his anger as well as his headache and sour stomach.

'Because I'm older and white. It's been that way since the beginning of time.'

This morning, he is impatient with Paul's jokes.

'You could have told me. I thought I was your best friend. You told Lucy things about you that I never knew.'

'I was very drunk. She was someone I would have been friends with back home. It was like I knew her already.'

Paul gets up off the bed.

'I'm late for work.'

He pauses in the doorway.

'You're Japanese. I guess I didn't think you'd understand. And besides . . .' He stops.

'Besides what?'

'Besides,' he continues as he walks down the hall, 'I've always been in love with you. That makes it difficult to talk to you about certain things.'

Later, when Paul is in the shower, Toshi goes into his bedroom and opens the dresser drawers. He doesn't really know what he's looking for. A photograph? Letters? I don't know Paul, he thinks. I thought I did, but I don't, not at all. What else don't I know about him?

He doesn't find anything. He leaves the drawers open and goes down the hall. He stands outside the open bathroom door and says, 'I'm going to move back to my apartment. I don't think I should stay here. Okay?'

Paul doesn't say anything.

'Did you hear me?'

Paul shuts the shower off. The murmur of the exhaust fan. Water dripping from the showerhead. In the kitchen, the radio is on.

'I heard you,' Paul says.

And then he turns the shower back on.

7

It has been raining for days. The snapshots on his wall and the pages of comic books scattered on the tatami curl up like waves. Exhausted and discouraged, Toshi leans into the wall for a moment, and leaves a damp handprint, and he remembers a cave in the hills of Shiretoko Peninsula, an hour's hike from the noodle shop. The walls of the cave were covered with phosphorescent moss. Toshi leaned his whole body into it, and when he walked away he left his shadow behind.

He's surprised that there are no red envelopes waiting for him. He turns his answering machine back on, vaguely hopeful. Could Jane possibly have given up, as worn out by her own persistence as he is? And what about Lucy, who has stepped into his life unexpectedly, stepping awkwardly between him and Paul?

His clothes and skin reek of cigarette smoke. Gathering up soap, shampoo, a towel, and his orange plastic basin, he walks past the 7-Eleven and the video store, his bare feet wet, sliding in and out of his rubber sandals. Rainwater rushes along the curb, tossing cigarette butts. He looks up through his clear plastic umbrella at the dark, wet sky. Apartment building lights twinkle like stars – the only stars he ever sees in Tokyo.

At the bathhouse, he sits naked on a stool and stares at

himself in the mirror. Mount Fuji, a mosaic of bath tiles, rises up in front of him to the wooden ceiling. He lets the faucet run until the hot water overflows his basin. All around him, naked men vigorously scrub their bodies with rough washcloths, shampoo their hair, rub pumice stones on the bottoms of their feet. They pull their razors across their wet cheeks, flicking the shaving cream onto the floor. Rows of faucets and showerheads gush water. So much water seems a luxury, even with the constant rain. He feels the hot vapor opening his pores, and the anxiety seeps out of him.

Toshi rinses off, then lowers himself into the vast tub, and he feels real heat – heat that aches, that enters his bones. Conjuring heat: His mother climbs the stairs after her bath, her pretty face flushed, her hair wrapped in a towel, a glass of cold tea in her hand. His first night in the college dormitory in Sapporo, he sits in the bath surrounded by unfamiliar faces, everyone too shy to speak, only nodding at one another. Toshi feels himself dissolve. He closes his eyes and he sees volcanic hot springs. Steam rises up over Japan and envelops the whole country in a cloud of sulphur. Women's voices drift over the low dividing wall of the bathhouse. A mother warns her daughter to be careful stepping into the tub. He hears a splash and opens his eyes. A bald, old man slides into the tub next to him.

'Ah, it feels good,' he sighs, nodding to Toshi.

'Yes, it does,' he says.

'Are you a college student?'

'No, I work.'

'But you're not from Tokyo. I can tell from your accent.'

'I'm from Hokkaido.'

'That's a good place. Clean air. Lots of trees.' The man nods again, then settles his shiny, wrinkled head back against the rim of the tub and closes his eyes.

We can sit naked together in the same tub even though

we're strangers, Toshi thinks. That's because we're Japanese. We understand each other. We trust each other. He is tired of Americans, of trying to know them. He feels devoured by them. Even Paul. Paul is in love with him. He knew that. He realizes now that he's always known it. But why did Paul have to spoil everything and say it aloud?

He closes his eyes again, surrenders again to the heat, and he sees Hokkaido. The flickering green light of the soft pines. The curling bark of the white birch. The sound of the forest when there is no wind.

The shadow of a small boy imprinted on a wall of luminous moss.

He shuts the balcony doors and turns on the air conditioner. Then he takes out his sketch pad and begins to draw. He is bored with Chocolate Girl. There are so many things he wants to draw. Tonight, he sketches from memory: a meteor shower in August. He's twelve, maybe thirteen years old. Lying on the dock at midnight, he searches the sky for shooting stars. Underneath him, the soothing sound of the sea. Above him, stars burn across the blackness like everything he desires.

Still sitting up, his sketchbook open in front of him, Toshi sleeps and dreams. His hand unfolds, and his pencil rolls across the table, drops onto the floor of the noodle shop. The shop is filled with customers. Behind the counter, his father works quickly, frying rice in the big wok. The room fills with oily smoke. His mother carries trays of steaming *ramen* bowls. Everyone Toshi knows is there. Paul and Jane and Lucy. The fishermen. Nakamura and Mami and Akira. And everyone is smoking cigarettes. Toshi starts to cough. Suddenly, he finds himself in a huge garage with Audrey Hepburn. She runs from car to car, turning on the engines. The windows are closed, and the garage fills up with exhaust. Toshi can't breathe.

He wakes up. His throat and lungs ache. The apartment is filled with smoke. He opens the balcony doors, gasps for air, and watches the smoke rush out into the hot, wet darkness. Neon lights flicker all across the city like rooftop campfires. Inside his apartment, small flames crackle by the front door. The tatami is on fire. Cockroaches stream out from behind his kitchen cabinets and dash up the walls. He grabs the kettle and pours water over the small flames, which sizzle and die.

He stands there naked, his heart pounding hard, his skin dripping smoke and sweat. The tatami smells like roasted tea. Someone bangs on his door.

'Okamoto-san! Okamoto-san! Are you in there? Wake up!'

He opens the door. Cockroaches swarm over his bare feet and out into the hallway. His next-door neighbor stands there in his summer long underwear, looking terrified. 'Oh, thank goodness. I was so frightened. I called the fire department.'

'I'm all right.' He hears sirens. Then he smells something else, stronger than tea. A wad of newspaper lies below the mail slot, smoldering. He picks it up. It's the *Japan Times*, the English-language daily. It's heavy, soaked with liquid. His neighbor leans over and sniffs it.

'Kerosene. It looks like someone tried to burn down your apartment.'

The firemen arrive, and then the police. Rainwater drips from their shiny slickers, forms small puddles in the corridor that reflect the fluorescent lights. A TV reporter appears with a cameraman, and bright light bounces off the walls, draining the night of any remaining color. Bare-chested and in his boxer shorts, Toshi shields his eyes, confused by the commotion. The elevator door opens and closes, disgorges strangers. The policemen pass the balled-up newspaper back and forth like a pork-stuffed bun while his next-door neighbor tells them about the foreign woman he saw banging on Toshi's door.

'It was a few days ago. Of course I don't know about foreigners at all, never even talked to one in my life, but for some reason, I thought she looked very upset.'

On the edge of the small crowd, the words *foreigner* and *arson* are taken up, woven into the texture of the night.

The TV reporter holds a microphone up to Toshi.

'I don't know anything about it. Probably she had the wrong apartment. I don't read the *Japan Times*. It's an English newspaper.'

'We've been having problems with foreigners here in Tokyo, you know. A foreigner crime wave,' one of the policemen says.

'Foreigner crime wave?' The newspaper reporter scribbles on his pad.

The policeman puts the kerosene-soaked newspaper in a shiny metallic bag and zips it up.

At dawn, Toshi's landlord arrives, walks through the apartment, and scowls.

'I'm not replacing the tatami. I'll send someone up to turn them later this week.'

'That's fine. I'm very sorry that you had to be disturbed in the middle of the night.'

'I don't like my tenants mixed up with foreigners. It only causes trouble for everybody.'

'I apologize. I'm sure it was a case of mistaken identity. From now on, I'll be careful.'

He bows deeply. But he wonders if his landlord might be right, if getting involved with foreigners will inevitably lead to trouble. And he also wonders: If it is too late to be careful.

* * *

Hours later, when he has finished cleaning up the apartment as best he can and is ready to take a nap, the phone rings. Jane. He knows he has to answer it. He has to talk to her. He lifts the receiver.

'Hello?'

'Good morning,' his mother says in a cheerful voice. 'I hope I didn't wake you.'

He doesn't tell her. It would be impossible to explain to her the turn his life has taken here in Tokyo.

'I wanted to let you know your father is coming to visit you.'

'Really? When?'

His father never left Hokkaido, rarely left the shop.

'I think he's on his way already.'

'Why is he coming? He didn't even call to tell me.'

'He didn't say. Only that he's driving down to Hakodate and then taking the ferry. I told him that it's such a long trip that way, but he said he didn't want to fly, and that he had plenty of time.' She pauses. 'He's been acting odd lately.'

'What do you mean?'

'I don't really know. He's been calling a lot, and wanting to talk. I think he's lonely.'

'Is everything all right?'

'Everything's fine. But please be kind to him. He's getting old, you know.'

'Don't worry. I'll take good care of him. How old is he?'

'Well, I'm sixty-five. So he would be . . . seventy-two.'

'He'll stay with me, won't he?'

'I suppose. He didn't say. He just called and said, "I'm going to visit Toshi-chan in Tokyo." You know how your father is.'

'Yes,' Toshi said. But, really, he didn't know.

In the early spring, Toshi graduated from college. He packed up his room, shipped his art books and supplies to Paul's apartment in Tokyo, said good-bye to his friends and teachers, and left Sapporo. His girlfriend, Patty Shapiro, had already returned to America, back to her American boyfriend. As he carried his duffel bag and suitcase through the bitter cold to the train station, the city seemed abandoned, his emotional attachments already severed.

He traveled up to Shiretoko Peninsula, changing trains at small, snow-swept stations, and moving northeast through familiar vistas. Billowing sulphur clouds hung motionless over hot springs resorts. Ski lifts crisscrossed mountains. A cross-country race. The skiers, in sheens of bright pink and green, their heads bowed and their numbers pinned on their backs, moved purposefully, rolling across the white hills like colorful beads.

His mother waited for him in front of the train station in Shari. Behind the steering wheel of Taro's car, she sipped a steaming cup of Mr Donut coffee.

Each time he saw his mother, he was confounded by the person she was still becoming. His father grew even more silent each year, shedding words like weight. But his mother, in the years since she'd left them, had become talkative, frequently cheerful. Sometimes he found himself resenting her. Had he and his father really made her so unhappy? Even her appearance: At the noodle shop, each morning she'd pulled her hair back into a tight bun. But after she'd moved to the inn, Taro teased her, called her 'Auntie,' until she loosened her hair and let it fall into a ponytail. Before Toshi went off to college, she'd untied the ponytail too. Now her thick hair, streaked with white, hung down her back. Her clothes were loose and plain, and as always hid the shape of her body. In the past few years, though, she often added something small and beautiful. Today, a man's sweater and pants, a down jacket. Silver wagon wheels with turquoise spokes swung tentatively from her ears.

Taro liked to entertain the inn's guests by telling them that he was descended from the Ainu, the aboriginal tribe that had once inhabited Hokkaido. One night, after drinking two flasks of sake, Taro had pointed at Toshi's mother and said to a group of young backpackers from Tokyo, 'This woman here is pure Ainu. Can't you tell by looking at her?'

She laughed at him as she served up a dinner of fish stew and mountain root vegetables. 'It's true,' she said. 'We Ainu have very thick hair, like animal fur. My own mother's hair grew right down to the ground. She wove fox bones and birds' feathers through it.'

The young guests stared up at her in wonder. Toshi looked at her with both astonishment and unexpected anger. She flushed at her own lie and hurried from the room.

He'd never known she was capable of lies. Yet she'd told one as quickly and easily as she told the truth, as if they were the same thing. He couldn't help but think, What else has she lied about? What don't I know about my mother?

They drove out of the drab town past frozen fields, rippling dark sheets that dipped down to the coast road.

'The inn is doing well?'

'This is the busiest winter ever. People can't afford to go abroad now, so they come up here to see the ice floes. Wait until you see the changes Taro's made. You know, he hired a Filipino girl.'

'Really?'

'It's hard to find young Japanese who want to work in an inn these days. They all want to move to the city and work in offices. He found her through an employment agency. She's very nice and hardworking.'

They drove without talking for a while.

Gusts of wind splattered pebbles against the windshield like rain.

'Your father and I were divorced last month.'

A strange numbness spread out abruptly from Toshi's chest into his limbs. Blood pounded behind his eyes. He stared straight ahead.

'Did you think we already were?' Her voice sounded dry, unfamiliar. She was a stranger to him.

'I didn't know.'

On Shiretoko Peninsula, people married young, had children right away. Toshi's mother was forty-two when he was born, his father forty-eight, old as grandparents. He'd never asked why they'd waited, or about the years before he was born. And after she left, nothing was ever said about their separation. Now, suddenly, his mother wanted to talk. But he didn't know what to say after so many years of silence.

'I asked for the divorce. Not your father. Please don't blame him.'

Toshi was angry. 'Why did you have to do it? You could have stayed married.' Even as the words tumbled out, he realized his foolishness. In his mind, they had remained together. But it had been fourteen years since she left.

'We couldn't have stayed married,' she said.

'Why not?'

She didn't answer him.

The road narrowed as the foothills pressed closer to the

sea. The mountains were solid white, the snow so deep that the treetops were only brief shadows on its surface.

'When the thaw comes, there'll be so much water pouring down to the sea. We'll be digging out of the mud until late May,' she said.

He would help her, give her time to say what she had to say. 'The streams and lakes will be high all summer,' he said.

'That means black flies and mosquitoes.'

And in the early morning hours, flocks of butterflies, he thought. Purple Emperors fluttering down from the treetops like startling dreams.

'Toshi-chan, you like Taro, don't you?'

'Yes' was all he said, still distracted. Taro's wife had died young – from cancer, Granny once told him. He'd quit his company job, moved up to Hokkaido. He'd never remarried, and he had no children. He'd taken Toshi fishing, had taught him how to salvage driftwood and build a shed from it.

She slowed the car, as if it was difficult for her to concentrate on what she wanted to say.

'Taro and I are going to be married.'

He was so taken by surprise that he couldn't say anything, even though he knew she was waiting. When he finally said, 'Mother, congratulations,' the words were automatic, simply good manners.

'Then it's all right with you?'

He heard the anxiety in her voice. She wanted his approval.

'Yes. Taro is a good man.' It was true. He knew that for her, this was good news.

'Thank you. Of course, I was worried about what you would think.'

The words spilled out. 'Why? Why were you worried? You never worried before. You always just do as you please, don't you?'

She pulled sharply onto the shoulder of the road and stopped the car. She stared straight ahead.

'Do you think your mother has been happy?'

She sounded as if she was going to cry. Already he was sorry he had spoken so harshly.

'Please forgive me,' he said, bowing his head.

'You don't know the truth. Someday I'll tell you.'

He raised his eyes, but she turned away and stared out the window.

'Truth? What truth?' What truth was she talking about? Why she left them?

'Not now.'

'Mother! Please!' he raised his voice.

'I can't. I can't.' She wiped her eyes on her sleeve and took a deep breath, composing herself. She pressed down on the gas pedal and slowly guided the car back onto the road.

He stared at his lap, still thinking, The truth? What does that word mean to them and to their lives? As they neared Rausu, he spoke again.

'Does Father know? About the marriage?'

'Of course. I told him right away.'

That was all she said. He didn't ask any more questions. He knew his silent father, the way he only nodded his head at all news, good or bad. He felt sorry for him, alone in his noodle shop at the end of the road. When he closed the shop at eight each night, there was no one there. First his wife had left him, then his son. Now his wife was marrying another man.

Out past the ice floes seagulls squawked as the strong wind pressed them back toward shore.

Taro took them out to a restaurant on the coast road that night. If his mother had told him about their conversation in the car, he didn't let on. He was in a celebratory mood. He ordered hot sake, and they held up their cups in a toast.

'It's taken me a long time to convince your mother to marry me. I finally told her that if she didn't say yes, I was going to find some other pretty young girl who would.'

He reached out his arm to pull her to him, but she leaned slightly away. Taro laughed and moved closer. 'I finally got her, and now I'm not letting her go.'

She shook her head. 'What a silly man I'm going to marry,' she said.

She was flustered by Taro's attention. Toshi saw her face color and he turned away. They were all silent for a while as they ate their dinners.

Taro spoke softly. 'Please don't blame your mother. It was my idea. We just want a chance to be happy together.'

'I understand,' Toshi said. And he did. For this was something he'd always wanted for his mother too, for as long as he could remember: happiness.

The bus and Mr Goto had gotten old together. The leather seats and the skin on the driver's face seemed to have sagged and settled into a similar pattern of folds and creases. Toshi opened his window to clear the cigarette smoke as the bus climbed up the mountain in fits and starts, wheezing on the sharp turns.

'So, you've finally come back home, Toshi-chan, have you? Going to help your father out?'

'Actually, I'm just visiting. I'm moving to Tokyo,' he said.

'Tokyo? Is that so? Tokyo's really a big city. Too crowded for me. I was there once, just after the war. I didn't like it. Does your father know?'

'Of course he does. I'm just here to visit,' he repeated.

'Is that so?'

Mr Goto didn't say anything else, just puffed on his cigarette and stared out at the road, as if driving took more of his concentration than it used to.

The parking lot on top of the ridge hadn't changed, except for the addition of three coin-operated binoculars. Mr Goto pulled in and stopped the bus, threw his cigarette out the window, and lit a new one.

'Your father's not such a young man anymore.'

'Yes, that's true.'

'I guess it gets pretty lonely, all by himself out there at the end of the road.'

'Yes, it must.'

Did he know about his mother and Taro? Of course he did. Everyone here knew everything about everyone. What had his father endured all these years since his mother left? For Toshi, as a child, it had been looks of pity from his teachers, the taunting of classmates, cruel remarks about his mother overheard in shops. All that had eventually stopped. And then Toshi left. Had it ever stopped for his father?

Mr Goto steered the bus out of the lot. Below them, a hawk rode the air currents, followed the contours of the mountain.

'Well, I guess none of us are getting any younger, isn't that so?' the bus driver said, and he started to cough. He pushed open his window, cleared his throat, and spit.

His father stood next to his polished white car at the Rausu bus stop, smoking a cigarette. Behind him, the frozen sea heaved and shuddered. Yellow clouds rushed across the horizon to spread a blanket over the sleepy Russian islands.

'Welcome back,' he said. He wasn't wearing his apron.

Toshi bowed. 'Thank you for coming to pick me up. Are you well, Father?'

He nodded. They got into the car, and his father headed back up the road toward the ridge.

'I thought we'd go to the hot spring pools above the falls.'

'What about the shop?'

'I don't open for lunch in the winter anymore. It's too much effort just for the few customers who show up. I make most of my money off the summer tourists. You'd be surprised how many we get these days.'

'What do you do all day?'

His father didn't answer. It wasn't a personal question, but it was the kind of question he had never asked. How did his father feel about his mother marrying Taro? He could never ask him that. He knew they would never discuss it.

The air was so dry he thought he could hear the clouds pass overhead. Dead leaves that had held on through the winter rattled on their branches like abandoned musical instruments. They undressed shyly, facing away from each other, folding their clothes on a dry, flat stone. The snow around the pool was flecked with tracks. Deer, foxes, and people. Toshi shivered. He covered his genitals with his hands and stepped quickly into the water. Aware of his own youth, he was shocked at how old his father had become. His pale skin hung on his frame like loose cloth, and his cropped hair had turned gray.

'Aaah, it feels so good,' his father said, closing his eyes as he lowered himself slowly into the pool. He listed like a fishing boat taking on water. Bubbles rose up around him and burst, releasing the strong smell of sulphur.

They sat for a long time without talking, looking at the winter woods: vertical lines, bare tree trunks, blanks waiting to be filled in when the spring came. Like one of Toshi's sketches – after the pencil, before the colors.

'So, you're going to Tokyo to live,' his father said finally. It wasn't a question.

'Yes.'

'That's good. There's nothing for a young person up here.'

'You'll be okay by yourself, Father? Running the shop?'

'No need to worry about me,' he said. 'You know people there?'

'My friend Paul. The American. You remember him?'

'Ah, yes. The foreigner.'

They were quiet again for a few minutes. Birches creaked and knocked against neighboring pines. Melting snow fell from branches in great clumps, thumping through the forest like footsteps.

His father said, 'It's important to know people in a big city like Tokyo.'

'Yes.'

That was the end of their conversation.

It occurred to him that he might not see his father again for a long time. There were things he wanted to ask him, to say to him about their life together, all those silent years in the two rooms above the noodle shop. And about his mother. But it was too late for that, he understood. Too late for them. Maybe it was already too late before he was born. He recalled his mother's words in the car. Did his father also know the truth?

He looked at him, a silent old man across the small pool. And it was like looking at him from across the sea.

Toshi was on a ship, moving farther and farther away.

Lined up in front of every doorway, umbrellas and bicycles clutter the narrow lane to Jane's apartment. Windows open and close, room lights are switched on and off. Water drips from drainpipes and air conditioners. Someone is practicing scales on a piano, and the musical notes leap out into the darkness like shafts of light.

Hemmed in by newer, higher apartment blocks, Jane's building hunches over, its wet tile roof sagging. Toshi stands in front of her door, hesitates, almost turns back, but then remembers: the tatami burning. He knocks. He hears footsteps, the doorknob turns, and his heart starts to beat fast. He takes a deep breath.

The door opens.

Jane clasps her bathrobe with one hand, brushes her hair out of her eyes with the other. Her face is puffy and flushed, and her skin radiates a heat he can feel. He is startled by her nearness, so much so that he forgets both his fear and his anger.

'Yes? What do you want?' she says, her face blank, impatient, as if he is a stranger. Doesn't she recognize him? Maybe he should have called first. But he didn't trust her. Prepared, what she might have done.

She loosens her grip on her robe and it slips open. A glimpse of her pale breasts, and then the green robe covers her again, like a wave rolling up onshore. Toshi is aroused, and dismayed by his excitement.

'I'm Toshi.'

'I know who you are,' she says, her voice too loud. 'Do you think something's wrong with me? Why are you here?'

She is agitated, already backing away, ready to close the door. Behind her, inside the apartment, a red lightbulb flickers.

'Well?'

'I wanted to talk to you,' he says, suddenly angry. 'About the fire.'

He is sure he sees it: A slight tremor runs across her face, just below the skin.

'Fire. What fire? You should have called first.' She laughs. 'I would have told you not to come.'

'Jane?'

A young Japanese man, naked except for his undershorts, stumbles to the door. He looks dazed. Drunk. His lips are swollen, and there are bruises on his chest.

Toshi turns and walks away.

The door slams shut behind him.

At the end of the lane, he stoops slightly to pass under a cluster of dripping hydrangea, and he realizes that he is holding his breath. He lets it out and inhales hot, damp air, the scent of wet leaves and soil. Night flowers bloom a pallid blue. In a misty circle of light cast by the street lamp, he stops to watch a motorcycle swing around the corner. Sheathed in a helmet and leather jumper, the rider looks like a human projectile, an acrobat who could turn somersaults in the air. The bike skids on the wet pavement, and a small gasp escapes Toshi's lips as it wobbles, defies gravity, and then rights itself. As it disappears down the street, the roar of the engine moves through Toshi, and he feels, inexplicably, abandoned.

He passes through the grounds of a large shrine, its paths lined with unlit stone lanterns and thick-leaved trees that block out the light from the street. In the darkness, Jane suddenly looms large. She opens her front door over and over again while Toshi looks for the source of his frustration in the angle of her head, in the light reflecting off her bared breasts.

In front of the shrine, he inserts a coin in a fortune vending machine, and a white slip of paper slides into his hand. He opens it and squints to read the characters. It is *kyo*, bad luck. Toshi ties the paper to the bough of a small tree next to the machine. The tree's branches are heavy with knotted slips of white paper. He walks away quickly without looking back, leaving his bad luck there.

Jane behind him.

8

Akira's computer game is wailing and beeping, Wan-chan is barking, and the phone is ringing. Toshi, bent over his desk, tries to ignore it all and draw: Lips puckered for a kiss. A hidden knife. Chocolate Girl's thoughts float in bubbles above her head as she lassoes a beached whale and tows it off a sandbar in Nagasaki Harbor.

His own thoughts? Boredom with work. Relief that Jane seems finally to be over. What to do about Lucy. He is bewildered by these Americans – fascinated, yet discouraged. Over dinner last night, their first meeting in weeks, Paul finally told him about Michael Aoi, his Japanese-American boyfriend who died of AIDS.

'I'm sorry I never told you. I was wrong, but you were so young when I met you, I thought you wouldn't understand,' Paul said. 'I know I'm a difficult person, but I'm trying hard not to be. You think I'm the strong one, but I depend on you.'

'You're my best friend,' Toshi said, thinking, Will we ever truly know each other? Do I see the same Paul as Lucy sees? Toshi grew up on a narrow peninsula, traveled coast to coast by bus in less than an hour. Paul grew up in America, a country so expansive that it spills over into the rest of the world. Is that why Americans spill out their thoughts and emotions so easily? Paul could never be confined in a six-tatami mat room.

Mami answers the phone, employing a string of words so polite and rarefied that Toshi has trouble understanding her. She passed the first audition, and soon she will be presented to the Crown Prince along with a thousand other girls at a huge garden party. She attends special classes at night to learn posture, deportment, and the arcane language of the Imperial Family.

'Toshi-chan, it's for you.'

He puts down his pen, stranding Chocolate Girl in the air above the Great Buddha of Kamakura. Inside the bronze Buddha, three young Thai girls cower in fear.

He picks up the phone. 'This is Okamoto.'

'Mr Toshi Okamoto?' A man. Officious.

'Yes.'

'This is the Tokyo Metropolitan Police.'

They've linked Jane to the fire. A grain of rice rolls down his forehead, catches in his right eyebrow.

Wan-chan barks, 'Yip, yip, yip.'

'Quiet, Wan-chan. Toshi-chan is on the phone. No bones for you,' Mami scolds.

'Your father is Fumio Okamoto, from Rausu, Hokkaido?'

'Yes.' His father?

'I'm sorry to have to give you this bad news.'

'Bad news?' Toshi repeats.

The office is suddenly quiet.

'Yes. Your father was found on the Yamanote line. He had a heart attack on the train.'

'A heart attack? He's here in Tokyo? Is he all right?' Sea wind whistles through the telephone. Clouds over the Russian islands rush toward him. If the wind blows loud enough he won't have to hear what he suddenly knows is coming next.

'I'm afraid he died on the train.'

'Died?'

His father stands in a cloud of dust outside the noodle shop, bowing.

His father sits alone at night in front of the TV, smoking a cigarette, lifting his glass of beer. Every night. Year after year.

'Yes. Your name and phone number were in his bag.'

Toshi picks the grain of rice out of his eyebrow and looks at it. His hand is shaking. Surely, there's been a mistake.

'Excuse me, but my father is dead?'

'I'm sorry to have to give you such terrible news over the telephone. We'd like you to please come down to the hospital to identify him.'

He hangs up the phone and stares at his drawings. There's a pounding of waves in his ears that drowns out everything around him. The Thai girls, their mouths wide open, wait for him to draw in their cries for help.

Nakamura, Akira, and Mami circle his desk and look at him as if he is someone to feel sorry for. Mami holds Wan-chan out to him.

Soldiers line the street in front of Shinjuku Station, their shining shields and batons held out in front of them like sacred objects. Behind them, people crawl over a mountain of rice, fill up their pockets and briefcases and shopping bags. The white mountain diminishes before Toshi's eyes. And in the plastic faceguards of the soldiers' helmets, he sees his own reflection, expanding and contracting, over and over again.

Taro meets Toshi's plane, and they wait together on the tarmac while the metal casket containing his father's body is unloaded and placed in the back of a van. He recalls what his father told him six years before, on the day he flew to Tokyo for his entrance examination. 'I've never been on an airplane,' he had said, handing Toshi an envelope filled with money.

So he'd finally flown on an airplane, but too late to enjoy it. And he'd come to Tokyo to see his son too late too. When Toshi began middle school, his father opened a special savings account for his college education. Every week, he drove to the bank and deposited money. He paid Toshi wages when he helped him in the shop during the dinner hour, and that money he deposited for him too.

'This is no place for you to spend your life,' his father had told him many times. 'There are better places. Get away from here and make a good life for yourself.'

Toshi had gotten away. But his father hadn't. Even after his mother left, and Toshi went off to college, he stayed. Why? Was it to be near his mother? Toshi would never know. His father was as silent in life as he now is in death.

The van with his father's body drives off, and he and Taro walk back toward the pickup truck. In front of them, the terminal building seems unanchored, as if it might float up into the wide, clear sky, higher and higher, until it disappears. Like his father. Toshi fights back tears of anger. The noodle shop, isolated and mute, at the end of the road. A giant wave might have swept the two-story building away at any time. The ground could have opened up suddenly beneath them. He'd learned about such things in school. Japan is constantly shifting beneath our feet, their science teacher calmly told them as he unrolled colored diagrams of the earth's crust. The girls played nervously with the buttons on their white shirts. The boys giggled and shook the legs of their wooden desks. Every Friday afternoon, the students filled buckets with soap and water, got down on their hands and knees, and scrubbed the wood-planked classroom floor, the hallways and staircases, always alert, anticipating motion. Volcanic eruptions and earthquakes. It can happen here, their teacher warned them. A terrifying sound like a roaring train, then people vanish into clouds of sulphur.

Toshi turns away from Taro and wipes his tears. Couldn't all of their lives have been different? If only someone had spoken, the words would have rent the silence in their house.

The tarmac continues to unroll before him, a dark carpet on the flat prairie.

His mother is already at the noodle shop. She and Zeni, the Filipino girl from the inn, are washing the floor when he arrives.

'Are you all right?' She steps outside into the sunlight and tugs off her rubber gloves. She's sweating.

'I'm fine.'

'It's so warm today.' Smiling briefly, she takes a handkerchief from her apron pocket, wipes her forehead and the back of her neck.

The trees on the slope behind the shop are thick with leaves, shiny and dark as pepper skins.

'And you, Mother?'

She nods. 'I'm okay.' She looks past him at the sea, and he turns to follow her gaze. The air is so transparent that the islands seem to have moved closer to shore, their usual haziness wiped away to reveal a glaring clarity. 'I'm okay,' she repeats.

The funeral will be held in the shop. Toshi, his mother, and Zeni scrub the grease off the walls and countertop. They carry two tables just outside the door, where Toshi's middle school English teacher, Mrs Hayashi, and two other women from town cover them with white cloth. They arrange the boxes and lists, ink and brushes. Every visitor will bring a black-rimmed white envelope filled with money. They'll sign their names, and their donations will be recorded.

Granny is too old now to move around much, but she sits in a chair in the sunlight, talking to them as they work.

'People will probably give three thousand yen. Maybe a few of the fishermen, five thousand,' Granny says.

His mother nods. 'Whatever.'

'Isn't there some family somewhere we should try to get in touch with?'

'No. You know there isn't. There's nobody left,' his mother says sharply, and she picks up a bucket of dirty water and carries it around to the back of the shop.

He's never heard her speak rudely to Granny before. But Granny doesn't seem to notice.

'Nobody left. Nobody at all. It must be lonely for you, Toshi-chan.' Granny closes her eyes, as if to better picture this nothingness that surrounds him.

The fresh bamboo shoots on the counter were still covered with damp, spring earth, filling the shop with the smell of the young forest. Carrots, onions, and eggplants were spread out on open newspaper, waiting to be washed and sliced. A pot of water boiled on the stove. Toshi, six years old, changed out of his school clothes and ran down the stairs barefoot. His mother stood behind the counter in an old T-shirt, peeling an apple for his snack. His father was drinking tea and watching his afternoon detective show.

'I told my teacher I have no relatives, but he says that's impossible, that all Japanese people have relatives living someplace,' he announced.

The sun streamed in the side window next to the stove. The window was always kept open, even in winter, to let out the cooking smoke and the smell of gas.

'Is it true? Do I have cousins? And aunts and uncles?'

'Ouch.' His mother dropped the small knife, put her thumb in her mouth. She looked at his father until he turned off the TV, then she went out the back screen door, letting it slam behind her.

Toshi sat down by his father, who slid his cup of green tea across the table. Toshi took a sip. It was cold.

'Is Mother all right?' he asked, afraid that he had said something wrong. Already at six, he knew that there were things about her he had to be careful of.

'She doesn't like to talk about what's past, that's all.' He got up and turned the flame off under the boiling water, then stood facing the open window, squinting at the sunlight.

'Your mother and I came here after the war. All of our relatives were killed in the war. Everybody. Parents. Brothers and sisters. Aunts and uncles too. There's nobody left. It makes your mother sad. Do you know what war I'm talking about?'

'Yes.' He knew. There had been a big war. America had dropped terrible bombs on Japan and had killed many people.

'The Americans killed my relatives?'

His father hesitated. 'That's right.'

'But where did you come from? Maybe there is somebody left and you don't know. Maybe I have cousins,' he said, longing for there to be more than just him and his mother and father. He wanted their house to be filled with people.

'We came from down south. A place you've never heard of. And there's nobody. So you can tell your teacher he's wrong.'

'Can't I at least tell my teacher the name of the place?'

His father didn't answer. He turned the TV back on, but the detective show was over. The news was on. A white-skinned foreigner in a suit and necktie was standing next to the Emperor. They shook hands, then the foreigner smiled at the camera.

'Is he an American?' Toshi asked. Was this the man who had killed his relatives?

'Yes.'

Toshi studied the American carefully. He looked friendly. He had a wide grin and big, open hands, and he towered over the Emperor, who looked tiny and stiff next to him.

His father dumped the vegetables into the sink and turned on the faucet. He was through talking with him.

Toshi stepped into his sneakers and went out the back door. His mother was sitting on the concrete stoop, weaving blades of grass around her cut thumb like a ring. He sat down next to her.

'I'm sorry, Mother. Does it hurt?'

'It's nothing. Just a small cut. You didn't do anything wrong. I just don't like to remember unhappy things,' she said, sliding the grass ring off. She took his hand in hers and tried the ring on each of his fingers, finally fitting it onto his thumb.

'You have your father and me. We all have each other. Isn't that enough?'

'Yes,' he said.

'Are you lonely?'

'No.'

Up on the slope, there was no wind at all. But on one branch of a single birch tree, he saw the leaves shimmer, as if nudged by a breeze. So he knew that something was alive up there. Maybe his mother and father were wrong. Maybe the three of them were not alone.

He finds his mother sitting on the stoop, her rubber gloves and the bucket of dirty water at her side. He dumps the water out on the grass, then sits down next to her.

'Are you all right?'

She nods, and looks up at the steep slope, as if searching for something. Toshi is worried about her. She hasn't said much since he called her from Tokyo and repeated the story they'd told him at the hospital: how his father had slumped over in his seat, but no one had paid any attention. 'There are so many homeless people sleeping on the trains these days,' the policeman had said. Dying, or already dead, his father circled the city for hours until the Rice Party tried to bomb the tracks outside of Ueno Station, and the train was evacuated. 'That's when we found him.'

What is his mother feeling? He wants to ask her, but he doesn't. And he wishes she would ask him what he's feeling. Because he doesn't know. On the plane ride up to Hokkaido, he replayed his father's death the way it had been described to him, the way he imagined it. Over and over again, he watched his father die, watched his face, searching for a clue to the man, to their relationship. But all he feels is horror, and guilt: The Yamanote line tracks are only about fifty meters away from Nakamura Studio. They could see the trains passing from the window. While Toshi was at his desk drawing silly cartoons, his father rode by again and again, dying, surrounded by strangers.

He leaves his mother sitting on the stoop, goes back inside and closes the door quietly behind him. Zeni is out front with Granny. He looks around the noodle shop, emptied of tables and chairs for the first time in memory, the smell of broth and soy sauce and cigarettes wiped away. The front door and windows are open. In the clean air and sunlight, the shop looks old and shabby, its walls and ceiling darkened by grease and smoke. It makes him sad to think that his father lived his life here.

Toshi opens the closet, thinking that there are things they'll have to sort through. Clothes, papers, some remnants of his father's life.

'There's hardly anything,' he says.

'Don't forget about his car,' his mother says.

They've both bathed and are drinking tea in the back room. In the front room, she's already laid out their mattresses.

'I don't need a car in Tokyo. Why don't you take it?'

'We could use another car. But I have no right to anything, you know. I'm not his wife anymore.'

'Take it, please. What about the shop?'

'Everything is yours. I guess you should sell it. Inheritance taxes are very high. I can ask Taro to take care of it for you if you'd like.'

'Please. If he doesn't mind.'

He looks around the room for something to take back to Tokyo with him, something to remind him of his life with his father. But nothing has changed upstairs or downstairs since his childhood, except for new counter stools when the old ones wore out, an occasional coat of paint rolled on right over the grease. He wonders if anyone else has ever been in these upstairs rooms except for him and his mother and his father.

'Your father was a man who didn't want many things.'

'Yes, I know. I wonder . . .'

'What?'

'Well, why he decided to come to Tokyo to visit me.'

He has been thinking about this ever since the phone call from the police. Was there something his father wanted to say to him?

'It seems we'll never know.'

'I suppose not,' he says, convinced he has missed something important. Something he needs to know.

'Toshi-chan? Do you think your father was an unhappy man?'

'Yes,' he says immediately, although he's never actually thought about it, and is as surprised by his quick answer as he is by her question. As a child, he watched his father move along so silently and predictably that even now it is difficult to think of him as anything other than his routines and habits. What time he got up in the morning. How often he bought a new car, or changed an item on the menu. Cold Chinese noodles in the summer, deep-fried oysters in the winter.

She opens her overnight bag and takes out a flat wooden box inscribed with faded calligraphy.

'It's true. He was unhappy. And it was my fault. That's why I left. I thought he still had time to make a happy life without me. To meet another woman and marry again.'

Toshi is startled by this, and wary. She's never spoken about his father in this way before, not in all the years since she left. He'd always assumed it was the other way around – that he and his father had made her unhappy. It was, after all, her unhappiness that they'd had to accommodate, around which they'd arranged their lives.

She opens up the box and hands him an old, black-and-white photograph. A handsome, young man standing in the rain. It is a moment before Toshi realizes that it is his father. He realizes that he's never seen a picture of him before. They never took pictures in their family, even on trips, or at his school sports events and graduations. They didn't own a camera. Except for Toshi's drawings, they had no narrative of their lives together. It was as if his parents had purposely eluded a visual record, had decided they would never want to look back.

'Your father was a wonderful man. He was always good to me. It was my fault our marriage didn't work.'

She stands up and stamps her feet to get the blood circulating.

'I left him too late. He was already so unhappy. I'm sorry for that. But I wanted you to know so you don't blame him.'

It occurs to him that she might be lying to protect his father now that he's dead. There is so much he wants to ask her, a lifetime of questions. But even now, as his father's death changes the rules between them, and as she reveals so much, he can't bring himself to ask her for more than she's offering. And after all, it was she and his father who taught him not to ask.

He looks down at the brittle photograph in his hand: His grinning father holds his hat out in front of him in both hands, upside down, catching the rain, as if he is offering it as a gift to the photographer. Behind him, hills that Toshi doesn't recognize curl like waves against a dark sea of a sky. His father looks happy. And he gazes at the camera, Toshi decides, as if he is very much in love with whoever is taking his picture.

'Who took this picture?'

'I did,' his mother says.

So once they did own a camera. 'Here.' He holds the photograph out to her.

'No. You keep it. Please. It's the way you should remember him.'

'This isn't my father. I never knew him this way. You did,' he says.

She turns away.

'Well, time for bed.' She shuts off the ceiling light, as if to hide her face from him, or his from her. 'We have a busy day tomorrow, so we should get a good night's sleep.'

She waits for a moment, perhaps for him to say something. When he doesn't, she walks through the darkness into the front room.

His mother is much younger than his father, so she must have been a girl when she took the picture he now holds so carefully in his hand. Like the best lacquerware, it seems to have no weight.

The clouds have rolled in off the sea, and it is dark

outside the window that faces the slope. If there was a moon, it would be shining on the white birch. His mother always avoided the front room; she liked sitting here in the back, looking out at the trees. Toshi preferred the front windows. The lights on fishing boats and, on clear nights, the shimmering lights on the islands. Those lights always looked like someplace he could go to.

The days of the wake and funeral are a blur: his father laid out in a dark suit Toshi never saw him wear, his face covered with a cloth and his hands folded neatly on his chest, his gold wristwatch still keeping time. The altar and his father's photograph set on top of the same counter where, each night after closing, he had lined up the bottles of soy sauce and refilled them from a big tin container. Later, Toshi and his mother sit in folding chairs and nod silently as, one by one, his father's old customers and the people he'd done business with for almost forty years bow to them, bow to his father's framed photograph, bring their hands together in prayer, offer incense, bow again. The Buddhist priest recites the sutras, drones on and on. The incense makes Toshi sleepy. Then his father's body is cremated. Together, Toshi and his mother guide a pair of long chopsticks over the ashes and pick out his bones. And finally, the cemetery, gravestones adorned with offerings of cigarettes, bottles of sake, and bright flowers. In front of a child's gravestone, someone has placed a small bottle of milk and a Snoopy doll. A colorful pinwheel spins in the damp breeze. On the other side of the coast road, past the bobbing fishing boats, rain clouds wait impatiently to come ashore.

There is sushi and sake and beer in the upstairs rooms. Outside the open windows, the rain has begun to fall. Seeing people in these rooms for the first time in his life, Toshi is oddly euphoric. He had worried that the rooms were too bare, that everyone would see how his father had spent all those years with nothing but sadness. But filled up with people, eating and drinking and smoking, filled up with conversation and laughter, the rooms don't seem lonely at all. Toshi and his father slept and drank tea together in these two rooms for ten years after his mother left them. But they never lived here, he now understands. They only occupied the rooms.

His father offers his upturned hat. He cradles it in his hands. A vessel. Is it filled with rainwater? With rice wine? The juice of mandarin oranges?

Back in his Tokyo apartment, Toshi props the snapshot up and he draws his father. Through the movement of his pencil on paper, he searches for the truth. He looks for explanations in the details of the photograph, as if following the roll of his father's shirtsleeve will describe the man. At the funeral, people talked to him about his father. He was kind, honest, hardworking, they said. But he was also a silent man, Toshi knew, a father who never spoke to his son.

And the girl with the camera. What was his mother like then? Why did his father marry her? He looks for her in the young man's eyes.

Hungry, he cuts the string around the big box his mother handed him when he left for the airport. Inside, she's packed apples, cucumbers, cans of tuna fish and sea urchin. Homemade rice balls with red pickled plums inside of them like red suns on white flags.

At the bottom of the box is an envelope with three

thousand yen. Such a small amount of money won't buy much in Tokyo. But this, he knows, is her way of taking care of him. Even after she left for the inn, she never stopped trying to take care of him. Every Sunday night, she walked him to the bus stop in Utoro. He crossed the peninsula and returned to his father's noodle shop carrying shopping bags and cartons tied up with string. His mother pressed on him bags of rice, fruit and vegetables, presents of underwear and pajamas and gloves, as if she believed that weight and volume might cancel out time and distance. But she had been wrong.

Toshi undresses, lays out his futon, and he remembers: Nights above the shop between his father and mother. His father snores. His mother's sleeping face suddenly contorts in pain. She murmurs, exhaling a bad dream. Disturbed, he gets up and looks out the balcony doors at the rain over Tokyo. But when he glances down at his own body, he is a small boy again, standing at the open window above the painted bowl of noodles. He looks out at the sea, at the bright moon, and his cotton pajamas flutter in the wind. A luminous flock of geese flies parallel to shore in a perfect diamond. The wind stretches the diamond out of shape, elongating it, but the geese snap back like an elastic band. He can't remember ever seeing anything quite so beautiful, and he turns to call his parents to the window. But they are gone, along with their bedding. He is back in his Tokyo apartment, and there is only one mattress. A cold white rectangle floating on the tatami, adrift.

9

Tokyo's streets are unnamed and unnumbered. Neighborhood maps mounted outside subway stations describe labyrinths, and even taxi drivers carry street guides thicker than phone books.

Toshi holds up Lucy's hand-drawn map, turns it sideways, then upside down, aligning it to reality so he can follow her penciled trail of landmarks from the station: A police box, a bicycle store. Turn left at the Kentucky Fried Chicken, right at the phone booth just past the rice cracker stand. A mailman on his red motor scooter and a cat leaping off a wall are only distractions.

It's a long way from the station, but he's glad to walk. The air is dry, the sky white and still – as if waiting for the next typhoon or, possibly, the first autumn winds to sweep across the Japan Sea, carrying cold desert air from China. As he walks, he notices the facades and lobbies of apartment buildings, the width of their balconies, imagines a new view from his windows. Toshi has started to look for a new apartment. Jane may have forgotten him, or replaced him, but some nights he still dreams of red envelopes shooting through the mail slot, edges sharp as razor blades. A few nights ago, there was a small earthquake, and he dreamed she was pounding on his front door. He woke up sweating.

A housewife pedals by on her bicycle, an empty child's

seat in back, a fat daikon radish sticking out of the basket in front. A display of plastic umbrellas in front of a convenience store, pink and yellow and blue, stops him in his tracks on this quiet morning. Set against a landscape of detergent boxes and toilet tissue rolls, they're bright wildflowers gathering sunlight.

On a magazine rack, every publication carries the same cover photo: The Crown Prince and the American actress Brooke Shields lean across a candlelit table, across champagne glasses and, according to the caption, plates of smoked Norwegian salmon and New Zealand kiwis, their hands – his small and delicate, hers large and tipped with polish – touching.

Lucy lives by herself in an old, one-story wooden house, hidden in the shadow of a shut-down Panasonic factory that is covered with graffiti – nationalistic slogans that have been appearing all over Japan recently. Spray painted on walls and on the curved shells of subway cars. Carved with knives into the great wooden platform of Kiyomizu Temple in Kyoto. After the press reported the Crown Prince's dinner with the American actress, a group of laid-off Toyota workers burned AMERICA = AIDS into the brush on the southern slope of Mount Fuji. The letters were five meters high and could be seen by passengers on passing bullet trains.

FOREIGN RICE IS POISON and LONG LIVE THE EMPEROR hang menacingly over Lucy's tile roof like storm clouds. But when Toshi walks through the wooden gate, he finds himself in a peaceful garden of dwarf bamboo and clipped shrubs. He is about to ring the doorbell when he hears voices inside, two people speaking Japanese.

An old woman's voice. 'Today is Wednesday, that means nonburnable garbage. Glass whiskey bottles and beer cans, for example.'

A man, a foreigner. 'I apologize. I didn't know. When should I put my burnable garbage out?'

Is he at the wrong house? She hadn't said anything about other people. Her landlady and Hugh? He thought they would be alone. He rings the bell, and the conversation abruptly stops. Lucy opens the door, smiles, and tugs at the black T-shirt that stretches down to her knees. Her legs and feet are bare, her short hair wet, as if she just stepped out of the bath. The smell of soap drifts down to him. She looks so pretty, her skin white as milk.

'Hi. I'm glad you're here. Come on in.'

As he steps up and out of his shoes, he holds out a bag of pastries he bought near the station.

'It's just a little gift.'

'Oh, thank you. You didn't have to.' She opens the bag. 'But actually, I'm starving. They look delicious. Thanks a lot. Was my map okay?'

He follows her into a tatami room that looks out onto the garden. There is no furniture, only cushions, a small table, and yellow flowers in a blue vase. Something he might have drawn.

'This is very nice,' he says, but he's disappointed. Toshi has never been out of Japan, so whenever he visits a foreigner at home, he imagines he is visiting another country. Americans' apartments are the best, for even when they're small, they arrange them so that there is always somewhere to go to, someplace you haven't seen yet. Americans seem to carry space around with them.

'I love living here, although you know how old Japanese houses are. Freezing in the winter and like an oven in the summer. I ran right out and bought this air conditioner the day after I moved in.'

She slides open a door, and they are in an air-conditioned room, carpeted, with Western furniture. More like what he'd expected. But where are the other people? Is there a back door?

'I'm sorry about the mess. I was going to clean up for you, but then I decided you should see it as it really is.'

'It's not a mess,' he says. And it isn't. The room is filled with audio equipment, one wall taken up by tape decks and amplifiers, equipment he doesn't recognize, black matt surfaces with rows of switches and dials. There are shelves filled with CD's and cassette tapes, an electronic keyboard, and speakers as big as refrigerators.

'Now you know why I have to live in a house. I make much too much noise for an apartment.'

'It must be expensive.' He couldn't imagine having an entire house to himself in Tokyo.

'Oh, no. Japanese people don't want to live in these old, drafty houses anymore. Only foreigners find them charming. I pay almost nothing. I'm sure the landlord will tear it down in a few years and put up a big, ugly apartment building. Come sit here.'

She leads him to an old wooden rocking chair, then sits in a plain chair opposite him.

'Isn't that chair great? I found it.'

'You found it?' He rocks back and forth, as a way of showing his appreciation. Where do people find chairs? Nobody he knows finds furniture.

'Uh-huh. On the street. Someone threw it out. My friend, Norma, she found a practically brand-new Sony CD player on a garbage pile. Japanese people just throw things out.'

'Yes,' he says, wondering if this is supposed to be a good or bad trait.

She jumps up so fast it startles him. She's so tall in this low-ceilinged room.

'Do you want coffee? You can have tea if you don't want coffee.'

'Coffee is fine.'

'Great. I have really good coffee.' She smiles, as if he's just paid her a compliment, and leaves the room.

He hears the coffee grinder, then the kettle whistling. He stands up and stares out at her small, neat garden. A pair of wooden sandals is lined up neatly on a flat rock on the other side of the glass door, and a stone path loops through the garden. The stones are swept clean and splashed with water. Did Lucy do that? Who is Lucy? he wonders. He reviews what he knows about her. An American woman. A composer. A married woman who is getting a divorce. Then he thinks, What don't I know about her? What do I need to know?

Lucy places a tray with coffee and the pastries on the table between them, then hands him a cracked ceramic mug.

'Help yourself to milk and sugar. I hope it's not too strong.'

She bites into one of the pastries, and powdered sugar falls like snow onto her black T-shirt. She wipes it away nonchalantly. 'Oh, this is good. I was so hungry. Usually I eat something in the morning, some toast or yogurt or something. But this morning I had no time.'

Was it because he was coming over that she had no time? Or was it because of her other guests? He sips his coffee. It's strong.

'Oh, I'm sorry. God, am I rude, eating without offering you any. Isn't that just like an American, I'll bet you're thinking.'

'No, I wasn't,' he says.

She laughs and holds out the plate of pastries. He chooses one without powdered sugar.

'Why don't I play you my music while we drink our coffee. Then we can talk about your design for the CD cover. That is, if you like the music. I want you to be truthful.'

She goes over to the wall of audio equipment and starts pressing buttons. The big speakers crackle, and the man's voice he heard earlier comes booming out: 'I see. Burnable garbage is Tuesdays, Thursdays, and Saturdays.'

She laughs and pushes another button.

'Oops, wrong tape. I'm trying to improve my Japanese, but I'm so lazy I only put it on when I'm in the bath or on the toilet.'

Toshi closes his eyes and listens, and he waits for something he will recognize. There's the peculiar but familiar twang of a koto, and then a shamisen being briskly plucked. Does Lucy play these Japanese instruments? Then he recognizes a piano, and a flute. But there's no familiar melody. It's nothing like either Japanese or Western music. It's not at all what he expected. What will he be able to say about it? But Lucy is not what he expected, either. And so, slowly, he relaxes. And the most extraordinary thing happens: The melody arranges itself into pictures inside his head, as if Lucy is drawing with music, each note a brush stroke. As the melody expands, colors appear and fill in the outlines. These are not cartoons. They are the pictures he wants to draw. They materialize inside his head, they come rushing at him, up and down the musical scale: His father's pale skin reflected on the surface of the water. His mother brushes out her long hair in her room at the inn. The music speeds up and the images move back through his life, then even further back. His mother and father walk on a thin stretch of rocky beach. Toshi isn't there, he isn't even born yet, but there is a wide space between his parents, as if they are making room for him. His father reaches out across the expanse of sky and sea to his mother, but with each step of her bare feet at the water's edge, she drifts away from him. His pants rolled up to his knees, his father kneels and scoops up a sand crab. His mother turns and laughs. Her loose hair billows in the sea wind. His father laughs too.

Unexpectedly, the music ends, and the image dissolves, seawater absorbed into the sand, leaving only a foamy residue of sadness behind. He opens his eyes, startled to find himself in Lucy's house. He needs to draw what he's seen before he forgets. Lucy is watching him. He feels so sad about his father's death and what his mother told him. How she turned away from his father. But now he knows what he needs to do: He'll draw his parents, and his own life growing up with them, shuttling back and forth across the narrow peninsula. That's how he can bring them all back together, give them a history.

'You don't like it?' she asks quietly. She searches his face, sees his sadness.

How could he explain to her how he feels? It's as if Lucy has visited the world he came from and brought something back in her music. 'I like it very much. Really. It's sad music.'

'No one ever said that.'

'I'm sorry.'

'No. It's not bad. I don't mind "sad."'

They sit silently for a few minutes, looking at each other. He wishes he could think of something else to say. He's afraid he's disappointed her. The music has ended, but he still feels disoriented, like he's moving, traversing the great distance between Shiretoko Peninsula and this room. Then Lucy smiles, and, unexpectedly, these two worlds merge in the line of her neck, in the contour of a snowy slope.

She takes him to a nearby *soba* restaurant for lunch. They stir the raw yolks of spotted quail eggs into the dark sauce with their chopsticks, add wasabi and green scallions, and they tell each other everything they can think of about their lives while they dip and slurp their noodles.

She tells him: 'Normal parents. Two weird, funny brothers. San Francisco schools. University in Berkeley. I met Hugh there. The Conservatory of Music. Some performing. Recording. Then Hugh got money to do the film on the rice riots, and I decided to come too. I mean, Japan. I didn't know anything at all. Zen, sushi, Sony.'

He picks out words. Place names. Ideas. He nods his head, wanting more.

'I started studying Japanese music, and so here I am. Still.' She takes a sip of her tea. 'An uneventful, reasonably happy life. My parents were very supportive so I guess I'm not too insecure.'

Supportive. To support. Holding something up so that it doesn't fall. The way, in the winter, he'd take Granny's arm to help her over icy patches on the road. Did anyone support him while he was growing up?

'What about you?' she asks.

He tells her things he thinks she might want to hear: The noodle shop. Snow. His mother and father. The inn in Utoro. The letter to Audrey Hepburn.

'Audrey Hepburn!' She claps her hands. 'I can't imagine it. Audrey Hepburn in Hokkaido.'

He's thirsty and drinks glass after glass of barley tea, for as he talks, he's still thinking about the drawings her music drew in his head. And he finds himself telling her more than he intended to: about his father's death, and the funeral, and what his mother said to him. Lucy listens quietly, nodding, encourages him to go on. The years when his mother was so silent, how she'd walk out the door without a word and not return for hours. And then, after she left, his father's silence.

When Toshi is done talking, he's curiously calm. He's never told this story before, not even to Paul. They stare at each other across the table until Lucy stands up and holds out her hand.

'Come on. I have a surprise for you.'

She leads him across a busy boulevard and under an expressway to the edge of a vista that makes Toshi laugh: Pedal boats shaped like swans drift in circles.

'A pond?'

'My secret pond,' she says. 'Do you like it?'

The dark water shimmers against a background of concrete apartment buildings – laundry hanging on every narrow balcony, underwear twirling in the breeze. A narrow footbridge leads out to a sumo-ring-size island where a tiny, run-down Shinto shrine sits, surrounded by willow trees. Toshi and Lucy rest in the shade there, their backs against a cigarette vending machine. An orchestral version of 'Home on the Range' floats across the water from speakers planted along the shoreline. Real swans drift by, and then the swan boats. A child's hand reaches out to scatter popcorn, and the water churns with the bright, flashing colors of carp.

'It's peaceful here, in an odd, Tokyo sort of way,' Lucy says in a sleepy voice.

He nods but doesn't reply. They sit for a long time like this, neither of them talking. He doesn't feel that he has to, or that she needs him to. A small movement catches his eye, and he looks down at the water's edge. A turtle emerges from the pond.

'Look!'

Possibly startled by his voice, the turtle skitters back down toward the water and rolls over onto its shell. It struggles to upright itself, unsuccessfully.

'The poor thing.' Lucy gets up, brushes off the back of her T-shirt.

'Careful. It could bite.'

'It won't bite me. It knows that I want to help.'

The turtle's head retreats into its shell. She picks it up and turns it over, places it at the water's edge.

'You can come out now,' she says, as if talking to a frightened child.

At that very moment, the late afternoon sunlight streams through the willow trees like a breeze, lighting up Lucy with colors that come right out of the air, colors that Toshi can't even name. And everything else disappears. The music, the swans. The four joggers on the opposite shore, stretching and smoking cigarettes. There is only Lucy and the turtle, which cautiously pokes its head out, finds its feet firmly on the ground, and slides with a splash back into the water. A splash that ripples in Toshi's chest.

He walks her home down dusky side streets. Each time a car passes, they have to move closer to the cinder block walls that conceal the neighborhood's small houses, and their bare arms brush. Beyond the high walls, dogs bark. Telephones ring. He smells rice steaming. Blue television light skims the tops of their heads to define their progress through the growing darkness.

They reach her front gate.

'Well, you have the cassette of my music. So when you come up with an idea, call me,' she says. But she doesn't go in.

'I'll make some drawings soon.'

He'd like to touch her, to kiss her, but he hesitates.

'You can fax them to me. Or we can meet. Whatever.'

'Okay.'

'Well . . .'

She slides open the gate.

In the garden, glass wind chimes tinkle. Above their heads, the Panasonic factory has faded to a benign shape in Tokyo's starless night sky.

'Would you like to come in?'

Yes, he would very much like to go in. But he wonders, Will she turn out to be like Jane? What will happen if he sleeps with her? Foreign women always surprise him, and tonight he doesn't want to be surprised. He needs to keep those drawings in his head.

She mistakes his hesitation for something else.

'I guess you have plans for tonight. I, well, let's just call each other, okay?'

He nods, distracted, for an image surfaces unexpectedly, a memory.

She smiles and waves, even though he is standing right in front of her, then ducks through the gate and slides it closed. 'Good night.'

'Good night,' he says, already mentally laying out a white sheet of paper before him. He watches the ice floes melt at the beginning of spring, hears the loud cracking.

Lucy steps up and removes her sandals, closes the door behind her.

The lights go on in her house, and festival bonfires flare up on the docks of Utoro.

And then he hears the old lady's voice.

'In your country, what do you do with your garbage? Do you have garbage in America?'

Every spring, the ice that girds Shiretoko Peninsula dissolves into blue crystals and washes ashore. The snowpack melts. The mountains swell like overripe fruit, pouring water and mud onto the towns. The fishermen lower their boats back into the sea, and return to work.

And in Utoro, at the first full moon in April, the towns-people hold a three-day festival to honor the Fishing God, a local Shinto deity who keeps watch over the town and sea from a two-and-a-half-meter-wide portable shrine sandwiched between the Yamazaki bakery and the prefectural administrative office on the coast road south. Year-round, the people of Utoro placate the Fishing God with offerings of mandarin oranges and apples, pounded rice cakes, packs of cigarettes, and cans of Sapporo beer from the vending machine in front of the shrine. Each spring, at festival time, they give the shrine a fresh coat of red and gold gilt paint and parade it through the streets on the shoulders of the fishermen. The festival runs through the weekend.

The first spring after his mother moved to the inn, she asked Toshi's father to let him come over on Friday, for the first night's procession.

The wives of the town's innkeepers and shopkeepers prepared food for the festival, which they sold in tents set up in the parking lot below the middle school. In the inn's kitchen, Toshi's mother and Granny simmered cauldrons of *oden* stew, dropped in chopped octopus tentacles, hard-boiled eggs, fish cakes round as baseballs. Thick slices of daikon radish. Tofu skins stuffed with ground meat and ginkgo nuts and tied into little pouches with seaweed string. They chopped up chickens for grilling, bones and innards as well, and threaded the pieces onto wooden skewers with whole cloves of garlic, shiitake mushrooms, and green peppers, then piled the skewers on platters and sprinkled them with salt.

The fishermen's wives took charge of their husbands' boats, scrubbed them clean, then dressed them up with banners and flags, and with long strips of white cloth ripped from old sheets and wrapped around the masts like scarves. Each year, they painted new banners: blue waves and so many fish that when the banners fluttered in the cold April gusts, the fish swam right off the edges. The flags were the Japanese flag, a red sun on a field of white. The fishermen's wives wrote their prayers in big black characters on the strips of white cloth: *Calm weather. An abundance of fish. Safe voyage.*

At sunset, drummers from all over the peninsula gathered on Utoro's main street. The fishermen and their sons, naked except for their loincloths, trudged down the muddy street, chanting in loud voices and balancing the cumbersome shrine of the Fishing God on pine logs, the heavy logs on their bare shoulders. The men's pale bodies were splattered with black mud and gleamed with sweat. Their loud, drunken voices thrilled Toshi. He stood outside the inn with his mother, who pulled him back as the men approached. He felt her grip on his arm tighten as women pushed through the crowd and poured flasks of hot sake into their husbands' and boyfriends' mouths, then splashed it over their heads. In the cold air, their shouts and laughter emerged as small clouds.

Friends and families joined the procession as it advanced, the splendid shrine teetering dangerously above their heads. By the time it reached the inn, the crowd threatened to crash through doorways and windows. In the flickering light of the paper lanterns that were strung all along the street, the men looked menacing, like an approaching army. His mother shrank back into the shadows. Closing her eyes, she edged her way toward the entrance to the inn. The men's wet faces careened in and out of the light. The town's fishermen. The bus driver, Mr Goto. The grocer. Toshi knew them all, and he wasn't afraid.

A strong arm swept Toshi up, and then he was sitting on Taro's bare shoulders, looking down at the parade. He could reach out and touch the swaying lanterns.

'Come on,' Taro yelled to Toshi's mother. 'Come along with us down to the dock.'

Toshi was riding right behind the shrine, and he felt dizzy with joy. He held on to Taro's head, his hair prickly and wet, and he looked up. The full moon swung alarmingly in the sky.

Toshi's mother shook her head and turned away from Taro's naked body. She looked frightened.

They moved forward, away from her.

'Come on,' Taro shouted.

'Mother! Mother, come with us! Don't be scared.'

But she stayed put, hugged herself as if she were cold. 'Be careful, Toshi-chan! I'll be waiting for you here.'

And then they were already past the inn, and her voice was swallowed up by the chanting.

'Your mother is an odd woman, but I like her,' Taro yelled over the din.

Toshi wondered what he meant by 'odd.' And why Taro liked her. It disturbed him. He hardly knew Taro, who treated him with an easier familiarity than his own father did.

The drummers had already arrived at the dock and climbed aboard the fishing boats, which were lit up with strings of lights. For every step the drunken fishermen managed to move forward, they seemed to take two back, wavering under the weight of the shrine. As they neared the edge of the dock, there was a collective gasp from the crowd as the shrine dipped forward. To Toshi, it seemed as if the Fishing God was trying to break free and dive into the black sea. Slowly, the men lowered the shrine to the dock, and then collapsed themselves. The drums started up again, louder and more insistent.

Taro lifted Toshi off his shoulders, and put him down.

'Are you all right?'

Toshi nodded. He was still shy with Taro. After all, Taro was his mother's boss. He owed him a lot.

'Don't get lost, okay? And don't go near the edge of the dock.'

'Yes, I understand,' he said, bowing slightly.

Taro laughed. 'As polite as your mother, aren't you.'

He patted him on the head and walked away, his pale shoulders still bearing the imprint of Toshi's legs. Taro joined the other men out at the end of the dock, where a vat of sake steamed over a charcoal fire. A Shinto priest wearing a boat-shaped hat dipped cups into the vat and handed them to the men. The sea was dark and still. When the men jumped in, the surface broke into millions of glass beads, children's marbles, the stars. The men splashed and paddled like seals. Their white loincloths unraveled and rose to the surface, drifted away like cigarette smoke.

The crowd pushed forward. Camera flashes lit up the men as they swam to the ladders and were lifted out, dripping and heavy as fishing nets.

Spitting out black water.

Their naked bodies blue as snow.

Wool blankets unfurled. The men shivered as they were led over to the oil-drum fires lit along the dock. Hot sake splashed on the wooden planks.

Toshi waited for Taro to be hoisted out of the dark water. He didn't see him anywhere. What if he had drowned? With so many men, it would be easy to lose someone, for a man to go under without anyone noticing. He ran from fire to fire, in and out of the light and the heat.

And then Toshi saw him, jumping up and down in front of the fire like a monkey, grinning, slapping his own flesh to warm himself. And stark naked. Girls giggled and turned away. The old fishermen's wives laughed and pointed at his penis, which had shrunk up so much from the cold it had disappeared into his bush of black hair.

'Another minute in the water, and you'd have turned into a girl,' one of them yelled, and they all howled.

Taro turned and shook his rear at the women. He saw Toshi standing alone in the dark and motioned for him to come join him. But Toshi didn't move. He wanted to go to Taro and the warmth of the fire. But he was too shy.

'Toshi-chan! Come here!' Taro called out.

Everyone turned to look at Toshi.

He ran into the firelight. Taro scooped him up and threw him over his shoulder like a sack of rice. Toshi felt the heat of the flames. He saw the full moon, then the black sea, then the water dripping down the backs of Taro's bare legs onto the dock. His own body swayed dangerously.

His mother was alone in the kitchen, watching TV. A man in a cowboy hat was playing 'The Tennessee Waltz' on his guitar.

'I embarrassed your son,' Taro said. He sat down at the table across from her.

Toshi's mother only glanced at him, then turned back to the TV. The guitarist walked off the stage with his guitar held high in the air as the audience applauded.

'Did you have a good time?'

He nodded. Something was wrong with her.

'Are you hungry?'

He shook his head. What was it?

'Well, go take a bath and get to bed. It's past your bedtime,' she said without looking at him.

Taro picked up the glass in front of her and sniffed it.

'What's this? Drinking whiskey all by yourself? Drinking alone is no good. I'll join you.'

He got up and took the whiskey bottle out of the cupboard.

Toshi's mother looked at him and smiled weakly, apologizing. She never drank. Toshi looked away from her, at the TV, as the news came on. Frightened people, handkerchiefs held over their mouths, raced through streets lined with soldiers, through clouds of smoke. There were gunshots.

'The riots in Korea,' Taro said. 'Things are really chaotic

there politically, aren't they?' He put the bottle and another glass on the table. 'Soldiers shooting students in the streets. It's still a backward country. Those Koreans aren't civilized.'

His mother jumped up from the table, knocking her glass over. She turned off the TV.

'Hey, I wanted to watch that,' Taro said.

She looked down at the table. The puddle of whiskey spread. The glass rolled toward the table's edge, but she didn't move.

Taro didn't move.

Toshi ran out of the room.

The glass shattered.

10

The TV quiz show is interrupted by a grim-faced newscaster.

'A devastating earthquake has just hit Hokkaido. Measuring seven point four on the Richter scale, the quake was centered east of Shiretoko Peninsula in the Sea of Okhotsk. Reports are just coming in.'

The waitress brings Toshi his potato salad and deep-fried pork cutlet sandwich. Everyone in the coffee shop turns toward the TV set.

'The earthquake was followed by a tsunami, with waves reaching twenty meters high in some areas on the eastern coast of Shiretoko Peninsula.'

Toshi runs out of the restaurant so fast that he doesn't realize he forgot to pay until he is on the Haneda Airport monorail, punching his mother's number into the train phone, and he notices the crumpled check in his hand. Above his head on a TV monitor, Rausu is consumed by flames. The topography of his childhood altered. A reporter shouts breathlessly over the commotion of helicopter blades: '. . . buried in the rubble of collapsed buildings or swept out to sea. Dozens of fishing boats capsized.'

Incredibly, the phone rings. Waiting for someone to answer at the inn, Toshi feels himself moving as fast as the train, faster, speeding past factories and crowded driving ranges, over a wide, dark river, past children dancing in a dusty schoolyard.

'Hello? Hello?'

'Mother!'

On TV, the governor of Hokkaido steps out of a helicopter. 'The fires are out of control. Residents are being evacuated on foot to safe, inland areas. Early estimates suggest that the damage could reach into the billions of yen.'

He can't get a seat on a plane until the next morning. At Nakashibetsu Airport, cargo planes disgorge supplies, medical teams, and digging equipment. Toshi rents a car and drives past fields tangled with green pumpkin. Up in the hills the air turns cold. Gold and red leaves sweep across the hood of his car as he listens to the radio news: Ruptured water mains and gas lines. Exploding rice cookers. The road swings out to the coast, and he sees smoke. Military helicopters hover offshore. Rausu's lighthouse is collapsed on the rocky promontory, its inner staircase a spiraling, bleached skeleton. Electrical poles, snapped off at their bases, lie across the road. He slows the car, bewildered by each new sight, thrown off balance, as if in a dream. Can a landscape really change so drastically in just a single moment in time? Could it ever go back to what it was? He searches for his past.

Then: Four old women stand by the sea and weep. They are connected in their poses of grief like a marble statue from antiquity, a photograph he might have seen in his art history books. One woman bent over, another with her head thrown back, two huddled together, they all press handkerchiefs to their weathered faces. The wreckage of households – refrigerators, television sets, microwave ovens – is strewn across the land. Balanced in midair between two telephone poles, a kitchen table levitates. The world Toshi remembers is turned upside down. He steps on the accelerator and watches in his rearview mirror as the old women, their frames already contorted by loss and sorrow, recede. Up ahead, the sea wall is crumbled. Trapped on the pavement, blowfish puff up like balloons, then burst.

On the dock near the end of the road, his mother moves among the fishermen with a thermos, pouring tea. Their boats are motionless, tossed up onto the shore like discarded toys – snapped masts, gaping holes, twisted rudders. Everywhere else, though, there's nervous movement: The dazed fishermen shake their heads and exchange cigarettes like words of comfort. Red foxes pace back and forth at the road's edge.

Bears hang from the treetops and bark like dogs.

He stops the car, and his mother hurries over. With her long, loose hair and oversize rain slicker, she looks like a young girl, not a woman in her sixties.

'Mother, are you all right? Is everything okay at the inn?' She looks well, despite his father's death, and now the earthquake.

'We're fine. There was almost no damage on our side of the peninsula. As I said on the phone, only a few cracks in the road, some broken windows and dishes, that's all.' She pauses, as if uncomfortable with her good fortune in the face of so much tragedy. 'I didn't expect to see you again so soon, and for something so terrible.'

Together they turn to look at the noodle shop. The rear has collapsed, so the shop leans back, and the front windows stare blankly at the sky, like an old man who sits down for a rest and then discovers that he can't get up again. Like his father slumped over on the train, circling Tokyo.

Seagulls squawk. Cigarette smoke drifts across the road.

'It's good that your father isn't here to see this.'

He doesn't say so, but he wonders if his father would have even cared.

'Shall we take a walk? The bulldozers are coming soon. I don't want to be here to watch.'

'Bulldozers?'

'Yes. They have to tear down all the buildings quickly that can't be repaired, because they're unsafe. They called this morning, after I'd already spoken to you. I told them that it wasn't my shop, that it was yours. But they said it had to be done right away. I'm sorry.'

'That's fine,' he says, but, to his surprise, he feels sad. He walks over and looks in the window. The back wall is buckled and splintered, and daylight pours into the empty room.

His mother comes up behind him and takes his elbow, an unfamiliar gesture that startles him.

'Come,' she says.

They start up the slope – for the last time, he thinks. The foxtail barley shudders, already bent flat against the hillside, as if anticipating the weight of coming snow. A crevice runs up the slope like a crack in a dinner plate, and neatly splits the roots and trunk of a single tall pine. Its upper branches still cling to one another over the chasm.

Out of habit, they search for edible plants as they walk. Ladder fern and jade-colored spoon fern. Nutty-tasting candleweed. And ghost mushrooms, which in the spring are translucent, but in the autumn turn a milky white. He has seen them in Tokyo's department stores, individually wrapped in damp sheets of moss, selling for exorbitant prices.

Taking a zigzag course, they stoop and dig the plants out with twigs, shaking the soil off the roots as they put them in the plastic bags his mother always carries in her pockets. They've done this together so many times, ever since Toshi was a small child, that they don't need to talk. And he finds it comforting to watch his mother's strong hands as she lifts the plants out of the earth. Her fingernails are cut short, and she wears no rings. The backs of her hands are the color of onion skins. They are hands that, even in faraway Tokyo, he can easily conjure up: They pour tea and smooth out blankets. They lift clumps of rice between two chopsticks and carry them to his mouth when he is sick.

Deep in the forest they stop in a familiar glade he hasn't visited in many years. As they enter the pool of light, he almost expects to encounter himself as a child – sitting very still, holding his breath as an antelope passes by. But the glade is empty. His mother sits on a fallen tree trunk and looks up. They are hemmed in by a circle of trees. There is only the blue sky, remote and aloof, above them.

'Sit down,' she says. 'I have something to tell you. Please sit next to me, so I won't have to look at you. This is a difficult story for me to tell.'

He settles down cross-legged at her feet, and the glade starts to spin under the still sky like a ride he once went on at the amusement park behind Tokyo Dome: It spun so fast that when it suddenly tipped onto its side, he didn't fall. But now he is falling. For he knows that his mother is finally going to give words to the unspoken story that filled up the noodle shop and the rooms above it his whole life. The story his father stirred each day into a pot on the stove top. The story his mother murmured every night in her sweaty dreams, then folded away each morning along with their mattresses. The story he's been trying to draw.

Suddenly, he's scared. Don't tell me! he cries silently. I don't want to know.

But she begins her story. And as she does, another story is coming to an end. He hears the distant rumble of the bulldozers as they roll down the coast road.

'My name was Kim Chung-Ja. I was not yet thirteen years old. I was walking home from school outside my village, the small village where I was born and raised, just north of Puyo, along the Kum River, where the red ginseng grows. My parents were farmers.' His mother begins in an even voice. And then she repeats this in the language of her dreams – in, he finally realizes, Korean.

'My name was Kim Chung-Ja. I was walking home from school with my little brothers, Man-Bok and Byung-Bok. It was spring, and even though the war was on and there was barely enough to eat – everything we grew the Japanese took from us – that day, the flooded rice paddies, the winter barley, the tender garlic and onion sprouts, everything was young and green. That day, I was full of hope. I carried my schoolbooks in my arms, and I started to skip with joy when I felt the scented breeze on my cheeks. 'There's nothing like the fragrance of young rice plants, is there?' I said, and my brothers laughed at me.

'That morning, our teacher had told us about the Japanese bombing Pearl Harbor, and how America had entered the war.

'"Pray for the Americans," she'd said very softly, afraid of who might overhear her, for there were spies everywhere – at school, working in the rice paddies, among the fishermen on the riverbanks. And I did pray, with all my might. But that afternoon, the world and the war seemed far away from us. We were still children. What did we need to know of bombs and sinking battleships? I thought. Foolishly.'

His mother stops speaking and stares into the dark woods. And he doesn't want her to go on, for he is still trying to grasp this one, single overwhelming fact: His mother is Korean. He is half-Korean. But she continues.

'A Japanese army truck appeared in the distance and moved toward us in a dark cloud of dust. We stopped laughing. There was nowhere to hide. We slowed down and walked with our heads bent. I had such an awful feeling in my stomach, worse than the hunger I always felt in those years. Suddenly, I couldn't breathe. I kept thinking, My brothers. I must take care of my little brothers.'

She takes a deep breath, and then another, and still another, before she goes on.

'We kept walking, slower and slower, watching each other's feet, listening to the truck approach. Then I saw the truck's muddy grille. It stopped right in front of us, blocking the road. We stood very still, and kept our heads down. Both doors opened. I remember the motor idling. I remember I thought, They didn't turn off the motor. That's a good sign.

'But then, I saw a pair of boots, and army pants.

'"What's your name?" a voice shouted at me in Japanese. A hand lifted my chin and squeezed until it hurt, and my eyes filled with tears. I stared into that soldier's face. I can still see it. I was so surprised because it was almost as young as my own.

'"Hiroko. Hiroko Kawaguchi," I said. Under Japanese colonial law, we all had to take Japanese names. We were forced to speak only Japanese at school. That was how they tried to destroy us, you see. By outlawing our culture and our language. Our history. As if we'd never existed.'

They. The Japanese, Toshi thinks, and the realization sickens him.

'Through my tears, I stared into that soldier's face, and all I could think was, Both truck doors opened. There's another soldier. Where is he? I was so worried about my brothers. But I didn't dare look around. The soldier was still squeezing my chin. He was hurting me.

'"You come with us," he said, and his voice quivered, as if he were afraid. He was just a boy, after all. Then two more hands grabbed my arms and pinned them behind me, and pushed me forward. The other soldier.'

Toshi can hardly bear to hear her story. He breathes in

the dark air from her past, and his lungs ache. He feels his own arms pinned behind him.

'That's when I really understood what he'd said to me. "You come with us." A few words that would change my whole life. I must have stared at him with such disbelief, for he repeated them. "You come with us." They pushed me toward the back of the truck. I tried to look back to say good-bye to my little brothers, but I couldn't. That was the worst part, for I suddenly knew in my heart that I would never see their faces again. "You come with us." The two soldiers lifted me up and tossed me through the canvas flaps like a sack of rice.'

She pauses. When she starts to speak again, her voice is strained and thin.

'And that was the end of my world as I knew it. My mother cooking in the kitchen of our house by the river. The green fields, the blue sky. Sunlight. All gone.

'I will never forget the inside of that truck. With the canvas flaps closed, I couldn't see anything, but there were others. Were they men, women, children? I didn't know. But their hands were all over me, grabbing at me. I cried out, I thought they were trying to hurt me. Then someone put a hand over my mouth. And I knew, all at once, whoever was there was afraid too. All those hands clutched me in terror. I could smell the fear. And worse, human smells. Vomit and excrement. I thought I'd suffocate.

'I heard the two doors slam shut, and the truck drove on. I never returned to my village. And I never saw my little brothers, or my parents, or my country again.'

The sound of trucks on the coast road travels through the forest and startles him.

'After the truck, there was a train. Then a ship. They sent me to an island off the coast of Hokkaido. One of the very same islands you grew up looking at from the front room window. That I had to look at every day until I left for Utoro.'

The past and present collide, but his mother doesn't stop. Each of her words is a blow he feels deep inside, shattering his bones. Light and noise pour into the noodle shop, demolishing it.

'In the factory there, another Korean girl told me, "They only take the pretty, healthy ones. We're unlucky in that way. Better to have dull hair and a pockmarked face." We were mostly Korean girls, all very young, but there were some Chinese, and even a few Japanese, who kept to themselves.

'They put us in freezing, filthy barracks. There weren't enough beds, so we slept two or three to a mattress with one thin blanket. We all had lice. And sickness.' She breathes deeply, then goes on. 'They didn't give us enough to eat. And what they did give us was bad. We had constant diarrhea from the food, and we got thinner and thinner. For toilets, we had to keep digging holes in the ground. The smell was everywhere, even where we ate and slept. We could never get clean.

'We were young girls. Still children. Always hungry, and cold, and frightened. And so homesick. I would wake up in the middle of the night and hear the girls around me crying out in their sleep. In the morning, we'd find that we had all dreamed the same dreams: Our mothers' faces. The ginseng that grew in the western hills. Hot, spicy cabbage and garlic. When we woke up our mouths were watering.

'What kind of factory was it? What were we assembling? Can you believe it, we never knew. The rooms were dark. The Japanese foremen told us nothing. When the time came that I could have found out the answers, I didn't want to know anymore. I knew only the weight and shape of the objects I touched, their cold metal surfaces. It was like working blind. Once, a door opened as I passed, and heat and smoke rushed out, almost knocking me over. I saw glowing cauldrons of liquid fire. Sparks flew through the air. I saw men working, stripped naked, their bodies black with soot. I remember thinking, Now I have seen hell.

'We had no radio, of course. The only news we had from the outside came to us from the soldiers, and they tried to take away all our hope. America was falling. Japan was winning the war in the Pacific. "All of Asia will soon belong to Japan!" the soldiers shouted. But I could see the desperation in their faces, and I knew they were lying.'

His mother stands up and walks across the glade into the shadow of the trees. 'This is the hardest part of my story to tell you. The very bad part,' she says, casting her words out under the cover of darkness.

The very bad part. He hugs himself tightly as the pain and bile rise up from his stomach. How could it be worse than what the Japanese, his own countrymen, did to his mother?

'Sometimes, girls were taken from the barracks in the middle of the night, carried off in their underclothes. We woke up in the morning, and their beds were empty. There was a building outside the factory compound, it was whispered. The soldiers and foremen stood in line outside this building every day, all day. Girls got pregnant. Some went crazy. Some took their own lives.

'I vowed I would kill myself before I would let them take me. But one night, after I'd been there for more than a year – it was spring again – they came for me. I'd seen how the soldiers had begun to look at me, so I was prepared. In my smock pocket, I carried a small pouch filled with metal filings and powdered chemicals I'd stolen. So when they led me away, I wasn't afraid. I had an escape. I would poison myself.

'But they stripped me and scrubbed my body with disinfectant and hard brushes. And they found the pouch.

Instead of death, which I had prayed so hard for, I got . . .' Her voice thins out into a single strand of anguish. 'They hurt me.'

The ground opens up, and Toshi is plunged into a black hole. He plummets past the Japanese soldiers, past the islands he'd looked out at every day. He tries to stop himself, he wants to stop his mother's story, to rescue her. He grabs onto the thread of her voice only to have it unravel further.

'It was worse than the worst nightmare. A room like a cage. And men, one after another, day and night. I was always in pain, always ashamed. I'm still ashamed. Ashamed to tell you this.'

He can't bear to listen. But her voice rises suddenly in anger, and pulls him back.

'I never once looked at any of them, those Japanese men. I'd decided that no matter what, I wouldn't give them that satisfaction. They were terrible men. What some of them did to me.'

Just as quickly, the anger in her voice dissipates, and he hears only exhaustion and defeat. Across the glade, his mother is a slumped shadow against the trees.

'I decided to die. I stopped eating. Without food, I grew weak. I fainted whenever I stood up. I must have been unconscious half the time, even when men were with me. Not that they cared. And so I drifted away from my body. Never to return to it was what I wanted.

'Then, one day, I woke up to hear a kind voice. A man whispered in my ear, "You'd better eat. They're talking about letting you die. Or worse. They don't want to waste anything on you if you're not able to work."

'I kept my eyes shut. I said, "But I want to die." He said, "Please look at me. I will help you."

'I don't know why I did, but I opened my eyes. A young soldier was kneeling by my bed. His was the first human face I'd looked at in months. I remember thinking, What a gentle face.

'"I will help you," he said again. And he did.

'He came to see me as often as he could without arousing suspicion. He smuggled rice balls and pickled radishes into my room and made me eat them to keep my strength up. And he never touched me. He only talked. He told me about himself. "Fumio Okamoto is my name," he said.'

'Father!' Toshi is horrified by his father's presence in this story. His whole body pitches forward in protest, and he struggles to keep his balance.

'Yes, the soldier was your father,' she says. 'But please listen. Your father brought me back from the dead. He brought me back by talking to me. "I am from Kyushu, just across the water from Korea," he said. "There are palm trees in my hometown, and in the distance, a smoking volcano." I listened, and I let myself imagine those places. He said he would take me there when the war was over, and we'd walk on the beach together. Then we'd find a boat and he would take me home. I listened and I cried. I didn't believe him. But his visits made my life bearable. Your father kept me alive.

'Then I was sent back to the factory. They did that, got tired of girls. The other girls wouldn't speak to me at first. They shunned me, as if it had been my choice, as if I'd enjoyed it. I had to eat alone. And sleep alone, on the floor. And if any man at the factory even looked at me, I'd be physically sick.

'And I never saw my soldier, your father, again. Only from a distance, and we couldn't acknowledge each other. "I promise I'll take care of you," he'd said. But that was all over. I'd have to take care of myself. Anyway, I couldn't imagine why he'd wanted to help me. I was a sick Korean girl, so thin you could see all my bones. And I'd never given him anything at all.

'It didn't seem possible, but our lives got even worse. Supplies ran out. There was no fuel for the machinery at the factory, so we stopped working. Every day was silent and empty, with nothing to fill the hours except fear and hunger. There wasn't even enough food for the soldiers. We killed bugs and ate them. And rats. And the soldiers took their own misery out on us in cruel ways. There were many more deaths.

'Then, one evening, we heard about the terrible bombs America dropped on Hiroshima and Nagasaki. And suddenly, the war was over.

'That night, all the girls dreamed one dream – of the sea around us in flames. In the morning we woke up in our barracks sweating and crying, and discovered that the soldiers had burned down the factory while we slept, and had fled in their boats. We were abandoned on that barren island with nothing at all.'

She turns around and walks back across the small glade to him, as if returning from a great distance, and from a great darkness.

'All the girls talked of escaping, of going home to Korea or China, or back to Japan, for the Japanese workers had been left behind too. But I thought that I could never leave, not after what had happened to me. Only a few years had passed, but it was like a century. I was no longer that girl who'd carried her schoolbooks down a country road, who felt the rush of spring in her blood. That girl was dead. I had become an old woman. I decided I would stay on the island. Someday I'd end up in the little cemetery that was already filled with the graves of young girls.'

He recognizes his mother's story as if he's always known it, as if he's been drawing it all his life, his hand and pencil searching for the truth. He's angry and ashamed. Angry at Japan, and ashamed to be Japanese. But he's not really

Japanese. He's half-Korean. A foreigner. He can't stop shaking, and his lack of control – over his own body and his own life – frightens him.

His mother sits down again, but he doesn't look up at her face, doesn't have the courage yet. He's surprised to hear himself speak.

'What happened? How did you get away from the island?'

'Your father came back for me. Months later. He came in a fishing boat. I still don't know how he managed it, how he paid the fisherman. I was so grateful, I never thought to ask. When I saw him coming down the road toward me, I fell to the ground and wept, and I couldn't stop. I cried for a full day, and then the next and the next. Your father had to carry me to the boat like a child. He thought I'd gone mad. Which I had.

'Shiretoko Peninsula was still very remote and unsettled back then. There was no airport, no road between Rausu and Utoro. After the war, the whole country was in shambles. It was easy for us to get by without family records. Your father told people we were from outside Nagasaki, and that our families had been wiped out by the bomb. Everybody was too worried about eating, about surviving, to bother to ask questions. Besides, we weren't the only ones. Lots of people used the war to hide things, to change their pasts.'

The bulldozers have stopped. It is so quiet that the rustling of branches startles him. Is this really the glade he visited so often as a child? He no longer recognizes it. Even the sky is unfamiliar. Everything has changed. By giving words to her past, his mother has destroyed his.

'I hardly spoke for the first few years. I wasn't a whole person, just a shell. You see, my soul was gone. It's true. On that island, I had let it go. I prayed for it to fly back to Korea, to my family.

'Your father had once promised to take me home. But I didn't remind him, and we were too poor to think about anything for a long time but feeding ourselves. Your father did different kinds of work. Eventually, we opened the noodle shop. And we kept to ourselves. No one thought it strange. The war wounded people in different ways. The people in Rausu were kind to me. Still, for a long time it was so difficult to live among the Japanese.'

She puts her hand on his shoulder. His mother's soul flying over the sea. Did it find its way back to Korea? What happened to her parents? And her brothers? Did they live to have children of their own? He might have uncles and aunts, and cousins.

'Toshi-chan? Please look at me.'

Finally, he looks up at his mother, whom he has always looked up at, and he is overcome by sorrow. He wants to see the girl she once was, the girl the Japanese soldiers killed. He struggles to hold back his tears, the convulsions of sadness rolling through his chest and throat. Even his own body is no longer recognizable.

'Toshi-chan, I loved your father. I owe him my life. And he gave up his for me. He had his parents and a sister. But he never went back home, he never even found out if they survived the war.'

She turns away from his gaze.

'I couldn't be a wife to him. Do you understand what I'm telling you? I tried, but I couldn't, not after what happened over there.' She nods in the direction of the sea and the Russian islands.

'As we got older, life got easier for us. Your father was such a patient, good man. Once, in the spring, he closed up the shop for a whole week, and we took a car trip across Hokkaido. It was one of the nicest times I can remember.' Her voice softens. 'Your father was very kind. Wherever we went, people liked him.'

He hears the longing in her voice. For the first time, he realizes that she misses his father.

'We decided to have a child before it was too late. I was already so old, and we didn't want to be cheated out of that too. Your father wanted you so badly. And so I was a wife to him.'

She stands up and bends over to rub her legs – the gesture reminds him that she is not young anymore.

'I never should have left that island. Your father was a brave and gentle man, and twice I ruined his life. The first time was when I let him rescue me and tie our fates together. The second time was when I gave him false hope. He never demanded anything from me. But I made him miserable by denying him what little he wanted. After I became pregnant, I turned away from him again. I will never forgive myself. And I can't ask you to forgive me.'

He stands too, but still he doesn't say anything. He knows she is waiting, but he can't speak. Not yet. It isn't just her past that she's revealed to him, but his own as well. He is still trembling, standing on unsteady ground that might open up beneath him without warning. And his father is there with them. He stands before them in the darkness, a spectral figure of pity and terrible sorrow.

She starts to walk, and Toshi silently follows, and soon they emerge from the forest. The evening sky is purple, and streaked with red. Out at sea the lights of fishing boats blink on like stars. Beyond them, the islands. Their past.

'I was glad when Japan lost those islands to Russia at the end of the war. But still, they were always there, always reminding me. When I started to work at the inn in Utoro on weekends, your father and I both thought it was only temporary, a good change for me. We thought it would help us.

'Then I discovered what a great relief it was to look out and see nothing but water. I told your father I was going to live at the inn. He understood. He didn't want me to go, but he didn't stop me.'

'But why didn't we all leave here? Go somewhere. Anywhere,' he cries, pleading, but too late. Only for a moment, he imagines them all together, a happy family.

'Your father knew why. I had to get away from him too.'

The cruel and terrible truth of her words nauseates him.

'He was on the island with me. Every time I looked at his face, I remembered. The pain was always there.'

They come to the top of the slope and look down. The noodle shop is gone, and the rubble has already been carted away in trucks. There is only a dark stain on the earth. Had it ever really been there? Doubt makes him unsteady.

'Your father only asked one thing of me. That I not take you. You were all he had, and he loved you so much. I wanted you with me, but I couldn't leave him all alone, down there at the end of the road.'

Yes, the noodle shop had been there. Toshi had lived his life at the end of the road. Even now, in the waning light, the memories are vivid: The school bus drives up, and a small boy in shorts, his tanned legs covered with cuts and insect bites, leaps down to the ground. His mother, waiting for him at the front door, smiles and wipes her hands on her apron. Toshi wants to run down the slope and in the back door of the shop, to find his father behind the counter, stacking just-washed bowls by the window to dry.

But it's too late.

He feels movement inside of him. A subterranean ache. Something splits open, and the streaked light and the starlight and the night air pour in.

And they both cry.

II ʃ

'You need healing, you need comforting. I will heal you. Close your eyes.'

His head is in Lucy's lap. She strokes his face with her long fingers. Softly. A current.

Water, rivulet.

Air, breeze.

It feels good. She draws everything out – disquiet, anger – through his skin.

Osmosis.

'You will heal me,' he says, wanting to believe her words.

It is evening. Waning light wafts silently over Lucy's garden wall and settles like snow on the tatami.

She whispers, 'Just relax now. It's all over.'

But suddenly he remembers: his mother pulled from her bed in the middle of the night by Japanese soldiers.

Toshi stayed on in Hokkaido for a week to be with his mother, and together they saw things he will never forget: A winged temple roof, detached, jammed like a knife blade into the sand. Scuba divers searching the pilings for drowned fishermen. A red fire truck roosting on top of a house.

And they talked. It was easier for them to talk now.

Taro and Granny already knew, she told him. They had known for years. Of course she had had to tell them.

'Why didn't you ever tell me?'

'I was afraid you might hate me if you learned the truth.'

'But you're my mother.'

They were in the inn's kitchen, drinking tea. On the far wall, still enclosed in a frame with her letter to Toshi, Audrey Hepburn smiled down on the dining room table.

'For a long time, I hated myself. Strange, isn't it? I forgave the Japanese long before I was able to forgive myself.' She stares down into her teacup. 'When your father came back to the island for me, I refused to go with him at first. I told him to leave me there. I knew if he didn't leave me then, he never would. And I was bound to make him unhappy.' A tear falls into her teacup, and she wipes her eyes on her sleeve. 'He didn't listen to me, and I was too weak to resist. Until you were born, I hated myself for that weakness.'

He called Lucy twice from the inn, and she offered to fly up. He said no, he'd be back soon. When he wasn't with his mother, he sat with Granny in her pottery shop. She spoke to him about her own life and losses, and as he listened he drew her portrait; following the lines of her face with his pencil, he understood how old she had become. A few afternoons a week, Zeni came over from the inn to help her out in the shop.

On his last morning, he took his father's white car and drove alone across the peninsula to Rausu. Whole sections of the town had already been razed, but the harbor was still in ruin. Plastic bath buckets and soy sauce bottles washed up onshore. What could be done? he thought, seeing how land and sea, past and present, had gotten so confused. He sat cross-legged on the hood of the car with his sketch pad and colored pencils in his lap. It was a brilliant autumn morning.

Across the shining water, the dark shadow of his mother's story was immutably etched into the islands, altering their shapes.

He began to draw.

Now here he is, in Lucy's house, his head resting in her lap. He's told her everything his mother had told him. While he talked, she fed him pasta and poured red wine. When he was finished, she led him into the dark room and told him, Lie down, put your head in my lap. He trusts her.

He opens his eyes and stares up at her beautiful face.

'I hate the Japanese.'

'Don't say that. You can never hate a whole race of people, a country. Your father was Japanese. He saved your mother. And he loved her so much he sacrificed his life for her. You're Japanese too. One half of you is.' She leans over, filling his vision, and kisses his right cheek. 'Is it this half?' She kisses his left cheek. 'Or this half?'

She slips out from under him, sliding a cushion under his head, and she goes into the other room. Music. The piece she played for him the first time he visited her house. Now it reminds him of Lucy, and of the swans gliding on the pond. She returns, a stack of white sheets in her arms, and he watches her unfurl them. She tacks them up on the walls, and over the open garden doors. When she is done, they are enclosed in a white room with music.

'This is our shrine,' she says, and he can hear in her voice her pleasure with her own invention. She kneels down and rolls his socks off. She pulls his sweatshirt up over his head. She unzips his jeans, and he lifts his hips. Outside, a fierce wind whips up. They both stop to listen to the rain move in their direction.

'The typhoon.' He reaches his hands up and under her shirt and cups her small breasts.

The white sheets tremble.

'Shh,' she says, a finger to his lips, a hand sliding down his bare belly. 'You're safe here.'

Lucy is asleep in his arms, her head on his chest, their legs entwined. The heat of her body keeps him warm even though a cold wind has entered the room.

The sheets flutter.

Images appear on the white sheets. A silent movie screen, the voices of his mother and father drowned out by the rain as they move through their lives together, unable to speak the truth. If only they'd told him their story, wouldn't all their lives have been different? Wouldn't his mother have stayed? They could have all gone away together, left Hokkaido. Another country.

The screen turns a lush green, the fields his mother walked through as a girl. Toshi smells the spring air and the young rice plants. He longs to go to Korea to find his mother's family. His family. And to his father's hometown in Kyushu. There are palm trees, his father had told his mother.

He drifts in and out of sleep, and his desires spread like the rain-splattered patterns on the rippling sheets. Audrey Hepburn's white-gloved hand rests on his arm. Under blazing chandeliers, they enter a crowded ballroom. Everyone applauds as they dance across a marble floor that reflects their gliding image like melting ice. Her neck, wrapped in diamonds, is luminous, a white birch branch trembling under the weight of new snow.

Toshi leaps into the landscape of Audrey Hepburn's neck.

'Please come over. Hurry.'

Paul's voice travels across Tokyo to pull Toshi out of a deep sleep, rolls him out of his futon onto the cool tatami. He looks up at the alarm clock. Nine.

'What is it? What's wrong?'

Lying on his back, he pulls open the curtain and considers the upside-down world. It's Sunday morning. A rainy day. His body is still asleep. He feels his limbs far away, barely responsive.

'Just come over. Please.'

'I'm sleeping.'

'Please.'

The subway is half-empty. Toshi wishes he were back in bed. Someone has left a copy of *Business Hip Hop* on the seat. He picks it up and flips through it. Chocolate Girl pushes a cargo ship filled with pesticide-tainted California rice out of Tokyo Bay. Rats swarm over the ship's deck. Four pages later, she's been captured and imprisoned in the ship's hold, her wrists and ankles bound with radioactive seaweed that saps her superpowers. Her bared, perfectly shaped breasts glow with contamination. As her eyes adjust to the darkness, she sees that the hold is filled with crates of amphetamines, Banana Republic sweatshirts, and assault weapons.

He shuts the comic book and leaves it on the seat, discarded for the second time. I won't do this anymore, he thinks.

He uses his key to let himself into Paul's apartment.

'Hello?'

'In here.'

Paul's in his bedroom. He's pulled out all of the dresser drawers and emptied the closet, and spread everything on the floor. There are piles of white dress shirts, Calvin Klein underwear, socks, martial arts and body-building magazines. Dozens of pairs of shoes and sneakers, rubber beach thongs, cowboy boots. Winter gloves and bathing suits. Bicycle shorts. Dumbbells and videotapes. Double-breasted business suits still on their hangers. Italian neckties fanned out like peacock feathers.

In the middle of all this, Paul, in his underpants, turns in slow circles. His bright red hair is uncombed and sticks up at disturbing angles. There's no room for Toshi to walk, no path between the piles, so he stays in the doorway.

'What are you doing? Are you moving?'

'Moving? God, no. Moving. No.' Paul keeps turning, throws his arms up in the air, then lets them drop. He repeats this motion. 'Oh, God.'

'What is it?'

'What is it? What is it?' He stops and smiles at Toshi, but then the smile fades, and he sinks to the floor.

'Well, it's my life. Of course.'

Toshi waits. Paul starts to cry. So he takes a tentative step into the room, places his foot on a pile of T-shirts.

Paul takes deep breaths. Beneath the palm of his hand, Toshi feels Paul's stomach swell up with air and then deflate, over and over again, as if in repeated sighs of defeat.

'Could you go in the kitchen and make some tea for me? That would be a help.'

Toshi rolls away from him and stands up. He goes into the kitchen. Spotlessly clean. Not even a dirty dish in the sink. A Filipino maid comes in twice a week.

When the kettle whistles, Paul appears in the doorway, watches him pour the hot water into the teapot.

'I'm sorry.'

'That's okay.' He brings the pot to the table, sits down. Paul's still standing, as if waiting for an invitation into his own kitchen.

'What were you doing?' Toshi asks.

'I was looking.' Paul lifts the lid of the teapot and looks inside.

'It's oolong. Looking for what?'

'I don't know.' Paul turns on the TV, and for a moment they both watch the news: A Japanese ship carrying plutonium has capsized two miles offshore of Manila in a typhoon.

'I started out looking for a photograph. I was lonely. So I wanted to see a picture, of Michael, from before he got sick. I'd put it away somewhere, hidden it, because there was a time when I didn't want to remember him, it was too painful. But I hid it so well I couldn't find it. I looked everywhere. All of a sudden, I was tearing the room apart, pulling everything out. I guess I panicked. I couldn't stop myself. I thought, If I just lay everything out so that I can see it, then it will make sense, be solved.'

He sits down at the table. Toshi pours the tea.

'Solved?'

'Answered. Resolved.'

'I don't understand.'

'My life.'

'Oh.'

Paul leans over his cup and blows softly on the surface of the tea. Toshi thinks, He's my best friend. I should be able to help him. But I don't know what I can do for him.

'I brought someone home last night. Waseda University. Swim team. Twenty-two years old. Good-looking. My usual. You know?'

'I know.'

'It was nice. But I woke up this morning and looked over at him in bed, and I realized that I'd picked him up before. About three years ago. I'd already had sex with him. And I didn't even recognize him.'

'So?' Is Paul concerned about his memory?

'So, last night I went through my whole seduction routine. Picked him up at the bar, charmed him, bought him a beer. Then took him down the street to Lamppost for more drinks. A taxi home. White wine. I could do it in my sleep, you know.'

Toshi recalls the first night they met. Paul took him to Lamppost and made him feel special. He didn't know then that it was a practiced performance.

'I'd already done it for him. And to him. But I didn't remember. And worse, he probably didn't either. And I just thought . . .'

'What?'

'I thought, What am I doing? If I can't even tell them apart, I'm doing something wrong, this isn't what I'd planned for my life. I'm not even having fun.'

'You're not?' This is actually a surprise to Toshi. Although he doesn't think much of the young men Paul chooses, he has at times envied him his busy love life.

'No. This isn't fun. What this is, is depressing. What this is, is exhausting. I'm getting too old to spend my nights in smoky bars.'

'Then why do you do it?'

'Because I'm looking. I'm looking for someone who wants to stay home at night with me. It's not easy, you know, to find that person. I did it once, who knows if I can do it again. I don't know, it just takes so much energy. Sometimes, I have to say this, I'm sorry, but sometimes I think I'm looking for you.'

Toshi doesn't want to talk about this, it won't do any good. 'I'm right here. You must be looking for someone else. Maybe you're looking for Michael again.'

Paul smiles sadly. 'Yes, you're right. I guess I must be.'

They're both silent for a while. They drink their tea.

'I'm sorry I called and woke you.'

'That's okay,' he says, and means it.

'Was Lucy there? Did I wake her? I forgot even to ask. You know me. Going crazy but still completely self-absorbed.'

'She was at the recording studio all night.'

'I don't see much of you these days, now that you're in love.'

Paul has been making remarks like this a lot lately, even though Toshi and Lucy do their best to include him in their new, shared life. Lucy and Paul even have their own telephone relationship. Paul calls from his office, Lucy takes off her headphones, and they talk for an hour. She offers him advice and sympathy.

'I'm sorry,' Toshi says.

'Of course you are. You're Japanese.'

'I'm not.'

'Not what?'

'Japanese.'

Paul drops his head into his hands. 'Oh, God. What a jerk. Now I'm sorry. Really I am. God.'

'Yes, you are a jerk,' Toshi says, and they smile at each other. Best friends. And then suddenly, there's Toshi's face on TV.

'There's been another attempted arson, identical to the one this summer at the Nakano apartment of a twenty-three-year-old *manga* artist,' the newscaster says. On the screen, Toshi stands bare-chested outside his old apartment.

Paul turns up the volume. 'Unbelievable. You're half-naked on national television.'

'The pattern is the same, according to the police. The victim is again a young, single Japanese man. The method, a kerosene-soaked English-language newspaper dropped through the mail slot.'

Toshi is replaced by a confused-looking man in pajamas.

'The police are pursuing reports of a Caucasian woman seen near the apartment of Kenji Morita, a twenty-five-year-old employee of Mitsui Pesticides, on the evening of the fire. According to witnesses, the woman is in her late twenties.'

'Wow. She's turned into a serial arsonist. This is too wild,' Paul says.

'The police believe this is the same woman spotted just before the Nakano fire.'

Toshi stares at the man on the TV. He knows that face.

'That man was at Jane's apartment the night I went to see her.'

'Are you sure?'

'Yes.'

'Are you going to tell the police?'

He considers this. Choices for his future. For Jane's future. Jane, with her awkward Japanese, trying to explain herself to the police. In court. Jane on the news. Or lighting more fires, pursuing more Japanese men. When she drove him to the airport, his mother said, 'There will be no more secrets. No more lies.' He believed her, and repeated this to Lucy back in Tokyo. 'No more secrets. No more lies.' But there would be one more secret.

'Let the police figure it out for themselves.'

'Hey, look at that,' Paul says, pointing to the TV screen.

Brooke Shields, accompanied by her mother, arrives at Narita Airport. Ringed by bodyguards, the giant American actress steps onto the moving walkway like the mythical Japanese goddess Amaterasu descending from heaven, her enormous head of hair a luminous halo.

'Incredible. It's the Occupation all over again,' Paul says.

Toshi's seen old newsreels of the American Occupation soldiers after the War: tall, smiling liberators handing out rice and chocolate bars to the gaunt Japanese children who followed them wherever they went. And powdered milk. Milk that made his mother cry.

Cameras flash. Microphones crowd the screen. Brooke Shields' smile is dazzling.

'Look at them go wild over her,' Paul laughs.

Paul's smile is dazzling too. Caught in its bright beam,

Toshi cannot help himself. He feels buoyed up, happy, optimistic about both of their futures.

Draped with the rising sun flag, the Rice Party's trucks roll through Tokyo's streets like tanks. Shoppers cover their ears and duck into stores to escape the loudspeakers' blaring message: 'We must preserve the purity of the Japanese race. We must not taint it with the AIDS-infected blood of immoral Americans. The Crown Prince must not marry the actress.'

Toshi pulls his knit cap down over his ears and hurries into Sanwa Bank. He is moving out of his apartment and needs to pay his final utility bills. The teller adds up the figures on her calculator, checks them on her abacus, then hands him a complimentary pack of facial tissues.

'You'll be wanting to arrange for direct payments for your next apartment, then?'

He smiles. 'No. I'm moving in with my girlfriend.'

Mami hangs up the phone and stares into space. Suddenly she bursts into tears.

'Oh, Toshi-chan, I've been so foolish. I've spent all my money and time training so hard at the Sunny Princess Deportment School. And it's all been a waste.'

'What's wrong? What happened?' He's so nervous this morning he can't concentrate on anything. Today's cartoon panels wait on his desk in front of him, still untouched. All he's done since he arrived is drink tea.

'I've been disqualified.'

'Disqualified? Why?'

'I don't know. They wouldn't say.' Sniffling, she dabs at her eyes with a handkerchief. 'Anyway, it doesn't matter. The Crown Prince is going to marry Brooke Shields.'

Nakamura steps out of the toilet in a cloud of cigarette smoke. 'The Imperial Household Agency will never allow it. She's a foreigner, and an actress. His father had a hard enough time marrying a Japanese commoner.'

He takes out his wallet and counts out bills. 'Mami-chan, why don't you take a break. You've been working too hard. Go out and get us all some lunch. And take Akira with you. He needs the exercise.'

'Huh?' Akira looks up from a computer screen filled with roaring dinosaurs. His head is shaved bare except for a long tuft in the back that's dyed orange. The rest is beginning to grow back in dark, asymmetrical clumps.

'Come on, Akira-kun. Sensei is trying to get rid of us,' Mami says, tucking her handkerchief into the sleeve of her tailored suit. She rips the matching pillbox hat from her head and tosses it in the wastebasket. 'At least I won't have to wear these stupid clothes anymore.'

'Her mother's brother is married to a Taiwanese woman,' Nakamura says after Mami and Akira leave.

'Who?'

'Mami's. That's why she was disqualified. I was afraid that they'd find out. Poor girl.'

'You knew?'

'Yes. I knew.'

'How?'

Nakamura doesn't answer him. He's looking intently at the drawings Toshi's laid out on his desk. 'So, this is what you've been working on all this time, is it?'

'Yes,' Toshi says. Months of work, and still just the beginning. Every night after Lucy falls asleep, he goes into the other room and draws. Listening to her music, he watches the story unfold on the white paper. With his colored pencils, he fills in details that often make him weep, he can't bear to be alone, and he slips back into bed beside Lucy, seeking the solace of her even breathing and the warm sleeping smell of her flesh.

Even now, in the bright fluorescent light of the studio, he can hardly stand to look at his own drawings.

'Sensei, I'd like your permission to develop this into a comic strip on my own. This is very important to me. I promise that it won't take time away from my work on "Chocolate Girl."'

Nakamura only nods, lights up another cigarette. He holds out the pack to Toshi.

'Green Earth. New brand. Menthol.'

'I don't smoke.'

'Of course you don't. Well, you're smart not to take it up. Not like Akira. He can draw, but his head is empty.' He laughs, then starts to cough.

Toshi walks away and stares out the window at the rain while Nakamura once again leafs through the cartoon panels, then through the individual drawings. This is the first time he's shown them. Even Lucy hasn't seen them yet: Still clutching her schoolbooks, a pretty Korean girl is tossed into the back of an army truck. A young Japanese soldier stands in the bow of a fishing boat, sailing toward a dark island. A small boy leans back into a wall of luminous moss, and leaves his shadow behind.

Not the whole story. But enough to give Nakamura an idea of what he wants to do. In the reflection in the window glass, Toshi watches him spread the panels out on the desk, then slowly walk around them – once, twice, three times, four times. What's Nakamura thinking? Three stories below on the crowded street, dark figures scurry along under dark umbrellas, taxi doors spring open and shut.

Finally, Nakamura speaks. 'This is very sensitive material. The war, you know. It will offend many people. It could be dangerous for you.'

'Yes, I understand that. And I don't want to endanger you.' Toshi's already decided. If Nakamura doesn't like it, he'll take it to another studio.

'So, if I don't let you do this, you'll look for another studio that will.'

'Sensei, I was just . . .'

Nakamura smiles. His teeth are stained brown. 'Yes, you were thinking that very thought. I know, I know. You see, I read minds. Being a good artist is not enough if you want to become a successful cartoonist. Many people have the technical skill to draw. So why, then, do you think I am so famous?'

'I don't know.'

'Sit down and I'll tell you.'

Toshi sits.

'Now listen carefully to me. I know that you and Akira and Mami think I'm a silly man.'

'No, Sensei—'

'Quiet. It's all right. It doesn't bother me. Why? Because I have abilities. I read minds, I see the truth. The past. Even the future. You think I'm crazy, but it's true. I just keep it to myself.'

He grinds his cigarette out, but doesn't light another one. Toshi has never seen him without a cigarette. He leans forward in his chair, nods, and waits.

'All the stories that I tell in my comic strips are true. These people I draw, even Chocolate Girl, they all exist.'

'But, Sensei—'

'Listen to me. There are many kinds of truth. Maybe they're not real people that you could meet on the street. But somewhere they do exist. Or did. Or will. Do you understand what I'm saying?'

'I'm not sure I do. I'm sorry.'

'What I'm saying is, if you need to do this comic strip of yours, go ahead. Don't worry about Chocolate Girl. Akira's lazy, he needs more to do anyhow. But I'll expect you to work very hard. I'm not blind, even with these filthy glasses. I know this story you're drawing is true. I know life. And I also know talent. So I want you to work hard, but be careful too.'

He leans forward until their faces are almost touching, and he waves his hands in the air around Toshi's head.

'Life swirls around us like a dangerous whirlpool.'

He leans back and straightens his glasses.

'I'll keep you on salary. You can work here, or at home if you like. When you think you're ready, and when I think you're ready, I'll arrange for publication.'

'Publication? You're not joking?'

'I don't joke about these things. Maybc *Business Hip Hop* will run it. If they don't have the courage, we'll find someone who does. People will be scared of this material. The government won't like it. Neither will the Rice Party. There could be trouble. You should be prepared.'

'I don't want to cause you any trouble, Sensei.'

'Don't worry about me. Just do a good job on this. And tell your story.'

'Thank you. Thank you very much, Sensei. I will work as hard as I can. I will try my best.'

Toshi stands and bows deeply, stays down, his hands gripping his legs tightly, and the blood rushes to his head. He can't believe that Nakamura is going to help him publish his story. He will be indebted to Nakamura for the rest of his life. He will owe him everything.

'You owe me nothing at all, except to do an excellent job,' Nakamura says, reading his mind again.

Hearing the door open, Toshi uncurls from his bow. He feels light-headed. Akira and Mami carry in three big McDonald's shopping bags. Mami's makeup is streaked from crying, or else from the rain.

'It's miserable out there,' Akira says. 'We should have ordered lunch brought in.'

'Never mind the weather. Come look at what Toshi-chan's

been working on at home. He's going to have his own comic strip.' Nakamura lights a cigarette.

'Your own comic strip? Really? Toshi-chan, that's wonderful. Congratulations!' Mami hurries over to the desk.

'What? Your own comic? You're a sneaky one, aren't you? While I'm out in the pouring rain getting your lunch, you're advancing your career,' Akira says. 'What if I caught a cold out there and died? Then you'd be sorry, wouldn't you.'

'I appreciate any help you will be able to give me. I already owe so much to you both.'

'Toshi-chan, these drawings are beautiful. But they're so . . . upsetting. Aren't you worried that they'll disturb people? Akira-kun, come look,' Mami says.

'If I look, I'll just get jealous. I know that Toshi's more talented than I am.'

'Maybe it will inspire you to work harder,' Nakamura says.

Akira empties the McDonald's bags out on his desk. 'If you get famous someday, you can hire me so that I don't have to work for mean old Sensei anymore.'

He spreads out the contents of the bags. Hamburgers, cheeseburgers, teriyaki burgers. French fries. Grilled rice balls and chicken nuggets. Corn soup. Milk shakes. Coca-Cola.

Toshi is suddenly hungry. He's ravenous. He looks at the food, and he sees ideas. He could eat everything, eat it all by himself. There are endless possibilities, he realizes. The future. What to eat first.

'To your beautiful and important art. To a story that needs to be told.' Lucy raises her champagne glass.

Toshi lifts his glass, touches it to hers. 'To your wonderful music.'

A Japanese woman and her French husband have opened

a small restaurant in the neighborhood. Lucy and Toshi made a reservation for New Year's Eve, spent that afternoon emptying out the closet and dressing each other up in odd combinations of clothes; laughing, they collapsed on the bed and made love, and had to take another bath.

Now their small table is covered with dishes, a special holiday menu. Creamy sea urchin soup. Shiitake mushrooms sauteed with garlic. Roast lamb. Grilled eggplant with miso. Toshi devours baskets of bread. Lately he's always hungry. He has never worked harder in his life, and he has never eaten more. His appetite is enormous. It's as if in drawing the story of his life he has created another person, someone who has to be fed. At Lucy's house when they cook together, they use enormous amounts of everything. They slice cucumbers and carrots, steam pumpkin, boil potatoes. The rice cooker is always full. All day long while he works, Toshi peels back the skins of mandarin oranges like the petals of flowers.

The amazing changes in his life in the space of a few months. The first installment of his story will be published in March, not by *Business Hip Hop* but by a small *manga* magazine, one not afraid of risky subject matter. Nakamura made the introductions. And Lucy's CD will be released soon. They're planning a trip to America in the spring to meet her family.

Toshi sips his champagne, the sharp bubbles another new sensation. Is there anything that doesn't occur to him right now? Everything seems possible. Drawings appear fully realized in his mind's eye at a furious rate, before he even picks up his pencil. He can hardly keep up. Places and events he's only imagined until now, or has never imagined. Korea, its borders, mountains, and rivers. A different life. And words! So many new words. There are Japanese-English dictionaries scattered throughout the house, on the kitchen table, by the bed, by the garden door.

Toshi reaches for the small dictionary in his jacket pocket. On the subway, Lucy's long fingers tap, tap, tap the keys of a Canon Wordtank, an electronic dictionary that displays the stroke order and meaning of thousands of *kanji*. Together they are mining two languages to express new, shared ideas and beliefs. To find out that you are not the person you thought you were is exhilarating but exhausting. Who will he become? Who will Lucy become?

'You look so busy inside your head,' she says. 'What are you thinking?'

'I was thinking that I know so many things that I didn't know a year ago,' he says, raising his voice above the din. The basement restaurant is crowded with Japanese and foreigners. Waiters lengthen their spines to squeeze between tables, hold aloft platters of raw oysters and earthenware pitchers of wine that graze the festive balloons dangling from the low ceiling.

'I can't imagine what it's like for you. Discovering your own history. So exciting, yet strange. I watch you change day by day, fitting in the pieces of a jigsaw puzzle.'

'What kind of puzzle?' he asks.

'Jigsaw. Like this.' Cutting into leftover pâté with her knife, she divides it into unsymmetrical, odd-shaped pieces. 'To see the whole picture, you have to fit them together.'

'Yes. That's a good word for me. *Fit*. I want to see where I fit. I want to find my father's family. And to go to Korea too. But when I asked my mother, she said she wouldn't go.'

'Did she say why?'

'She said, "It's gone."'

'Gone?'

'Yes. I asked her, "What's gone?" And she told me, "Korea. I had no choice. In my mind, I had to let it go."'

'You know, there are many women like your mother. Not just Koreans. Chinese, and Filipinos too. She's not alone. There are organizations.'

Toshi shakes his head. 'No. It's impossible. She's still too ashamed.'

'Your poor mother.'

'Yes. But it's my family too. I need to find out who I am.'

She reaches across the table to squeeze his hand. 'I know who you are. And I love who you are.'

In the center of a crowded bar in Shinjuku, white lights twinkle on a white Christmas tree. As soon as they enter, they spot Paul across the room, tying a red ribbon around the neck of a handsome young man.

'This is Malcolm. Malcolm is a student from Singapore.' With a flourish, Paul fashions a big bow. Malcolm grins. Introductions are made. Paul hovers over him as if he is an expensive present he's given himself. Lucy, as always, has a list of questions, and Malcolm surprises them with his answers. He's not as young as he looks, and he's an architecture student at Tokyo University. 'I already have a degree in engineering from Singapore,' he says, and Lucy raises her eyebrows. Toshi thinks, Maybe Paul's changing also.

Just before midnight, the four of them hurry through the freezing rain to a nearby shrine, Paul and Malcolm huddled under one umbrella, Toshi and Lucy under another.

'I like Malcolm,' Lucy whispers.

'Yes. So do I.'

She squeezes his arm. 'Wouldn't it be wonderful if Paul did too.'

They eat New Year's noodles at a street stall, then follow the crowds, thousands of people, up the steps to the shrine. They toss in their coins, ring the bell that calls the gods, clap their hands, and pray. His head bowed, Toshi makes his wishes for the coming year. His mother. Granny. Taro. Paul. And then a memory flickers: Lucy leans over the candles on

Toshi's birthday cake. She is his wish for himself, has been since that night, he realizes.

The subway is packed with loud, drunken women in plush winter coats, and with red-faced men who stagger up and down the car, or sleep fitfully, heads on strangers' shoulders. Toshi and Lucy squeeze into a single seat. Across the aisle, a young girl vomits quietly into a Harrods shopping bag. The train stops at Roppongi. On the crowded platform, a woman in familiar red cowboy boots has her arms around a Japanese man. She hangs from his neck and sways. Toshi can't see her face.

'What?' Lucy says, perhaps feeling the sudden tensing of his body.

But the train doors close, the crowd shifts, and she's gone.

The next afternoon, they meet Paul at Haneda Airport.

'How's Malcolm?' Lucy asks. Toshi hadn't even thought of asking. Most of Paul's dates disappear after one night.

'Actually, he wanted to come to see me off. I told him it was silly, I'd be back in a few days.' Paul looks embarrassed.

'He's nice,' she says.

'Yes, he's nice,' Toshi says.

'Well.' Paul shrugs.

Lucy hugs him. 'It's all right that he's nice. That's a good thing, you know.'

On the plane, Paul sits next to the window. Looking down on Tokyo, they see small fires bloom all over the city.

'I heard it on the news this morning,' Lucy says. 'They're firebombing supermarkets that sell American rice.'

Toshi thinks, Jane.

Paul falls asleep.

On Lucy's lap, an apple pie she's baked for Toshi's mother.

In the overhead bin, long underwear, wool hats and scarves, and fur-lined gloves.

Utoro is concealed and reduced by the snow, postboxes and signposts buried until spring. Toshi's mother and Lucy take long walks together through white tunnels shaped by plows, the tunnels curving up and over them. The sky is white or blue. They walk close together, talking in low voices, sometimes laughing. Other times, they are silent and pensive.

Toshi is helping Taro carry in firewood, and they both stop to watch the two women come down the street, Lucy bent over Toshi's mother, so that it almost looks as if they are embracing. His mother and Lucy. The two foreign women. Did his mother have a close friend when she was a girl, someone she still thinks about?

Paul has gone with Zeni to look at the ice floes, Granny tells them when they all squeeze into the entranceway, stamping their cold feet. Bundled up in sweaters, her legs hidden under a quilt, Granny looks shrunken, diminished by age.

'Let's join them,' his mother says.

'Not me. I see plenty of ice,' Taro says.

'You're coming too,' she says. 'Don't be lazy.'

'Only if you'll keep me warm.' He puts his arm around her. She starts to slip away, but Taro holds her tight. 'Your mother's always trying to run away from me. But I'm stronger than she is.'

Toshi watches his mother's face move rapidly through a sequence of emotions. Embarrassment, then acquiescence, then pleasure.

The last tour buses of the day roll out of the parking lot

on their massive snow tires, tailpipes breathing clouds of exhaust, ghost faces behind the fogged windows. They all stand at the edge of the pier, hunched over against the bitter wind. The ice floes shift and grind, and the noise is unsettling.

'This is so incredible. How far out does the ice go?' Lucy asks.

'All the way to Russia. You could walk. The Ainu used to. They'd catch fish and seabirds for food,' Taro tells her.

'No!' She laughs and turns to Toshi.

'It's true,' he says, even though it's not. And he can picture this: Out on the ice with Lucy, they leap from floe to floe. They never take a false step, never fall in.

'Paul told me that you're a composer,' Zeni says to Lucy. 'I used to play music before I left the Philippines.'

'Really? I love Asian music. I have some recordings of Philippine music. What instruments do you play?'

Lucy is excited, she's forgotten the ice.

Toshi's mother takes his arm and leads him away from the others. 'Come walk with me to the end of the pier.'

In front of them, the sun sinks below the horizon, and the world is salmon pink, then plum, the colors arcing from sky to ice.

The first stars appear.

'I like Lucy. I can tell she has a kind heart,' she says.

'Yes, she does.'

She tucks her graying hair into her wool hat and tightens her scarf around her neck and chin. For the first time, he can see that she, too, is getting old.

'You're lucky. Don't you think you're lucky?' she asks.

'Yes, I think I'm lucky. But don't you think you're lucky too? Taro is a good man. And the inn is doing so well.'

She looks out to sea. There is nothing to cast a shadow. The ice floes have almost disappeared. Shapes and ideas dissolve, and only sound remains. The sound is wind and ice. Restless and mournful. Above them, the win bob on the surface of the sky.

Toshi sticks his gloved hands in his parka pockets, ...es his toes in his boots, and waits for her reply. When she finally speaks, her voice is as sad as the wind.

'Taro is a wonderful man. He's very good to me. And I have you. And Granny. And now, maybe Lucy. These things make me happy. I didn't think I would ever be happy again.'

Once more, she takes his arm, and she guides him down the pier as if one of them, or each of them, needs the other for support.

'But lucky? No, I'm not lucky. A long time ago, it was already too late for me to be lucky.'

Epilogue

Early spring rains sweep through Tokyo to reveal tight clumps of pale pink plum blossoms. Azaleas unfold across the city like bright afterthoughts of color. The Crown Prince's fiancée has given up her career at the Foreign Ministry and commutes daily to the Imperial Palace compound, where she studies haiku poetry and learns to bow, how many degrees. To wave to crowds, the correct angle of the hand. A June wedding date is announced. Two representatives from the Imperial Household Agency, dressed in morning coats and top hats, visit the fiancée and her family at their suburban Tokyo home and present them with the traditional engagement gifts, including a bolt of shiny silk, and a fresh sea bream. The fiancée and her mother both wear kimonos. Toshi and Lucy look at the pictures in the morning paper while they drink their coffee. Lucy hums and sings snatches of songs, strings them together as she eats, reads, moves around the kitchen. There's always melody in the house.

A wave of nationalism is sweeping the country. Also in the morning paper: The Rice Party bombed the new Toys 'R' Us store in Nagano. Dockworkers are striking, refuse to unload American rice, and an Agriculture minister holds up a dead rat which, according to the photo's caption, was found in a rice shipment.

And in the Entertainment section: A movie theater in the Ginza has been renamed the Audrey Hepburn Theater, in memory of the actress, who died of cancer in January at her home in Switzerland.

'I'm taking you out tonight,' Lucy says unexpectedly. He's washing the breakfast dishes, she's halfheartedly drying – swiping at them with a towel, then balancing the mugs and plates in the dish rack.

'Really? Where to?'

'I'm not telling. It's a surprise.'

'You've never done this before.'

She drapes the dish towel around his neck and dances out of the kitchen. 'Just wait. There are many things I've never done that I will do someday.'

She leads him through a warren of dark, narrow footpaths lined with bar signs. FRESH POTATO. PINK GAL. FOOTBALL. MEATBALL. *Doors slide open and shut on the smell of* oden *stew and cigarettes, murmuring voices, plaintive karaoke songs. A transvestite in a kimono and glossy wig eyes them from under a street lamp.*

There is no sign outside to attract customers, nothing to indicate a place of business. Lucy knocks, and the door opens a crack. Jazz music drifts out. 'Noda sent us,' she says in Japanese. At the mention of her musician friend's name, the door opens wider to reveal a middle-aged man with a thin mustache.

'Come in. Welcome.' He bows slightly.

'Welcome, welcome.' The master, who looks just like the waiter, smiles at them from behind a narrow bar. Two small tables are squeezed into the tiny room. 'How is Noda? We haven't seen him for a while. I hope he hasn't forgotten us.'

Toshi stops in the doorway and stares. The walls and the ceiling are covered with photographs of Audrey Hepburn. Behind the bar, a life-size poster of Holly Golightly from Breakfast at Tiffany's *is draped in black cloth. Below it, a stick of incense and a burning candle illuminate offerings of apples, a tin of imported biscuits, glass bottles of perfume, French wine. A shrine.*

'Do you like it?' Lucy asks, squeezing his hand.

It's another place he's never been to, couldn't have imagined. His world keeps expanding.

The waiter seats them at the unoccupied table. Two tall women with matching haircuts and heavy eye makeup are the only other customers. The bar serves only vodka. 'The master lived in Paris once,' the waiter tells them, setting two glasses on their table, as if this is a reasonable explanation. The vodka is iced. The room is hot and damp. Underneath the music, the rain beats down on the pavement outside. The two women smoke clove cigarettes and sing along in deep voices with the tapes the master plays. Opera, and old American rock and roll. Jazz. Songs in Italian, English, and French. 'Callas.' 'Dinah Washington.' They call out in unison, identifying every singer. And they know the words to every song. They have thick bangs cut low across their foreheads. The tiny bar fills up with their cigarette smoke, and they smile at each other as they sing.

'They look like they live in this bar,' Lucy whispers. She sits with her arm around Toshi and smiles with pleasure at everything. The music and the women. The stories the waiter tells them. Toshi is comforted by the weight of her arm across his shoulders, and by the outline of her face in the smoky light. Her long fingers rest on his chest, sometimes moving, tapping out the music. He is happily drunk. Edith Piaf is singing.

'We're in Paris,' he whispers, imagining that they really might be.

'Paris? We are?'

'Yes. I'm Cary Grant. You're Audrey Hepburn. We're on a boat cruising down the Seine.'

She laughs.

'My boyfriend was in love with Audrey Hepburn,' she tells the waiter when the music stops. The master stands behind the bar, slowly rewinding a cassette tape with his finger. She tells the waiter this as if it is a delightful secret she is sharing, but everyone hears her.

'She was the very best,' the waiter says. 'Still beautiful until the day she died.'

The women stop smoking.

'Master, please play it. You must,' they say in one husky voice.

The waiter joins the master, and they both put on big sunglasses. The master takes a cassette from the stack on the shelf and inserts it.

Audrey Hepburn sings 'Moon River.' Just like she sang it in Breakfast at Tiffany's. *Toshi knows the scene well. Audrey sits on the fire escape strumming her guitar, looking sad and yet hopeful at the same time. Everyone in the bar sings along. Toshi feels sad and hopeful. Lucy puts her head on his shoulder, and at that very moment, Audrey whispers to him.*

'Oh, how I love you,' Audrey Hepburn whispers.

It's her voice. He's sure of it. He can smell her expensive perfume.

'Love you, love you, love you, love you,' she says in one long, sweet exhalation.

He feels her breath on his neck. She's that close. He turns, but the song ends. The bar is silent except for the hiss of the stereo speakers.

Audrey vanishes.

'Wait,' he whispers.

'What?' Lucy says, lifting her head.

The two women sob.

Lucy kisses his cheek.

The master comes out from behind the bar and sits down with Toshi and Lucy at their small table. He takes off his sunglasses and points to the poster of Audrey Hepburn, her beautiful hair piled up high on top of her head. Her big eyes looking bravely out at the world.

And her wonderful neck.

'Look at that neck,' the master says. 'No Japanese woman has a neck like that.'

He says this in the same wistful voice that Toshi's mother used so many years ago, on his ninth birthday, in that movie theater in Hokkaido.